The Diamond Murder

Tracy Diane

Giverny Press

Published by Giverny Press, a division of The Giverny Group, Inc.

Giverny Press
www.GivernyPress.com
Asheville, North Carolina

Paperback ISBN: 978-1-7325685-8-7
Digital ISBN: 978-1-7325685-9-4

Also by Tracy Diane

Middle-Grade Adventure

Blue John's Cavern
Rusher's Gold
Black's Opal
Egeran's Mountain

Psychological Thriller

Outtake – Coming October 2025

Chapter One

The sting of three-inch heels nipped at Penelope's feet as she sprinted across the brick sidewalk toward the smoke billowing from the crystal shop's windows. She flung open the glass door, its rusty hinges crying out.

Penelope heard the jingling of the door's agate wind chimes, but could see nothing through the bitter, reddish-gray cloud that filled the store. Jasper bolted through the room, barking and sniffing for Clara and Midnight. The three-month-old husky howled louder than most adult dogs.

"Mom, where are you?" Penelope yelled over the wailing fire alarm. She waved her arms to clear the smoke from around her face, gagging on the cinnamon-scented fumes that invaded her lungs. Penelope saw no flames in The Crystal Cove, just a blanket of haze that made her eyes water. She blinked and squinted through the spicy air as tears sent her mascara sliding down her cheeks.

"Penelope, I'm here." Clara Lake emerged from the back room of the rock and gem shop, waving a broom as she made her way through the fume-filled store. She found the smoke alarm, then smashed it with the broom's wooden handle. "Keep the door open so I can push the smoke out."

Jasper and Midnight trailed behind Clara, then curled up on their fluffy beds beneath the shelving along the back wall. Penelope's new husky had become fast friends with Midnight, her mother's stout black cat. She propped the door open with a large quartz crystal while her mother swatted at the burning haze. Penelope sniffed the sleeve of her burgundy dress. "Oh, Mom, I smell like soot." She wrapped a long auburn curl under her nose, grimaced, and threw her hair behind her shoulder. "What happened here?"

Penelope surveyed her mother from head to toe. She didn't appear injured, and Penelope was happy about that, but sensed she wouldn't like her mother's answer.

"Now, Penelope, don't get angry with me. You're going to get wrinkles on your forehead and you're too young for that." Her mother pushed the last of the smoke spirals through the door and into the fresh Sierra Springs air. Clara wore a long black gown with purple accents of gemstones and ribbons throughout the bodice that accented her petite frame. Penelope recognized what that meant.

"Mom, have you been casting spells again?"

Clara shook her head, but Penelope knew she was guilty. "Mom," she cautioned.

"Okay, I was, but it was only a quick spell. That candle shop across the street is trying to steal my customers. She's got candles with gemstones, like the ones that I sell. It isn't fair." Clara propped the broom in the corner behind the register, then fixed her hands on her hips.

"Mom, Sierra Springs is big enough for both shops. We've known Tessa for years. She's a candlemaker, nothing more." Penelope pulled a tissue and compact mirror from her bag, attempting to fix her makeup.

"Hmm. I'm not so sure." Clara found Midnight and Jasper snuggled together. She ran her hands over their fur, checking for soot residue.

"This may be a small town, but people love to come to your shop. You have the best rocks and gems in town, plus your daughter is a real geologist and knows everything about them."

"And I know lots about crystals too...for witchcraft." Clara scooped Midnight into her arms like a baby.

Penelope rolled her eyes. "Okay, Mom. If you're a witch, why was there so much smoke in the rock shop from your spell? Did it backfire again? Like all the others?" She slid the doorstop away and the rock shop's thick, mahogany wood-framed door eased to a close. Inlaid quartz, garnet, amethyst, and amazonite crystals surrounded an interior glass panel that bent the sunlight into rainbows across the shop floor. Just as the door clicked shut, it flew open again as Penelope's sister, Olivia, and best friend, Laurel, barreled into the shop like the bulls in Pamplona.

"Penelope. Clara. Are you guys okay? I saw the smoke from the cafe," Laurel said, gasping to catch her breath.

"We came as fast as we could." Olivia scanned the shop and fixed her gaze on Clara as her concern turned to dismay. "Oh, I think I get it. You did another *spell*, didn't you?" she asked, forming air quotes with her pointer and index fingers.

Clara put her hands on her hips. "I was trying to stop people from shopping at Tessa's candle shop."

"You tried to put the candle store out of business by doing a spell that set your crystal shop on fire?" Olivia teased. Penelope stifled a laugh. Her younger sister had a way of making the obvious funny.

"Oh, stop, Olivia. I was walking by Tessa's store this morning and saw that she had some candles that looked like they had gems just like my crystals inside them. So, I mixed up a little spell with a pinch of cinnamon to steer customers to my shop instead of hers, but something went wrong, and all this smoke started pouring out of my pot and it smelled like a burned snickerdoodle."

Penelope, Olivia, and Laurel erupted in laughter.

"It's okay, Clara," Laurel said. "I'm sure the cinnamon and smoke stench will fade soon." Her light brown hair swirled around her waist. Penelope was envious of Laurel's straight hair. She loved her curls, but they left her with few styling options.

Skepticism crossed Clara's face. "Let's hope so, sweetie."

"Mom, don't worry about the candle store. Everyone loves your shop. You've been here for thirty years. Tessa could never take away your business." Olivia squeezed her mother's shoulder.

"Olivia is right. Tessa only sells candles. Even if they have crystals in them, I'm sure she wouldn't sell loose stones," Laurel agreed, her faint French accent lingered.

Penelope and Laurel were inseparable from the moment they met. Laurel's older brother, Andre, watched out for them when they were young, and then became Penelope's boyfriend in high school. The Beaumont family moved to North Carolina from France before the girls started middle school.

Penelope pulled her hair into a high ponytail, wrapped the ends around her fingers, and tucked them through, resulting in a loose bun. She found a soft yellow dusting cloth under the display cabinets and tossed it to her mother. "Clean."

"Don't you have to get to work?" Clara wiped down the edges of the crystal bins on the center tables.

Penelope Lake was the Earth Science curator and resident geologist at the Sierra Springs Natural History Museum. During graduate school, Penelope realized that a mineral sample she collected during a hike near her hometown years earlier was, in fact, the first discovery of a rare mineral. The new mineral thrust Penelope into the scientific spotlight at a very young age. In just fifteen days, she would unveil a new rock and mineral display at the museum, showcasing years of work sparked by that initial discovery. The museum's owner was throwing a gala for the unveiling and using it as a platform to solicit donations to build an entirely new children's wing. Penelope was nervous and excited but thrived on the pressure.

"Yes, but I can take a minute to help you get the shop back in order. I'm just going to spend the day in the rock workroom prepping the samples for the new display. Are you okay with keeping Jasper here again?" Amid the strain of the impending gala, Penelope had bought herself a puppy.

"Sure. Midnight and I both love the company." Clara found Midnight as an eight-week-old kitten sleeping at the back door of The Crystal Cove on a frosty winter night. The veterinarian said that Midnight's twelve-week teeth were erupting, and Clara fell in love with his pure black fur and piercing green eyes, which gleamed like two moons floating in his round face. Clara kept Jasper and Midnight in the store with her during the day to keep her company. They were as big a delight to her customers as the colorful crystals and geodes that filled the shop.

"How is the new display coming?" Olivia asked.

"Good. I have two weeks to finish the research, prep and clean the remaining samples, install the display cases, and get my speech ready for the gala." Penelope's stomach churned as she rattled off her to-do list. She was the expert in town on rocks, minerals, and fossils. The owners of the Sierra Springs Natural History Museum hired her before she graduated from the University of North Carolina, and before Clara could ask Penelope to join her at The Crystal Cove.

"So, not much going on?" Laurel joked with her trademark high-pitched laugh.

"Not at all." Penelope grabbed a broom and swept the floor.

Everybody in town came to Penelope for advice on what to get their children or grandkids for Christmas or birthdays. Penelope always had a suggestion for something exciting that would make the kids interested in science, like a fun rock and mineral kit with experiments that made bubbles or created optical illusions. She was the best salesperson for both the museum gift shop and The Crystal Cove.

"Hey Olivia, why don't you run down to the cafe, get some of those new pastries you made, and ask Tristan for a thermos of coffee? Penelope and your mom can all try your new treats, and we can help get the rock shop cleaned up quickly."

Laurel's cafe offered a caffeine jolt in the morning and soothing wine in the evenings. The Tipsy Java was Sierra Springs' most popular bakery and bar rolled into one. Olivia's delicious sandwiches, pastries, and sinful desserts kept the customers happy and Laurel on a chronic diet.

"Sure thing, Laurel," Olivia replied as she slipped out of the door. Penelope's younger sister was a baking genius. She began working for Laurel right after graduating from pastry school. A constant overachiever, Olivia took enough classes to almost earn a culinary degree as well.

"Oh no, ladies, you all have jobs and businesses to run. I can clean the shop," Clara offered.

"Clara, you're like a second mother to me, and Tristan can manage the cafe for a bit," Laurel said. "We're going to stay and help you out. Plus, you need to be the first to try Olivia's new pastries. She's amazingly creative."

For the next few minutes, Clara, Penelope, and Laurel cleared the countertops and rock and mineral specimens of the cinnamon-scented soot. This wasn't the first time that Clara botched a spell that ended in smoke and grime coating everything in the store. But after their cleaning blitz, the shop sparkled once again.

Over the years, Clara's store has become the top destination for locals and tourists searching for crystals, oils, herbs, and books on the mystical properties of crystals. She also had a reputation as the town kook because she openly told customers she was a witch when they entered the shop during one of her often-failed attempts at a spell.

The agate door chimes welcomed Olivia back as she swept in with two bags of pastries and a large container of coffee. Clara brought four disposable cups from her office, filled them with coffee, and added Olivia's homemade vanilla oat milk creamer.

The Tipsy Java cafe was a short two blocks east of The Crystal Cove on Main Street, the heart and soul of Sierra Springs. It was Laurel's dream to own a business where her friends and neighbors could spend time together. She and

Penelope had spent many hours during college working on a business plan when they were home during school breaks.

Penelope often wished her office at the museum was closer, but with just a short detour, she could drive by her mother's shop and the cafe on her way to work for a quick cup of coffee or simply to say good morning and drop off Jasper.

"Oh good, the smell of cinnamon smoke is almost gone." Olivia winked as she lined four napkins along the counter and topped each with a fist-sized apple cream tart. Her auburn ponytail spilled over her shoulder as she served. Olivia's crystal blue eyes mirrored her mother's and sister's—a sure sign they were family, their grandmother used to say.

"Thank you. These look amazing," Clara said, taking a dainty bite from the rim of the tart. "Ooh, raspberry cream."

"Your favorite flavor." Olivia plopped onto the stool behind the gem case and skimmed her fingers across the glass top. "So, Mom, that must have been a big spell this time. The glass still feels a little sooty."

Clara tilted her head. "No, young lady, it was just the right size. I must have just mixed something wrong. It wasn't supposed to smoke."

"I'm just kidding." Olivia raised her eyebrows at Penelope and whispered, "When will she realize that she's not a witch?"

"I heard that, Olivia." Clara tossed a yellow cleaning cloth, hitting her youngest daughter in the belly.

Olivia grabbed the cloth and tossed it back at her mother, but missed, landing it across Midnight's face. Jasper bit the cloth and scampered into the back room, Midnight close on her heels.

"I've got to make sure that I have plenty of customers. Tessa's crystal candles might steal mine," Clara said, exasperated.

"Mom, stop." Penelope groaned. "We just talked about this. I can promise you that Tessa's candles won't harm your sales, plus you've been selling crystals to her husband's jewelry business for years. Why would Tessa do anything to hurt your store?"

"Well, you could be right. Robby buys a lot of raw gemstones from me." Clara sipped her coffee.

Tessa's husband, Robby McCaul, cut, polished, and turned the gems into unique handmade jewelry. Robby and Tessa moved to Sierra Springs when Penelope was in high school. Before she opened the candle store, Tessa was a substitute art teacher during Penelope's senior year. When Robby opened his jewelry store on the other side of town, he became one of Clara's best customers.

"Have you talked with Tessa about what she's selling? Maybe they're the crystals Robby bought from you." Laurel stuffed the last bite of apple cream tart in her mouth.

"I haven't been inside. I just looked through the window this morning." Clara shrugged.

"I think it's time we go. You have a few minutes before you need to open." Penelope hopped off her stool and seized Clara's hand, leading her to the front door. "Come on, ladies," she said, pushing the door open. "Let's check out the competition."

Banishing Spell for Unwanted Competition

When you want to fight against unwanted business competition, create a batch of banishing potion and keep your enemies from stealing your customers.

Spell Supplies

Rainwater | Cauldron | Candle | Glass Bottle | Cinnamon Sticks | Peppercorns | Cloves | Paper and Pen

Heat the rainwater, peppercorns, cinnamon sticks, and cloves in the cauldron. Do not let the cinnamon sticks touch an open flame, because they will smoke! (Just ask Clara!) Write the name of your business competitor or their store name on the paper. Fold and twist the paper then place it in the bottle. Fill the bottle with your banishing water and seal a stopper. Repeat the following chant as you "dispose" of the bottle by tossing it in the trash. *You've declared a war on me, but triumph isn't yours to see. I am strong. My spirit's free. I will claim the victory. So mote it be!*

Chakra Stones for Protection

Use protection stones while you do the spell. You can also wear jewelry made with these crystals or keep them in your pockets until your competitor is banished.

Black Tourmaline | Amethyst | Rose Quartz

Chapter Two

A warm spring breeze hit Penelope's face as she emerged onto the Main Street sidewalk. "You two watch the shop," she told Jasper and Midnight before locking the door to The Crystal Cove.

The puppy and her feline buddy watched through the glass door as the foursome hustled across the road toward the candle shop. Penelope glanced sideways at her mother and chuckled at the sight of her grimace. She could tell that Clara was uncomfortable as they approached The Drip Shack.

"Oh, Mom, it's going to be fine. You should put a smile on your face and just ask Tessa about her new candles," Penelope said. "I don't think this is a big deal."

Clara smiled and nodded slightly. "Okay, Penelope, I'll keep an open mind just for you."

Penelope reached for the door just as it swung violently outward and smacked her hand. Almost instantly, a woman burst past her and down the sidewalk, her hand covering her mouth and dark hair whipping in the breeze. Penelope could hear the woman grumbling as she hurried away from the candle shop.

Penelope turned to Laurel with one raised eyebrow. "Weird."

"Who is that?" Olivia asked.

"Never seen her before," Penelope debated if inquiring about the woman would be friendly or nosey. "Tessa!" Penelope called as she entered the store.

Tessa McCaul stepped from the back of the shop with a short wave to her visitors and a cell phone jammed tight to her right ear. She placed her left hand over her mouth, muffling her words.

Nosey, Penelope decided, but her curiosity languished.

The foursome wandered through the candle shop, admiring the handcrafted collections.

Tessa cut off her call, and with a deep breath, greeted her guests.

"Hi, Penelope! It's great to see you, Clara. Robby said that the last batch of rough gems you sold him was fantastic. You should stop by the jewelry store and see some necklaces he made from them. They're super rustic and cute."

"I'll do that, Tessa," Clara snapped as she scoped out the front shop window display.

Penelope caught Clara's eye. If her mother was the witch she claimed to be, Penelope hoped she could read her mind at that moment because it was telling Clara to calm down.

Tessa's fiery red curls cascaded over her shoulders toward her waist. She pasted on a smile and gave Penelope a brief hug. Tessa was pretty, with tanned skin and green eyes that made her appear younger than her thirty-nine years. Her billowing hobo skirt accentuated her tall, thin frame.

"Is everything okay?" Penelope whispered. "Who was that woman?"

Tessa waved her hand. "Everything's fine. She used to work for me, but I had to let her go. Bygones and all."

Penelope wasn't sure what Tessa meant by 'bygones,' but clearly, the conversation was over.

Tessa cleared her throat. "It's nice to see you all. I don't get out of the store much these days. What brings you ladies here today?"

"You have an extensive selection here." Clara strode between the tables. Her eyes never left the candles.

"Yes, I'm really proud of my candles. I make each one of them by hand now. That's why I've been so busy. I quit buying from other candle suppliers and make them all myself."

"Everything smells so good, and the colors are so vibrant," Olivia said. "What types of wax do you use?"

"Everything from soy wax to beeswax and almost everything in between." Tessa's eyes gleamed as she surveyed the room. "I've spent the past few months studying how to make the perfect candle with the delicate balance of strong and light fragrances with different burn times and wick types."

"Wow, you've done a lot of work on your craft," Laurel commented. "You should bring some of your candles with a stack of business cards to The Tipsy Java, and I can make a small display for you by the register."

"That would be amazing. Thank you. And I'll pick up a stack of your cards and hand them out to my customers as well. We business owners need to stick together, right?"

"Absolutely, you do. Right, Mom?" Penelope pivoted to find Clara ogling Tessa's gemstone candles.

The inside of The Drip Shack resembled the layout of Clara's store. Mahogany wood shelves lined the walls while antique tables scattered throughout the interior showed off different groupings of candles and ways customers could create home displays. Clara and Tessa were always friendly. Penelope wondered why these new candles so visibly upset her mother.

"You have a creative eye," Clara commented. "I can see that you spend a lot of time thinking about your designs." Her demeanor softened as she examined each of the candles.

Tessa joined Clara at the window display. "I just made this new line this week." She picked up a large purple candle from the display.

Penelope thought she saw a flicker of worry cross Tessa's face as she sighed, her fingers tentatively tracing the dripping wax and gemstones peeking from the sides of the candle.

"Before I married Robby, I lived in a tiny apartment. I tried to save money on the electric bill by using candles in the evening. Robby and I spent last weekend cleaning out our storage closet and ran across a box full of used candles that had wax dripping down the sides from the hours and hours of burning."

Penelope, Olivia, and Laurel gathered around the display as Tessa continued, "Robby thought the candles looked cool with the wax already dripping down the sides and that gave me the idea of creating candles that look like they were already burned even though they were brand new. I have seen similar candles on the internet but realized I could create something new and exciting by layering the interior wax color and fragrances. As you burn them, the colors change and the fragrances mingle to create something new."

"That is so clever." Penelope wished she had the same creativity as Tessa with candles and Olivia with pastry. But she would have to settle for her ability to solve the Earth's rocky puzzles and leave the artistry to others.

"I just love this deep purple color for the outside." Tessa pulled a pair of scissors from her pocket and used one blade to slice through the top of the candle, revealing six intricate layers of wax. "Each layer is a lighter and lighter shade of purple until you reach a pale lavender in the center."

"They are just beautiful, Tessa," Clara said. "I can imagine how pretty it burns, revealing each additional layer."

Tessa lifted an eight-inch-tall candle from the display, handing it to Clara. "I call this line my Amethyst Falls candles. I'd like you to have this. There's something special inside."

"Thank you. It reminds you of the way amethyst crystals have a darker purple on the tips and then fade to a lighter color the further back you go toward the crystal's base." A thin smile hovered on Clara's lips. Penelope could tell her mother desperately wanted to disapprove of Tessa and her candle shop, but the beautiful candles and the delicious smells were winning her over.

Clara touched the sides of the candle. "What do I feel on the edges?" Penelope sensed she was fishing for details about the gems. They were easily visible along the sides of the candle.

"That is the extra-special part of the candle. I put diamonds inside. Just a few that I got from Robby's shop."

Clara raised an eyebrow. "Really? These must be the world's most expensive candles."

"Diamonds are inside the candle?" Laurel's eyes widened as she examined the gems.

"Oh, just poor-quality diamonds. Robby didn't want to use them in his jewelry. They aren't worth anything." Tessa waved her hand across her body as if she were pushing away a problem. "I like the way they sparkle along the edges as the candle burns."

"If you are calling the line Amethyst Falls, why not have real amethysts inside, instead," Penelope asked.

"I tried, but they didn't sparkle as well, so I switched to the diamonds but kept the name because of the purple wax color. I think I just need to get some better quality amethysts next time and try again."

"Tessa, I can't take this candle knowing that there are diamonds inside," Clara said, placing the candle on the window display table.

"Clara, I insist. Trust me. Robby's business partner had to agree to buy a bunch of small stones to get the bigger, high-quality ones. Anyway, this candle was just an experiment. I think it would be better with larger crystals, anyway. Maybe we can team up and I can use some crystals that you sell in your shop, like clear quartz or some better-quality amethysts, and we can both sell the candles to advertise for each other, like Laurel and I are going to do." Tessa retrieved the candle and shoved it into Clara's hand. "Promise me you'll keep the candle in your shop."

"Oh, okay. If you insist. I'll find the best crystals for your candles. We can experiment with different types to see which transmit the most light from the flame." Lifting the candle to the overhead light, Clara watched the diamonds shimmer from their waxy cocoon.

Tessa smiled. "That would be great, thank you."

Olivia leaned toward a table blanketed in white candles covered with glitter. "Yummy, these smell delicious."

"I was experimenting with the fragrances and that one ended up smelling like a sugar cookie."

"No wonder I like it. Cookies are my favorite pastry." Olivia cradled a sugar cookie candle in her arm. "I'm buying this."

"Awesome! The one that Penelope is holding smells like lavender and the others smell like cherry, merlot, and roses. I'm not sure which one the customers would like the most."

They spent the next few minutes chatting with Tessa about the different methods that she used to make her candles and admired the unique flare each one had that set it apart from the typical candles you could buy in any chain store. Before long, each of them had a full bag to take home.

"It sure has been nice visiting, but I better get back to the shop. I may have some extra cleaning left to do before opening." Clara shook Tessa's hand.

Tessa leaned close to Penelope and lowered her voice. "New spell?"

"Yep." Penelope wondered if Clara was ever tired of cleaning soot from the rock shop. Her spells rarely seemed to go as planned.

Tessa's smile faded quickly. "So, you'll keep the Amethyst Falls in your shop, right?"

"I certainly will. And I'll start gathering some crystals for you to work with. This is exciting to work together." Clara reached for the door handle.

As they meandered across the street back to the rock shop, Penelope felt relieved that her mother and Tessa were collaborating. Her mind turned to her to-do list for the day. She loved her work, but this spring was unusually busy with planning for the museum gala and the simultaneous unveiling of her new rock collection, on top of all her daily duties at the museum and her work with the city engineers now and again.

"We need to get back to the cafe." Laurel nudged Olivia. "The last time I left Tristan in charge this long, he tried to start Karaoke Night at The Tipsy Java."

Laurel's cafe manager was excellent at his job for his youthful age. Tristan Conner started working at Tipsy Java before he was legally old enough to serve drinks in the evening, so Laurel had to keep him on the morning coffee shift until his twenty-first birthday.

"I'd have to be tipsy to do karaoke again," Penelope said, remembering one drunken night at her favorite college hangout.

"The candles with the wax melting down the sides gave me an idea for a new dessert. How about individual tower cakes with dripping icing that looks like hot candle wax?" Olivia glanced toward Laurel for approval.

"Like tiny candle petit fours." Penelope loved cake, especially Olivia's cakes. Penelope's baking skills lacked finesse and, often, flavor. After the last time she tried to surprise her little sister by baking her a birthday cake, Olivia made Laurel promise to keep her out of the kitchen. Only Penelope could make a chocolate cake taste bland.

Clara smiled. "That sounds like a great idea. Save some for me and Penelope."

"Agreed. That sounds outstanding, Olivia," Laurel said.

Olivia and Laurel said their goodbyes, then trotted off toward The Tipsy Java.

Clara watched her youngest daughter bounce with excitement for her new dessert idea. "That girl is going to be a famous chef one day."

When Olivia moved back to town after finishing pastry school, Laurel offered her a job as her chef and baker. Olivia created all the pastries, sandwiches, and a line of handcrafted creamers for the cafe. Laurel let Olivia use the commercial kitchen for private catering clients. Penelope was proud of the business that her best friend and sister had built. They credited Clara's inspiration with The Crystal Cove as their roadmap to success.

Penelope opened the shop door to a rousing game of tag between Jasper and Midnight.

"See, Mom. I told you Tessa isn't trying to steal your business." Penelope caught Jasper mid-leap and snuggled the puppy. "She wants to work with you."

"This *is* beautiful," Clara said, admiring the candle as she set it on the corner shelf near the display of amethyst geodes.

Jasper leaped from Penelope's grasp, instigating a fresh round of tag as Midnight scampered through the shop. Penelope ran her hand across the surface of the candle toward the rough patches of pre-melted wax that appeared to be sliding down the sides. The purple shade reminded her of the lavender fields near her grandmother's home, east of Charlotte. She raised the candle and took a slow breath. The fragrance sent her mind reeling to summer visits and picking flowers in the fields.

"You're still planning to help me at the Spring Festival tomorrow, right?"

"Sure, Mom. I'll be there. Can I hand out some fliers about the gala?"

"Of course. I'm happy to spread the word about my brilliant daughter and her rare new rock and mineral exhibit. Hopefully, we can sell a few tickets and get some donations for the museum, too.”

“Thanks.” Penelope wrinkled her nose. “It still smells a little funky in here.”

She and her mother scanned the gem shop. Most of the soot from the earlier botched spell was gone, but a faint odor of burned herbs and cinnamon remained. “I’ll light Tessa’s candle and see if the fragrance smell covers up the stench from my spell this morning,” Clara said.

Penelope’s phone chimed. Her assistant, Lucy, had texted that the new display cases were in, so they needed to get the crew going on the installation. “I’d better get to the museum. I’ll stop by later and get Jasper.” Penelope kneeled and ruffled her pup’s fur, then scooped her up. “You be good, you hear? Play nice with Midnight and don’t let Grandma try any more spells.”

“How about just one spell?”

“I thought you were over this Tessa thing.”

“I am. It’s a spell for making money at the festival. Now shoo. Go to the museum. There are rock displays that need you.” Clara flashed a mischievous smile as she disappeared behind the curtains.

“Mom! I’m not coming back to help you clean again.”

“I’ll see you later,” Clara yelled.

Penelope plopped Jasper on the floor next to Midnight. “You two are in charge.” She wagged her finger at the furry pals. “Make sure she doesn’t burn this place down.”

Chapter Three

Penelope's bedroom sounded like a five-alarm fire before the sun rose above the North Carolina mountains. She always struggled to get up in the mornings and finally resorted to setting the alarm on her phone to chime at five-minute intervals. If the phone didn't wake her, the extra alarm clock on the dresser would demand she put her feet on the floor and get moving. Some mornings, like today, Penelope needed her backup alarm clock in the bathroom to scream, too. With three alarms clanging and chiming in patterned noises and rhythms, Penelope's eyes slowly opened. When she was a teenager, her mother wielded a metal music triangle like a weapon, clanging it inches above her head when she refused to rise. Over ten years later, Penelope still wasn't sure which sound was more unbearable.

Jasper leaped from the floor and landed squarely on Penelope's stomach.

"Ouch, Jasper, keep your claws in when you do that." The playful pup bounced on the bed, almost rolling Penelope to the floor. She wrapped her arm around the three-month-old puppy who stole her heart when a museum patron showed her a picture of a new litter her dog had just a month before. The day Jasper turned eight weeks old, Penelope picked her up and then spent two hours in the pet shop choosing enough leashes, bowls, toys, food, and treats for a houseful of puppies rather than just one. She loved Jasper's energy and looked forward to their daily jogs and playtime, although she preferred when the rough-housing started after she awoke.

Jasper flopped onto Penelope's stomach and licked her face. Penelope scooped up the pup and cradled her like a baby. She loved having a new puppy. Penelope hadn't had a pet of her own since she was in high school and always wanted a husky to run and play with at the park. When the crystal shop was quiet, Clara taught her basic commands, like sit and stay.

"We better get moving. The festival starts soon," Penelope told the squirming pup before kissing her muzzle and plopping her to the floor. She slipped on a flannel robe covered with colorful cartoon dinosaurs she purchased at the Smithsonian Museum's gift shop during a graduate school trip. Penelope patted barefoot to the kitchen and opened the back door to the tiny, fenced yard attached to her condominium. Jasper sprinted through the doorway to run laps around the shrubs. She had only flicked on her coffee machine when Jasper was scratching the door, asking to come in for breakfast.

Penelope scooped canned chicken entrée for puppies into a green ceramic dog bowl that read 'Jasper' across the front in a silver script. As the pup circled Penelope's feet, rubbing against her legs, the constant whimpering insinuated she was moving too slowly. Jasper head-butted her ankle.

"Okay, Jasper, okay." Penelope set the bowl on top of the paw print placemat on the floor. She cleaned Jasper's water bowl and dry food bowl and refilled them. Finally, Penelope slipped back to the coffeemaker to brew her first cup of the day.

Every Saturday in April and May, the town threw a huge festival and farmer's market in the park at the center of downtown, filled with food and craft vendors, and games for the kids. Every year, Clara set up a tent for her gem shop and Penelope helped her man the booth while Olivia kept them stocked with sugar-coated chocolate rocks to give to customers.

This year Penelope was bringing a small display of her rare samples from the new museum exhibit that was opening in just two short weeks. The discovery of the new mineral in the North Carolina mountains led Penelope on a quest to find more unique rocks and minerals from around the world. The samples in the museum display reflected over five years of searching and discovery. Penelope had a few sneak peek samples to show off at the festival, but the main attraction, the lavender and magenta striped mineral that everyone was waiting to see, was locked up tight in her laboratory safe.

The festival attracted an amazing crowd, but Penelope hated having to get up at five o'clock in the morning to help her mother set up the tent so they were ready to sell when the festival opened at eight. Last year, The Crystal Cove had a prime tent location near one of the main entrances adjoining the food trucks, where most attendees spent most of their time.

A long stretch of green grass extended from the food trucks through the park entrance and acted as a funnel for the lucky vendors who claimed one of these first-come-first-served spots. Penelope jumped in the shower, then dressed in her most comfortable jeans and navy wool sweater layered over her green The Crystal Cove branded T-shirt that Clara ordered just for festivals. Springtime in western North Carolina meant layers. The air felt like winter in the morning and summer by the afternoon.

"Let's go, Jasper. Do you want to wear your sweater today? You're going to have to be a good girl and stick close to the booth."

Some people in town considered it strange, but Jasper liked to wear sweaters. She paired well with Midnight, who wore capes when he was in public. Everyone in town knew the cat that ran around the festival in a black cape with a red monogrammed letter 'M' and a fur collar. It was one way Clara could keep track of him because there was an abundance of black cats in town. Jasper and Midnight were quite a sight with their sweater and cape.

Penelope slipped the sweater over Jasper's neck and pulled her paws through the leg openings. The purple cotton sweater with embroidered flowers was fitting for the first day of the Spring Festival. Penelope and Jasper rushed out the door and settled in the SUV. Penelope had always wanted a sporty little Corvette, but they weren't good for hauling boxes of rocks, so she settled on a Hummer, the best geologist's vehicle she could find. It could travel over any terrain and tote her samples and equipment from the museum to the field and back again. The Hummer was a deep purple color, shimmering with flecks of green and gold that reminded Penelope of one of her favorite crystals, the peacock ore.

She arrived at the gem shop just in time to see her mother crawl out of a slick black Audi with Midnight in her arms. Penelope didn't recognize the driver and wasn't sure she wanted to. Her mother had many *confidants,* as Clara called them, and that was more than Penelope wanted to know about her mother's social life.

"Morning, darling." Clara rushed to draw Penelope into a quick hug. "And good morning to you, Jasper. You look beautiful today in your sweater. Are you ready for the festival?"

"Mom, you understand she can't talk to you, right?"

"Yes, dear, but we communicate in other ways, just like Midnight and I do." Clara gave Penelope a quick wink and took Jasper from her arms, securing harnesses and leashes on their furry friends. Penelope propped the front door open and loaded the tent and banners from the back of the shop into her waiting car.

"We need to hurry so we can get the spot that we had last year," Clara said.

"That's exactly what I was thinking."

"I put all my chakra crystals in boxes last night. Do you have your samples from the museum?"

"Yep." Penelope pointed to the plastic totes in the Hummer's trunk.

In a few brief minutes, Penelope and Clara finished loading the car with the festival supplies. Jasper and Midnight sat strapped into the back seat, ready for adventure.

Penelope locked the shop door and hopped into the driver's seat. She glanced up and down the street for cars, but it was so early that only festival vendors were active. "Oh, Tessa's shop is lit up. She must be exhibiting again this year."

"I wonder if she will have her own tent or share one with Robby?"

"It would make more financial sense to share. The booth spaces do cost a lot. That's why I appreciate you letting me bring a few samples to advertise the museum." Penelope jumped on the gas. The engine roared as their heads jolted backward, smacking the headrests.

"Honestly, Penelope, you drive like a stock car racer." Clara rubbed her neck.

Penelope chuckled. "Then I guess you should have hired a better driving teacher when I was a kid."

"Hey, I taught you how to drive!"

"Exactly!" Penelope laughed.

Less than fifteen minutes later, Penelope and Clara had claimed their favorite spot on the promenade. They had been exhibiting for so many years they were experts at raising the tent, arranging the banners and tables, and unpacking the rocks and minerals they hoped to sell. Penelope had a stack of geology kits she had designed for the museum gift store to thank donors and gala ticket holders who stopped by. Penelope secured the loops of two long leashes beneath one of the tent poles. Jasper and Midnight had plenty of room to run and play, but would be close enough for Penelope and Clara to monitor them.

"I'll go get us some coffee." Penelope scanned the food vendors, looking for The Tipsy Java.

While Clara relaxed in a director's chair emblazoned with The Crystal Cove logo across the fabric back, Penelope strolled through the park among the tents that her fellow vendors were erecting. The new vendors struggled to set up their canopies and place their items just so, while the veterans had their procedures down to a precise set of movements. Tristan had The Tipsy Java tent set up early so he could sell coffee and pastries to the vendors before the park flooded with guests.

This was Penelope's favorite time of year. The entire town was awakening from its wintry slumber and joyfully welcoming the spring warmth and sunshine. A wall of white tents lined the park, their temporary shelves and tables overflowing with handcrafted treasures. Pottery, paintings, jewelry, and carved wood pieces beckoned to be admired and purchased.

The budding trees lining the park's edges swayed gently in the warm spring breeze, their pale green leaves playing a welcoming chorus to the arriving vendors. The air was thick with the perfume of new blossoms—roses and violets mingling in a floral melody.

Dandelions dotted the lush grass underfoot. Penelope inhaled deeply, savoring the scents. A smile played across her lips as the mouthwatering aroma of coffee and sugary funnel cakes being fried to crispy perfection from the food trucks made her stomach growl.

As Penelope scanned the sea of vendors, she saw a familiar sight in the back row. "Hi, guys." Penelope approached Robby and Tessa. "Your tent looks great. I love your candles and jewelry."

She moved along the edges of the table, admiring her friends' handiwork. Robby had helped at the museum when he graduated from the gemological program at Sierra Springs Technical College, though his love was never in the rocks and minerals themselves, but in what he could create with his lapidary equipment. He was happy when the museum hired Penelope as the resident geologist because it left him free to focus solely on his jewelry store.

"Hi, Penelope, are you all set up?" Tessa's new melted candle creations lined the back of the tables, letting the jewelry stand prominently up front.

"Yep, just fetching some coffee before the crowds arrive. Mom is watching the tent and trying to keep Midnight and Jasper in line."

"I'm sorry I'm missing opening day this year." Robby stretched his back as if he were stiff from carrying the jewelry from the store to the park. At first glance, Robby and Tessa didn't seem like a match with her whimsical style and flowing red curls and his stocky frame with sandy hair that was prematurely graying at the temples. But they had been married for over twelve years, and the longer Penelope knew them, the more she realized that they just fit together, like pieces in a jigsaw puzzle.

"You aren't staying?" Penelope eyed an obsidian and fluorite bracelet on the table. The smaller black obsidian cabochons made the swirls of purple and green in the larger fluorites look like waves in the ocean. Penelope thought the bracelet would be the perfect complement to a new sundress she recently ordered from an online catalog.

"No, Katia took a last-minute meeting with a new vendor out of town, so I have to meet with a different vendor at the store and then the accountant is stopping by to pick up the paperwork she left for our quarterly taxes. I don't know why these people insist on meeting over the weekend." Robby stashed the empty product boxes beneath the display tables.

Katia Lazofsky was Robby's business partner in the jewelry shop. Penelope had only met her a few times, as she seemed to travel constantly looking for new gemstone merchants.

"That doesn't sound like fun." Penelope picked up the bracelet. "I'll take it. How much?"

"For you Penelope, it's on the house. And I would much rather be here than with an accountant." Robby waved his hand as he retrieved his car keys and jacket from the tent floor. "Even though we're stuck in the back this year."

"Hopefully not out of sight, out of mind," Tessa mumbled.

"I'm so sorry, love. I need to meet the vendor at the store in a few minutes." Robby gave Tessa a quick kiss on the cheek. Penelope watched her pull back slightly. "I'll see you later, ladies," Robby slipped through the back flap and disappeared into the sea of tents.

Penelope watched Tessa's face as Robby left. She seemed tense...or sad. Penelope wasn't sure which, but she certainly did not look happy.

"You okay? You can always text me if you need help today."

"It's not that. Robby's—"

"Hey, candle woman, what are you doing here with jewelry? Are you trying to steal my customers?" a gravelly voice shouted.

A tiny woman, not even five feet tall with a mop of mousy brown hair whizzed before Penelope as her index finger jabbed at Tessa.

"Hi Jessie, what is wrong with the world's most obnoxious vendor now? Did your cheap jewelry turn your customers' fingers green again?" Tessa snapped.

"Whoa, what's going on here?" Penelope asked. She had known Jessie since high school, although they were a few years apart. Penelope remembered her as one of Olivia's friends from the band.

Jessie whirled around and scrutinized Penelope. "Oh, another one of you."

"Another one of what, Jessie?" Penelope asked.

"Pretty people who think they can come in here and steal all of my business."

Penelope raised her hands. "Hey! We're all friends here. Tessa sells candles and I help my mother sell rocks. How could we possibly steal your business?"

"I've been battling against that husband of hers for years at this festival, but he's usually across the park. Today, he comes and sets up right next to my tent selling his fancy jewelry and she puts out her candles to distract everyone away from my tent."

"I think you mean he sells quality jewelry," Tessa quipped.

"Come on, guys. It's eight in the morning. If we supported each other rather than bickering, we could all make more sales." Penelope hoped to soothe tempers, but neither Tessa nor Jessie relented.

"We set up here as a last resort. We got here too late to grab a spot on the main walkway." Tessa's ears turned crimson as she spoke.

"I don't believe you." Jessie smacked her arm. "Damn mosquitoes. They're just like you. A pain in my ass!"

"Don't test me, Jessie." Tessa's body tensed.

Penelope's mind scrambled for a way to defuse the tension as the two women faced off, like two snorting bulls raring to charge. She took a few steps back and peered around the side flap of Tessa's tent into Jessie's. "I haven't even had my morning coffee yet, but from ten feet away, I can tell that your jewelry is completely different from

Robby's. His are more jewelry store items and yours are bold, colorful, and obviously handmade with love."

Jessie's hands slowed from a full shake to a slight tremble. "Well, I guess they are different."

"They're a lot different," Tessa said. "You little imp," she muttered.

"Let's all take a deep breath, calm down, and you guys can work together. After customers purchase at your tent, you can suggest that they check out the other." Penelope was feeling the lack of caffeine. She detested being the unofficial referee.

"I don't need your help. I'm going to outsell you today, anyway." Jessie spun on her heels and charged out of the tent.

"Wow, she is just delightful this morning. I think she needs coffee more than I do!" Penelope peeked around the tent flaps and saw Jessie flop into a beach chair, which made her look like a child struggling to see over the tables. Penelope stifled a laugh.

"I can't believe Robby left me alone to deal with *her*."

"Don't worry about Jessie. Her stuff isn't nearly as nice as Robby's," Penelope whispered as she clasped the obsidian and fluorite bracelet around her arm. The line of shiny polished stones danced around her delicate wrist, adding a touch of color to her otherwise pale skin.

Tessa cracked her knuckles. "This is my first time exhibiting my new drip candles and Robby left me all alone to handle everything for both of our shops."

"You'll be great. You can handle the customers and I'm just a text away."

"The customers are fine. The rejection, if they don't like my new candles, is another thing."

Penelope put her hand on Tessa's arm. "You can do this. Plus, your candles are gorgeous, and they smell great." Penelope picked up an Amethyst Falls candle and slowly inhaled the lavender scent. The thick candle bobbled in her hand, leaving her scrambling to catch it before it tumbled to the grass.

"Oh, no!" Tessa leaned over the table, snatched the candle from Penelope, and knocked over a dozen other candles and bracelet displays. "This one is special. I need to keep it in one piece."

"I'm so sorry. You have more, right?"

"Yes, but not like this one." Tessa hesitated. "It's the match to the one I gave your mother. It's a display only, not for sale. I was hoping it would be my signature piece, kind of like Robby's pyrite rings are for him. But I've only made the two with diamonds so far."

"I get it. Robby's fool's gold rings are a show-stopper. Your candles will be, too. I know it." Penelope helped Tessa replace the candle onto the tallest stand and adjust it so the customers would see the perfectly dripped wax cascading down the sides, making it appear elegant and rustic simultaneously.

"Thanks, Penelope. I'm just nervous." Tessa's hands quivered as they finished readjusting the entire display.

"No worries. I'd better get those coffees before the festival opens. I'll check in with you later. But text me if you need any help."

"I will. Thank you."

"See you later," Penelope called as she headed toward The Tipsy Java canopy.

After a quick hello to Tristan, Penelope returned to The Crystal Cove tent carrying two vanilla hazelnut lattes, raspberry danishes, and a plain croissant for Midnight and Jasper to share. She recounted Jessie's meltdown to her mother.

"I'm not sure how she and Olivia were ever friends. Jessie Hanlon is like a dark cloud at every event," Clara remarked. "I bet I have a spell that would fix her."

Penelope clamped her hands to her ears. "I didn't hear that!"

"Were Laurel and Olivia over there?"

"No, Tristan said that Laurel is at the cafe and Olivia is running more coffee and food between the store and the festival all day."

The crowds were gathering, and Penelope and Clara soon became preoccupied with showing off their rock samples and mineral crystals. Penelope had no time to worry about anyone else's problems. As usual, Clara's chakra stones were popular, and sales were brisk throughout the morning. Penelope had even secured the sale of a handful of tickets to the museum gala and over three hundred dollars in cash donations from out-of-town visitors, leaving her elated.

Penelope hummed as she moved from one side of the tent to the other, talking with the customers. Typically, the festival attracted people from around the region, and Penelope enjoyed handing out business cards for the shop and the museum and directing visitors to their websites for future sales.

***

As lunchtime arrived, Clara offered to get sandwiches from the food trucks. "Do you want your usual?" she asked, rummaging through her purse, searching for her wallet.

"Ooh, yes, please. That would be great. Thank you, Mom."

"No problem. I'll get something for Tessa and drop it by her tent and check on her. If she's been as busy as we have, I'm sure she could use a break."

"Awe, Mom. That is awfully nice of you." Penelope poured water into two metal bowls and set them on a blanket with piles of dog and cat treats for Jasper and Midnight.

"I texted Olivia earlier and asked her to bring more baggies of chocolate rocks for the kids. We're getting low."

Penelope peeked into the wicker basket by the cash box. "Oh, we're down to only two left. I hope she gets here soon."

"I'll text her again while I wait for the sandwiches. Be back in a few minutes."

"Tell Tessa I said hi and that I'll come by later to help her pack up."

"Will do." Clara sauntered toward the sandwich truck.

Louis Black launched the food truck five years earlier, and it was the first of its kind in Sierra Springs. He'd contemplated opening a physical location when his son, Jack, graduated from culinary school, but Louis told Penelope they enjoyed being food nomads and invested in more trucks instead. Each Spring Festival, LB's Deli stationed themselves at the entrance to the park, and each year, Clara and Penelope ordered the same Reuben sandwiches—Penelope's with extra dill slices and Clara's with a side of coleslaw.

"Hi, Penelope. The festival must be going well. Mom asked for more chocolate rocks." Olivia plunked a plastic tub overflowing with cute bags of candy on the table.

"Wow, Olivia, thanks. We're down to just two and have the entire afternoon to go." Penelope began refilling the wicker basket with her sister's sweet creations. She stuck a treat sack in her messenger bag, anticipating the need for a mid-afternoon sugar rush.

"I have something to show you." Olivia pulled a plastic bag off her arm and removed a pastry box.

Penelope peered through the clear top and squealed. "Petit fours! My favorite."

"I know!" Olivia pushed a box of crystals to the edge of the display table and gingerly set the box in its place.

"Thanks, you're the best sister I've ever had."

"I'm the only sister you've ever had." Olivia tossed a pile of napkins into Penelope's lap.

"Oh yeah. That's right." Penelope snapped her fingers. She opened the pastry box and inhaled the sweet aroma of cake and icing. "Oh, my gosh! You did it," she exclaimed as she examined the petit fours. Two dozen perfect, 3-inch-tall cylinders of fluffy cake, raspberry filling, and almond icing sat in rows on top of a pretty paisley parchment lining. Penelope could smell each layer. "These look just like Tessa's candles with the icing dripping down the sides. How cool!"

Olivia beamed. "I worked on them all day yesterday and Laurel sold out in under fifteen minutes during the dessert rush last night. I've got to get back to the cafe soon to make more for tonight."

Penelope snatched a petit four, popped it in her mouth, and reached for another one.

"Hey, only one. The rest are to sell!" Olivia smacked her sister's hand and quickly closed the box.

"Tell Laurel that I'm coming by to hang out after the festival. I have a feeling that I'm going to need some of that tipsy java if you get me." Penelope laughed through a mouthful of cake.

"Where's Mom? I was hoping to say hello."

"She went to get us sandwiches. She was also going to drop off some food for Tessa."

"Oh, where is Tessa?"

Penelope pointed to the rear of the park near the water fountain. "I feel bad for her. Jessie Hanlon is next to her and is in a nasty mood."

"Really? Jessie's usually nice. I wonder what's going on with her?"

"She practically attacked poor Tessa this morning, accusing her of trying to steal her customers with Robby's jewelry."

"Hmm, that's odd." Olivia placed one petit four on a napkin. "That's for mom."

"Can't I have one more?" Penelope asked, reaching for a second cake bite.

Olivia relented and opened the box, letting Penelope choose another. "You should eat your sandwich before dessert," Olivia scolded.

"Yes, ma'am. If you didn't want me to eat all your treats, you shouldn't have become a pastry chef," Penelope called as Olivia disappeared into the crowd.

***

Visitors swarmed the festival again after lunchtime. Children darted about in the dappled sunshine; their faces smeared blue and pink from the fluffy clouds of cotton candy grasped in sticky hands.

Penelope and Clara spent the afternoon helping customers at the tent and taking turns eating their sandwiches and petit fours.

"I think this is the busiest we've ever been at a Spring Festival opening day," Penelope said. "How was Tessa when you went to see her?"

"She was good. A little overwhelmed, which is why I stayed so long while she ate to give her a break. Her candles are a big hit. Everyone kept trying to buy the Amethyst Falls that she brought for display, but she was adamant that it was only for show until she and I could get a full line done with my raw crystals."

"Midnight and Jasper have certainly been entertainment for the customers today," Penelope said as the cat leaped through the air in pursuit of a runaway leaf.

Midnight was normally a relaxed cat, but on this spring day, he was running and playing like a toddler on a sugar high. Every acorn and dry leaf became an instant cat toy as he batted, swatted, chased, and leaped through the grass. One customer even gave him a bouncy ball that he found for sale at a toy vendor nearby. As the crowds wound down, Penelope looked around the tent and realized they had sold most of the crystal samples that they had brought. All the museum's rock and mineral kits were gone, and she was almost out of business cards.

As the late afternoon drew near, the crowds began filing out of the park and heading back to their cars with bags full of crafts, crystals, and food.

"I'm going to go check on Tessa and see if she needs any help packing up," Penelope said. "Do you think you can handle it here for a few minutes?"

"Sure thing, honey. Midnight, Jasper, and I will get things cleaned up." Clara surveyed the little merchandise left on the tables.

"Thanks. The car keys are in my messenger bag under the table if you need them." Penelope slipped around the table and headed toward Tessa's candle tent. She hoped her day went well since it was her first festival handling the candles and jewelry alone.

As Penelope neared Tessa's tent, she could see a sign hanging from the top banner that read 'Gone for a few minutes. Back soon.'

Penelope spun in a circle, slowing her gait. Perhaps Tessa was just off browsing at other vendors or moving her car closer for loading. As Penelope closed in on Tessa's tent, she noticed that most of the inventory was replaced, showing that Tessa had a successful day of sales. Something seemed off. An unexpected chill washed over Penelope, making her shiver.

"Tessa!" Penelope called as she entered the tent. Boxes Robby earlier stashed beneath the display tables sat stacked like soldiers at the back of the canopy. She glanced around and saw the cash box lying on the ground, open and empty.

"Jessie, where is Tessa?" Penelope hollered into the adjacent tent.

"How would I know?" Jessie retorted.

"You didn't notice that the vendor right next to you was gone? Someone took all the money from the cash box."

"I can't see through the tent flaps, and I didn't talk to her after this morning." Jessie was still yelling. Penelope wondered how Olivia was friends with someone so uncaring.

"Tessa!" Penelope slithered between the table and the boxes, feeling uneasy. "This isn't right," she muttered. As Penelope slipped through the opening, her foot caught on something hard, sending her tumbling to the ground.

"What was that?" Penelope rolled over on the grass. Tessa's body lay curled beneath the boxes, her lifeless eyes silently pleading for help.

Penelope screamed.

Chapter Four

Penelope scrambled to her hands and knees, lunging forward, toppling the empty boxes to the ground. As she pushed the bottom box, Penelope's heart skipped a beat. Tessa's pale body lay crumpled on the ground, crudely covered in partially crushed, cardboard. The toe of her boot escaping the box flap had caused Penelope's fall.

"Tessa!" Penelope shook her friend's shoulder. Tessa's entire body rocked. She had never seen a dead body in person, but Tessa's pale, cold skin looked worse than the corpses she had seen in horror movies. Tessa's eyes were open as if she were searching for someone.

Penelope scrambled to Tessa's side, rolling her flat. "Jessie, help!"

Jessie poked her head around the side flap. "What are you doing on the...oh my gosh. Is she okay?"

"No. Call 9-1-1." Penelope frantically pushed on Tessa's chest with the heel of her hand. Her brain flipped through the images of the CPR instruction manual from the class she took when she started working with kids at the museum. She couldn't think straight. Penelope's trembling fingers searched for a pulse on Tessa's neck.

Jessie yanked the phone from her back pocket. Penelope could hear words like 'help' and 'police,' but her mind was spinning.

Tessa never blinked. She never took a breath. Penelope never stopped compressions.

Shock was setting in and Penelope quaked. Jessie clasped Penelope's right hand and elbow, hauling her off the ground and onto a cold, gray metal chair in the booth's corner.

"I...I think she's dead." Penelope's eyes searched for Jessie to disagree, to say no, that Tessa was fine, and the ambulance was on the way.

Jessie simply nodded in agreement.

"How? You were right there all day?"

"I can't see in her booth unless I walk around to the front. I was helping customers all day." Jessie stared at Tessa. "The police will be here soon," she mumbled. "I should pack up."

"You're leaving?" Penelope watched Jessie sprint to her tent. The clatter of jewelry displays being thrown into boxes drifted through the still air. In less than a minute, Jessie wheeled a hand cart stacked with merchandise out of the front of her tent and hustled toward the vendor parking area as quickly as her stubby legs would move.

The blare of sirens snapped Penelope's attention back to Tessa. She texted Clara.

Tessa's tent—now!

***

Half of the Sierra Springs police force arrived at the festival in under ten minutes.

"I didn't expect so many cops to respond," Penelope said as the detective approached the tent. A crowd quickly gathered.

"Penelope?"

She stared at the detective for a split second before images of high school football games, chemistry class, and track practice flooded her brain. She gasped. "Ryan Snow." Penelope leaped from the chair and extended her hand before deciding to go for an awkward hug. Despite aging over ten years, he looked the same as he did in high school with his dirty blond hair still shaggy, the perfect frame for his deep green eyes.

"What are you doing here? I thought you lived in Maine," she said, releasing her grasp.

"I did, but I missed being near family. I just started as a detective with the Sierra Springs police yesterday." He turned toward Tessa.

"I wish I had run into you for a different reason. She's dead," Penelope pointed to Tessa's body.

Ryan instructed two of the officers to cordon off the area surrounding the tent and checked for a pulse on Tessa's neck. He looked to Penelope, "Is Jessie Hanlon here?"

"No. She left."

"Did you see what happened? Dispatch said that Jessie called in an accident."

"Yes. I came over to see if Tessa needed any help packing up and I found her like that." Penelope searched for her mother through the gawkers hovering around the police tape. She could use a genuine hug. "I tried to do CPR."

"Where is Jessie?"

"She was in the tent next door. I asked her to call 9-1-1, but I think seeing Tessa freaked her out, and she ran off toward the parking lot."

"Hmm." Ryan scribbled in his leather-bound pocket notebook.

Penelope pointed to the cash box. "It's empty."

The chaotic sound of the crowd gathering grew louder as a WAIY Channel News 2 van rolled along the pathway through the festival.

"How did they get here so fast?" Ryan slipped on a pair of latex gloves and picked up the cash box.

"They were already here reporting on the festival." Penelope watched as the weekend news anchor and a camera operator leaped from the van and sprinted toward the police tape.

Ryan called to the nearest patrolman. "Officer, can you push everyone back?"

The officer nodded and instructed the onlookers and reporter to move away as he strung additional neon yellow police barricade tape in a second circle around Tessa's tent area.

Ryan retrieved a plastic evidence bag from his pocket and gently placed the cash box inside. He inspected Tessa's body without touching potential evidence, then radioed the police station, asking for a crime scene unit and photographer to join him as quickly as possible.

"She looks familiar," Ryan commented.

"Tessa taught art classes at the high school when we were seniors, remember?"

Penelope could tell that Ryan had made the connection as his face softened. "Oh yeah. She was nice."

"She was. When I came back here after college, we became friends. Her store is across the street from my mother's." Penelope hadn't seen Ryan since the summer after high school graduation when the air between them shifted. Penelope suspected throughout school that Ryan had a crush on her, but he waited until that summer to say so and when Penelope said that she wasn't willing to break up with her boyfriend, Ryan disappeared into college and out of Penelope's life.

Penelope sank into the corner chair as the detective found a second seat and settled beside her. As the shock of finding Tessa wore off, Penelope's body relaxed, allowing tears to fall. Ryan pulled a handkerchief from his shirt pocket and handed it to her.

"Can you tell me everything that you remember? Start with the first time that you saw Tessa today and take me through finding her body."

"I'm not sure how much help I can be. I saw her and Robby here this morning when they were setting up. Robby was leaving Tessa to handle the booth alone, and I wanted to help, but we were so swamped with customers today that I couldn't get back here to check in on her until a few minutes ago."

"Robby is her husband?"

"Yes. Robby McCaul. He owns a jewelry store. We have to tell him."

"I'll notify him when we're done." Ryan scribbled in his notebook. "You had a tent here, too?"

"Yes. My mother's rock shop always has a tent, and I help her. She lets me give out materials about the natural history museum where I work. Mom saw Tessa at lunch. She brought her a sandwich since she was working alone."

"Okay, I'll have to interview her, too."

"She should be here somewhere." Penelope gazed at the crowd, her eyes blurring from her tears.

"So, you came back here when the festival was wrapping up and that's when you found her?"

"That's when I *tripped* over her." Penelope moaned. "She was right there under all those boxes. It was awful." Penelope's body was exhausted. The shock of adrenaline from finding Tessa's body was wearing off, and the horror was setting in.

Ryan reached for Penelope's hand and squeezed it. She squeezed back, slightly comforted, but her heart felt shattered.

"Penelope!" Clara was jogging toward her daughter, waving wildly. Her jog was more of a fast waddle.

"Here comes your mom." Ryan stood. He motioned for the officers to let Clara into the taped area.

"This is just terrible." Clara hurried toward Penelope and Ryan. Midnight and Jasper trailed behind, attached to long leashes. Clara pulled her daughter into a suffocating hug. "I can't believe that you found her. Are you okay?"

"Yes, Mom, I'm fine." Penelope rubbed her hands across her face. She wasn't used to finding the dead body of a friend. "How did you already know that I found her? I didn't tell you that."

"Oh, honey, the Sierra Springs gossip train has already left the station." Clara fastened her gaze to the detective. "Ryan? Ryan Snow, is that you?"

Ryan nodded. "Yes, Ms. Lake. It's good to see you." A puzzled expression glanced across his face as he watched the sweater and cape-clad pets settle at Clara's feet.

"Your mom didn't tell me you were back in town." Clara gripped Ryan's arm.

"It just happened recently. I was working in Maine and an opening for a detective came up here and I jumped at the chance to get back home."

"Well, that's wonderful, and you look fabulous." Clara eyed his six-foot one-inch frame.

"Mom. Stop." Penelope shook her head. "Tessa's dead."

"You've had a shock, sweety. Calm down and breathe. You need to center yourself. Besides, Ryan here looks delicious, and you're single now."

Penelope looked at Ryan and mouthed, "I'm sorry."

She could sense that her mother's wildly inappropriate comments were her way of keeping Penelope from sliding further into shock. As awkward as Clara made Penelope's reunion with Ryan, it had worked. The wooziness subsided, and Penelope felt stronger. Her mother was right. Even through her blurry, tear-filled eyes, Ryan was a welcome sight during one of the most horrific moments of her life.

Penelope took a deep breath. "Alright, Mother, leave Ryan alone. We have to figure out who killed Tessa." Now was not the time to fall apart, she told herself. Her logical, puzzle-solving brain took over. She needed to be tough and find out who would want Tessa dead.

Ryan's head swiveled. "You mean I must figure out how she died. Not we. Me. And I don't know for sure that she was murdered. It could have been natural causes."

"No way. Tessa was murdered. I tripped over her foot because there were boxes stacked over her body. She couldn't have done that herself. Plus, someone stole her money."

Ryan nodded. "I'll agree with you. It's suspicious. But that's all I'll agree to."

Penelope and Clara stood watching the police scour the area for clues. Soon, the ambulance arrived to transfer Tessa's body to the morgue. Dr. Beatrice Long and her technician hurried from the ambulance with a stretcher between them. They approached Tessa's body with practiced efficiency, their faces somber but professional. Dr. Long was the most popular family physician in Sierra Springs, and she pulled double duty as the county medical examiner, appointed by the Chief Medical Examiner in Raleigh over twenty years ago.

"We need to document everything before we move her," Dr. Long said, pulling a camera from her bag and handing it to the technician. He carefully photographed Tessa's position and the immediate surroundings, ensuring a visual record for the investigation. Dr. Long spoke quietly with Ryan near the crime scene tape furthest from the reporters. Penelope strained to hear the conversation, but she could barely make out a few random words.

"Beatrice," Clara called. Dr. Long flashed a comforting glance at Penelope and her mother as if she was reassuring them she would take good care of Tessa. Clara and Beatrice were childhood friends, and Penelope knew her well. Beatrice took her job seriously and would do nothing that could jeopardize finding Tessa's killer.

"Come on, Mom. Let's let them work." Penelope pulled her mother to a corner of the tent, never moving her eyes from Tessa.

Dr. Long donned a pair of latex gloves and began collecting trace evidence from Tessa's clothing and exposed skin, using sterile swabs, and placing each sample in indi-

vidually labeled evidence bags. She paid particular attention to Tessa's hands, scraping under the nails for potential
DNA evidence.

"There's some unusual residue on the sleeve of her
dress," Dr. Long said, gesturing for Ryan to come closer.
"We'll make sure the lab analyzes it thoroughly."

After the initial evidence collection, they carefully lifted
Tessa onto the stretcher, taking care not to disturb her position more than necessary. The technician secured a paper
bag over each of Tessa's hands, protecting any additional
evidence that might be present, and then zipped her into a
plastic body bag, preserving her dignity even in death.

As they prepared to place Tessa on the stretcher, Dr.
Long turned to the detective. "We'll preserve her clothing
and personal effects for your team at the morgue. I will
conduct a more thorough examination for trace evidence
during the autopsy."

Penelope could hear the stretcher's wheels squeak as the
technician secured Tessa's body for the trip across town.
The finality suddenly felt like a weight on Penelope's
shoulders. "I was having the best day I've ever had at the
festival, and I came over here and found my friend murdered. It's just unbelievable." Tears inched down Penelope's face. "This doesn't seem real."

"Honey, you don't know she was murdered. Maybe she
just was sick and died of natural causes, like Ryan said."
Clara put her arms around her daughter's shoulders.

It surprised Penelope that her mother would consider
someone in their late thirties able to die of natural causes
without warning. "Seriously, Mom, I've seen enough TV
shows to know that nobody dies a natural death and hides

their own body underneath a bunch of boxes with a 'Back Soon' sign hung on the tent to keep people away."

"What do you think, Ryan?" Clara asked as he returned from speaking with the officers, instructing them to pack up the contents of Tessa's tent.

"It's too soon to know anything." Ryan closed his notebook. "You should both go home. I'll need formal statements from you both tomorrow. You can come to the station, or I can come to your homes."

Penelope shrugged. "Okay, but I don't know what else I can tell you. Tessa was fine this morning, even with Robby having to work at his store."

"And she seemed to handle everything fine at lunch." Clara rubbed her daughter's arm. "Has anybody told Robby?"

"I have officers out looking for him now, but—"

"Tessa!" Robby screamed as he ran. The closer he got, the more Penelope could see the tears streaming down his face. Robby's eyes were red and puffy. Two police officers followed close on his heels.

As Robby staggered toward the tent, Ryan grasped him by the shoulders. The officers packing the tent contents jumped to Ryan's side, helping to restrain Robby as he fought their grip. "You can't go near her. Let the medical examiner take care of her."

Robby struggled to push his way toward Tessa. He strained to see past the officers as Dr. Long and her technician rolled Tessa away on the stretcher.

"I have to see her. What happened?" The waterfall of tears steadily poured down Robby's face. His visible pain made Penelope hurt inside.

A pair of young officers arrived on the scene. They seemed too young to be in the police force. When Penelope looked closely at them, she could tell that they were identical twins. And both were completely out of breath.

"We're sorry, Detective," one twin said. "We found him near the parking lot. When he saw the lights, he freaked out and started running before we could even talk to him."

"That's okay, guys. I've got it from here. Why don't you help the other officers pack up all the merchandise from the tent? We need to take it all as evidence." Ryan was still holding onto Robby, who teetered as if he might collapse. The officers disappeared into the tent.

"Let me get you a chair, Robby." Clara dragged a folding chair across the grass and eased him into the seat. Penelope sat on the ground, rubbing his hand.

She and Clara exchanged glances as the ambulance drove away, its lights flashing silently. Penelope knew that Tessa's last journey might hold the key to unraveling this mysterious tragedy that had befallen their quiet town.

Clara pulled Jasper and Midnight close and drifted into Tessa's tent unnoticed.

"We're going to find out what happened to Tessa," Penelope promised. Anguish blanketed Robby's face, making Penelope's heart ache. Murders happen in books and on television. Not in real life to her friends. The day felt surreal, like an impossible dream, and Penelope hoped she would soon wake up in her bed. Her logical mind knew better. The friend that she talked to just a few short hours before was gone.

Ryan crouched beside Robby. "Mr. McCaul, I promise I will do my best to solve this. I'm going to need you to come to the police station and make a formal statement at some point soon. But I need to ask you a couple of questions before we leave the festival."

Robby nodded. "What can I tell you?"

"Do you know anyone who would have wanted to harm Tessa?"

"No. Everybody loves, er.... loved Tessa."

"And when did you leave the festival today?"

"I helped Tessa set up the booth, but then I had some business to take care of and she said she could handle the sales for the day by herself, so I left before the crowds started showing up around seven forty-five." Robby looked at Penelope.

Penelope interjected, "I was here when Robby left this morning. Tessa had everything under control. She might have been a little nervous because she's never done the festival alone before, but she knows how to handle customers, so I figured she'd be fine."

Ryan scribbled in his notebook again, and Penelope wondered what he was writing.

"Why don't you ride to the station with me, Robby? We can get your statement over with. You'll be more comfortable that way, and we can get you something to drink and eat."

"Okay." Robby turned to Penelope. "Will you come, too?"

"Sure."

Ryan and Penelope pulled Robby to standing and slung his arms around their shoulders.

Clara rambled around the inside of the tent, impeding the officers who were packing the merchandise. She pulled the Amethyst Falls from the tall display, holding it close.

"Ma'am, please leave the area and let us finish," one twin said. Clara sighed and stepped out of the tent, wrapping her long cardigan around her waist.

"What can I do?" Clara asked as she watched Penelope and Ryan struggle to keep Robby upright.

"Will you take care of Jasper?" Penelope asked over her shoulder.

"No problem." Clara pulled tight on the leashes.

As they slowly trudged toward Ryan's cruiser, images of boxes, candles, jewelry, Jessie, and Tessa's lifeless body flipped through Penelope's mind. Her stomach churned. She tried to calm her mind as she did before a competition or big presentation. She had to be strong for Robby now.

As they helped him to the police cruiser, Penelope was thankful she lifted weights. They practically carried Robby to the squad car, making the hundred-meter walk feel much farther. Ryan opened the back door of the cruiser, and Penelope guided Robby into the waiting seat and locked the belt around his waist. Robby stared straight ahead; his eyes clouded with tears.

"Sit up front with me, Penelope." Ryan opened the front passenger door.

Penelope slumped into the leather-bound passenger seat, her curiosity piqued by the unfamiliar surroundings. The leather seat crackled beneath her as she adjusted her position, taking in the array of gadgets and gizmos that adorned the dashboard.

A chunky laptop was mounted to her left, its screen glowing with a map of Sierra Springs. The radio crackled softly, spewing occasional bursts of police jargon that sounded like a foreign language to her ears.

A tiny pair of running shoes hanging from the rearview mirror caught her eye. It was an unexpected touch of whimsy in an otherwise serious vehicle. A clipboard rested between the seats, filled with forms and notes in a hasty scrawl.

She noticed a thermos of coffee wedged into a cup holder, the faint aroma of hazelnut wafting through the air. A half-eaten tuna sandwich sat on a napkin nearby—evidence of the detective's interrupted dinner.

"Yuck. It smells like a rotten fish in here." Penelope covered her nose as the overwhelming stench of tuna and coffee invaded her nostrils.

"Sorry, I was on a break when I got the call. I didn't have time to throw the second half of my sandwich away." Ryan grabbed the open sandwich and wrapped the foil tightly, halting the assault of fish and mayonnaise on Penelope's sense of smell.

"That reminds me of high school bus rides to track meets and you would bring that awful tuna salad." Penelope smiled, a fleeting break in her thoughts about Tessa.

As Ryan started the engine, the car hummed to life around her. The car ride quickly became silent as Ryan guided the police car through the parking lot littered with cars and looky-loos trying to get a glimpse of the hubbub at the candle tent. The crowd was slow to move, so Ryan flashed his lights. *Whoop*, the siren cried through the somber air.

Penelope couldn't help but feel a mix of excitement and trepidation. This was certainly not how she had planned to spend her Saturday evening, but she hoped that by tagging along with Ryan and Robby, she might learn something that could help her solve her friend's murder.

"So, what do you think?" Penelope leaned toward Ryan and tried not to touch any of the buttons and switches on the console between them.

"I think you're a witness, not my partner. I've got this. Trust me."

"I can help you. I came back right after college. I know lots of people in town." Penelope turned to check on Robby. His eyes were open, but his mind seemed to be shut down.

"Penelope, I've got this," Ryan repeated.

"I just want to help. I could be your partner. Do you have a partner?"

Ryan's eyes widened. "Um. No. I'm going to be working with An..., uh, the new chief for now."

"The new chief?"

"Yeah, uh. Didn't you hear that Chief Wilson retired to Hawaii with his secretary a couple of weeks ago?"

"No. How did I not hear about that?" Penelope had been so busy locked away in her laboratory, working on her new rock display for the gala that the town gossip had completely missed her.

"You don't know who the new chief is?"

"No. Who?"

A sudden cry from the back seat was met with the guttural sound of spewing vomit.

The stench hit Penelope like a wave, sharp and acrid, filling the air with a nauseating intensity. It was a foul cocktail of sour milk and rotten eggs, tinged with the bitter tang of bile. Penelope's fingers scrambled to roll down her window before she revisited her lunch.

Ryan hit the gas, and the cruiser sped through the Sierra Springs streets.

Chapter Five

Penelope was relieved when the police station came into view. She sprang onto the sidewalk and gulped a huge breath of fresh air as the car came to an abrupt stop. The police station was housed in an immense building with the other town government offices.

The Sierra Springs Municipal Building loomed over Park Street, its weathered stone facade a stark contrast to the lush green hills surrounding it. Perched atop a gentle slope, the three-story structure bore the weight of small-town governance with quiet dignity.

Wide stone steps led up to heavy oak doors, flanked by stacked stone columns, their inevitable patina a reminder of the town's history. A weathered bronze plaque declared the building's construction date as 1932. Newly budded rhododendron lined the building's base, their evergreen leaves a year-round reminder of the town's natural beauty. Penelope wondered if the landscape architect who designed the building's foliage thought twice about the toxicity of the leaves.

The expansive parking lot sprawled below, its asphalt surface crisscrossed with faded white lines and dotted with the occasional oil stain—each mark a silent testament to the comings and goings of the town's citizens. Winding concrete sidewalks snaked their way up the hill, offering a less steep alternative to the main staircase.

The roof, a patchwork of faded green copper and newer, brighter sections, hinted at years of necessary repairs. Dormer windows peeked out from the sloped surface, their panes reflecting the late afternoon sun like winking eyes. As evening approached, warm light spilled from the windows, and the old clock tower atop the building chimed the hour, its sonorous tones echoing across the town.

Penelope consulted the building and engineering departments when they were planning to blast through the mountainside to create fresh cuts through the rock to build new hiking trails or roads. Her expertise in geology ensured that new construction didn't trigger a landslide, jeopardizing the residents living among the hills. She spent many hours in the building over the years, but never under such somber circumstances.

The interior of the Sierra Springs Municipal Building was a study in contrasts, its two halves as different as night and day. Upon entering, visitors found themselves in a spacious foyer with soaring ceilings and gleaming marble floors. A central information desk, manned by a jovial receptionist, served as the building's nerve center. To the left, a wide corridor led to the various government offices, to the right, a set of secure doors marked the entrance to the police station.

The government side exuded an air of faded grandeur. Wood-paneled walls lined corridors that echoed with the click of sensible shoes on linoleum. The scent of old paper and coffee permeated the air. Frosted glass doors bore the name of each department, including City Planning, Engineering, Tax Assessor, and Parks and Recreation. Despite attempts at modernization, an undercurrent of small-town charm persisted in the creaky filing cabinets and vintage wall clocks.

Contrarily, the police station side bristled with modern security. Reinforced doors required not just a key card, but also a fingerprint scan for entry. The atmosphere here was more clinical, with stark white walls, fluorescent lighting, and the low hum of computers. A bullpen of desks occupied the center, surrounded by interrogation rooms, evidence lockers, and corner offices for the detectives and chief. The faint smell of gun oil mingled with that of stale coffee.

Throughout the building, key card readers flanked every door, their small red lights a constant reminder of the separation between public and private spaces. Even the elevators required proper clearance to access certain floors.

Despite the security measures, there was an undeniable small-town feel to the place. Personal touches, including family photos on desks, a dartboard in the break room, and hand-knitted quilts draped over the backs of chairs, hinted at the close-knit community that worked within these walls.

As day turned to evening, the building gradually emptied, leaving behind only the evening shift at the police station and the ever-present purr of electronics, along with the occasional creak of old pipes and the whisper of secrets hidden in dusty filing cabinets.

Ryan led Robby into the conference room at the end of a long hallway lined with pictures of the police chiefs throughout the town's history. His legs were much steadier by the time they had arrived at the station. The realization of Tessa's death seemed to seep into Robby's consciousness. Penelope watched him from the doorway, exhausted after a day of selling at the fair and then finding one of her friends dead. She felt a tinge of selfishness for thinking about herself when Robby's pain was so visible.

Ryan asked Penelope to wait in his office while he spoke with Robby alone. Just a few doors down, she sank into a black linen-covered chair. A young officer brought her a cup of coffee with milk and sugar. Penelope thanked him and took a generous, slow sip. She winced. The small cup held at least four sugar packets. Still, she appreciated the caffeine and warmth while she waited.

Penelope pulled her phone from her pocket and texted Laurel.

Penelope: I'm at the police station sitting in Detective Ryan Snow's office. Yes, THAT Ryan from high school.

Laurel: OMG! What did you do?

Penelope realized her mistake.

Penelope: Nothing. Haven't you heard?

Laurel: No.

Penelope: I found Tessa dead in her tent.

Penelope watched the ellipses dance on the screen. She could feel the anxiety rising from the pit of her stomach again.

Laurel: What? What are you talking about?

Penelope was mid-way through typing a lengthy reply when her phone rang.

"What happened?" Laurel demanded.

Penelope's mind flipped through a carousel of images surrounding the moment she found Tessa. "Laurel, it was awful. I went to see if Tessa was going to need any help to close up her tent and I literally tripped over her."

Penelope's mind thought in puzzle pieces. Her early field workdays as a geologist taught Penelope to find pieces of information and solve the mystery. The truth of what a rock formation looks like is often hidden under years of dirt accumulation covered by grass and tree growth. You find the outcrops, those rare spots where boulders poke their head out at the surface. You take a sample, test it, learn from it, and put each piece of information together, ultimately showing you the bigger picture. The outcrops of information surrounding Tessa's murder were scarce for now.

"That's terrible! Are you okay?" Laurel's voice pitched higher.

"I'm fine, but Robby showed up. He had a complete breakdown. I feel horrible for him."

"Where is he now?"

"He's in the conference room, talking with Ryan." Penelope set the phone on speaker and laid it on her knee. She rubbed her temples, slumping back in the chair.

"How did she die? She wasn't very old."

"It wasn't natural. I'm certain she was murdered."

Penelope could hear Laurel gasp.

The line went silent. Penelope tried to piece together the few clues she had, but nothing fit. Yet her methodical brain and dogged loyalty took over. She was determined to find the killer.

Laurel broke the silence. "Tell me everything."

"Someone emptied her cash box." Penelope took another sip of the sugary coffee.

"She was killed in a robbery in broad daylight?"

"I guess. That seems awfully daring though," Penelope's voice trailed off.

"Hey P, have you run into anyone else at the police station?"

"Just other police officers. Why?"

"There's something that I have been needing to tell you all week and I haven't been able to figure out how, but now that you're there, you need to know."

Penelope could detect the nervousness in her friend's voice. "Laurel, you are freaking me out."

"Andre is back in town. And he's the new police chief." Laurel raced through the words so quickly that Penelope was unsure if she heard correctly.

"What? Why didn't you tell me?" A shiver washed through Penelope's body from her head to her toes. Her hands suddenly felt clammy as her heart raced. She glanced at her running watch and saw her heart rate spike.

Ryan stepped through the door. "Are you ready for me to take your statement now?"

"I got to go. We'll talk later." Penelope cut off the call and shoved the phone into her pocket as she rose from the chair. "Uh, huh."

Ryan closed the door and sat behind his desk, and motioned for Penelope to sit. "The new Chief of Police is already pressuring me to solve this as quickly as possible."

"You mean Andre is pressuring you? Laurel just told me." Penelope rarely had control of her facial expressions, and she was sure that Ryan saw a mix of anger, hurt, surprise, and shock all rolled into one. This day was getting worse and worse.

"I'm sorry. I started to say something earlier, but I wasn't sure if you knew or what I could say. I heard through the grapevine that things didn't end well between you." Ryan's eyes focused on his notebook.

Penelope cleared her throat. "Well. Now. That is an understatement." Penelope sat up straight in her chair, feet together and hands clasped in her lap. She was still shaking and desperately wanted to stop. Immediately.

"Are you okay with giving your statement now?" Ryan turned on his cell phone recorder.

"Yes, I'm just a little overwhelmed. But I'm fine. I need to do this for Tessa."

"All right, Miss Lake, take me through your day at the festival." Ryan spoke in his official police investigator's voice.

Penelope's nerves immediately subsided, and she leaned back in her chair. "Miss Lake? Since when am I, Miss Lake?"

Ryan stopped the recording. "While I take your statement. You can go back to being Penelope after we finish." He started a new recording and repeated his question.

Penelope sat upright. "Okay, Detective Snow, this is what happened."

For exactly twenty minutes, Penelope recounted every step of her day, from the minute she woke up to the time she reached the gem shop to the second she arrived at the festival with her mother to set up their tent and merchandise. She looked at her watch and tried to estimate the exact time when she walked to Tessa's tent and saw Robby and her setting up for the day. Ryan wanted as many details as Penelope could remember, but when she woke up that morning, giving a minute-by-minute statement about her day was not on her to-do list. There was only so much she could recall.

Ryan filled four pages in his notebook. When they finished, he said an assistant would type up her statement and asked that she return the next day to sign it.

As Penelope rose and turned toward the door to his office, Ryan jumped from his seat and cleared his throat.

"You're anxious. You need to go home, have a glass of wine, and watch a movie. Don't think about anything that happened today."

She closed her eyes for just a moment. How nice it would be to curl on her couch underneath her warm, weighted blanket with Jasper, watch one of her favorite shows, and forget that today ever happened. "I think I'll do just that, Ryan."

Penelope heard herself lying. She did trust Ryan. They were close friends in high school, but he had been gone since they were eighteen and he was the one who made a clean break. Even though Tessa and Robby were almost ten years older, Penelope felt more connected to them than to Ryan at this moment.

Ryan guided Penelope through the station halls. The layout was a mirror image of the engineering department that Penelope often visited. The stark walls did nothing to elevate Penelope's mood.

"Do you still run?" he asked. "Maybe we could go jogging sometime."

Penelope wondered if Ryan was trying to distract her from the day's events or if he was simply trying to renew their friendship. "I do. I've started doing aquathlons."

"What's that?"

"It's like a triathlon with no biking. You run, then swim, and then run again, or sometimes just swim and run. I run with a running group some days and I train with the master's swim team at the rec pool." Penelope's eyes darted up and down the hallway. She didn't want to be caught unaware if Andre was nearby.

"That sounds ambitious." Ryan smiled. At that moment, Penelope realized how much she had missed her friend.

"It's fun. I've always liked both sports." Penelope turned and gave Ryan a quick hug as they reached the door to the lobby. She pushed the lock release button on the wall. The automatic door revealed Laurel pacing the waiting area.

"I figured you would need a ride," she said. "Are you okay?" She clamped Penelope in a bear hug.

"I'm fine." Penelope wiggled free.

"Hi, Laurel," Ryan interjected.

"Hi, Ryan. Penelope says you're a detective here now."

"Yeah, I just started yesterday."

"Come on, Penelope, let's get you home. Bye, Ryan. We'll catch up sometime." Laurel clutched Penelope's forearm and hurried her toward the front door.

Penelope turned and gave a silent wave to Ryan.

Laurel flung open the oak door and almost ran them both headfirst into a man reaching for the door handle. He jumped back.

"Hey, sis! Oh, uh. Hi, Penelope," Andre Beaumont said quietly. "I figured you had already left."

"Andre." Penelope gulped, unable to form additional words at the sight of her ex-boyfriend. Penelope stared at his chiseled features. Her body shivered as an icy wave rushed through her veins, leaving her flushed. Andre looked identical to the last time Penelope saw him. Her sporadic glimpses into his social media accounts paled in comparison. A flood of emotions sprang from her heart and brain all at once. Hurt. Love. Heartbreak. Sadness.

"We were just leaving," Laurel said quickly. "I'm taking Penelope home."

Laurel rushed Penelope down the stone steps and ushered her into the parking lot. Penelope stopped in the middle of a sea of police cruisers, yanking her arm free of Laurel's tight grip.

"He knew we were here?"

"I texted him and told him to stay away." Laurel winced. "I'm so sorry. I've done such a good job, until now, keeping you two apart."

"Until now?"

"You know. Holidays. His move back last week," Laurel's voice quieted.

"Last week?" Anxiety swirled through Penelope's body, lodging itself deep in her belly. When she awoke this morning, she thought her Saturday would be a fun day hanging out at the festival with her mother, selling a few rocks and tickets to the gala, and then going for drinks at The Tipsy Java. Instead, she had tripped over her dead friend's body, been questioned by the police, and almost physically ran into the love of her life...the one who got away trampling her heart. She wanted to go home. Penelope resented Laurel hadn't warned her of Andre's permanent return to town.

"I realize I should have told you." Laurel's eyes pleaded for forgiveness.

"You bet you should have told me. Your brother. My ex-boyfriend. My first love who crushed my heart, moved back to town, and you didn't tell me? You let me literally almost run into him!" Penelope wiped her hand down her face. She was a little surprised at her own reaction. She wanted to throw up. Could it be that after all these years, she was still in love with Andre? She hoped not.

Laurel groaned. "I know! What can I do to make it up to you?"

"You owe me Tipsy coffee." Penelope let out a deep breath. "Lots of it."

"As much as you want."

Penelope couldn't stay mad at her best friend. Especially after today. "Let's go. I'm exhausted." Penelope spun around, looking for Laurel's car.

Laurel locked arms with her friend and guided her to the back of the parking lot. "I am so sorry P. He's my brother and I love him, but I wish he hadn't been such a jerk to my best friend. Although... that was a long time ago," Laurel added quietly.

"It's okay. Nothing that happened between me and Andre was your fault. And you're right. I should be over him. I thought I was over him. This is the first time I've seen him in person in years and I just wasn't ready." Penelope winced. She paused. *It can't be*, she thought.

"Am I forgiven?" Laurel pulled her car key from her jeans pocket.

"I think I'm not over him." Penelope let her head fall backward. The evening stars were peeking through the clouds.

Laurel grinned. "Do you want me to tell you he asked me how you were doing?"

Penelope cast an inquisitive glance at Laurel. "No. Yes. He did? He looked good. Oof. I hate myself for thinking that. I'm still mad at him for breaking up with me the way he did."

"You guys were together for five years. That's understandable."

"But most of that time, he was in college in Colorado, I was in high school, and then at UNC. I know I should let it go. Seriously though, he broke up with me by text." Penelope could still remember the moment the text arrived. She expected Andre to send his flight information so that she could pick him up at the airport for a fun weekend together, but instead, it was a ten-word breakup.

Andre: The distance is too hard. I found someone else. Sorry.

Penelope had sat on her bed staring at the phone, her entire body trembling. She was too stunned to cry. Penelope remembered copying the text and sending it to Laurel, who was quick to scold her brother. Since then, Penelope never had a relationship that lasted more than a few months.

"Yeah, I let him have it for that." Laurel squeezed the key fob, and the car chirped as the doors unlocked.

"I appreciate that."

"I'm glad that his stupidity never came between us."

"That would never happen. I know it's been hard on you having to compartmentalize us." Over the years, Olivia and Clara warned her when Andre was in town visiting. Laurel never tried to force them to see one another.

"He's my brother. Your ex. But since he is in charge of the police, we're stuck with him being in town now. And it *has* been a long time since you guys broke up. I hope you guys can be friends."

"Humph. Maybe," Penelope replied, shaking her head. "I'll work on it." Penelope slipped into the front passenger seat of Laurel's car, bumping her head on the roof. "Geez,

I appreciate you're environmentally conscious, but do you have to drive such a teeny tiny car?" Penelope rubbed her head.

"You're the one with the earth science degree. I would think that you would be in favor of compact cars. They don't use too much gas or have too many emissions. You should think about that as you drive that massive Hummer around."

"Hmm," Penelope grunted. She was too tired and upset to worry about her car now. She closed her eyes as Laurel whizzed along the road toward her house.

The women sat in silence, although Penelope could sense Laurel wanted to talk more. She just didn't have the energy to discuss Andre again but couldn't stop herself from asking.

"What Laurel?" Penelope opened her eyes. She watched the dashed lines on the roadway fly by.

"Was it awful finding Tessa?" Laurel stared at the road ahead.

Penelope detected tears in Laurel's eyes and fought back her own. She had held her emotions together for the past few hours and Penelope didn't want to lose control now.

"Yes. But I really don't want to talk about it anymore tonight." She flipped on the radio.

A nineties grunge band droned on. Penelope gazed into the side mirror, listening to the sad guitar chords. She had never liked grunge music but did not have the energy to change the station, as the gravity of the day weighed on her. While Laurel wove through the street, Penelope spotted a black sport utility vehicle taking the same turns behind them. She wondered what kind of car it was with a thick, smiling grill, slanted slits for headlights, and dark tinted windows. She squinted into the rearview mirror, trying to read the logo emblem, but she could barely make out a shape that looked like a rectangle with bumpy edges.

"Huh." Penelope's stomach turned as she remembered seeing a similar-looking car parked in the back corner of the lot at the police station.

"Huh, what?" Laurel glanced at Penelope.

"Hey, Laurel, can you take Sycamore Street to my house?"

"That's longer. Why?"

"Just turn." Penelope pointed to the perpendicular road ahead.

"Okay." Laurel hooked a quick right.

Penelope kept her eyes fixated on the rearview mirror. The headlights turned behind them, making the pit of her stomach queasy. "Laurel, I think we're being followed."

Laurel's gaze darted between her mirrors. "What do you mean, being followed?"

Penelope glanced back to the road. Kids were playing basketball under the streetlights. The SUV eased past the children.

"I saw that SUV in the police station parking lot, and it has made our last three turns. Have you ever seen a car like that?"

Laurel glanced in the mirror. "Looks fancy, but there are a lot of SUVs in town." She took another left turn, followed by a right and another quick right and a left, zigzagging her way to Penelope's house. "Why would someone follow us?" The evening light surrendered to overwhelming darkness, reducing the black SUV to merely a pair of glowing headlights.

"Good question. But they didn't take that last turn. They're gone," Penelope said, checking the mirrors.

"I think you're just being paranoid because you've had a stressful day."

"Maybe I'm just so tired I'm just seeing things." Penelope rubbed her eyes, unable to shake the haunting sensation of someone watching from afar.

Laurel slowed to a stop in front of Penelope's house. "Your lights are on."

"Mom dropped Jasper off."

"Come by the cafe tomorrow for brunch. I'll have mimosas ready."

"Sounds good. Thanks for the ride home." Penelope got out of the car and watched her friend zip down the road.

As she retreated to her house, she could see Jasper waiting for her in the window. Thankfully, Clara left the Hummer in the driveway and her keys under the welcome mat. She turned a key in the solid wooden door as an engine revved down the street. Penelope whirled around just as the smiling grill of a black SUV sped away from the intersection.

Chapter Six

Penelope woke Sunday morning, feeling drained. The excitement and horror of Saturday's festival weighed on her mind. She was up late texting her mother to reassure Clara that she was okay and telling Olivia the details of Andre's return to town.

Penelope omitted the mysterious SUV that followed her home. Laurel believed that Penelope seeing the SUV behind them was just a coincidence, so she promised to put it out of her mind. But her attention kept falling back to the thick, grinning grill that led to the ominous headlamps. *A little online investigating couldn't hurt*, she thought.

With Jasper fed and the coffee brewed, Penelope cracked open her laptop and let her fingers do some searching. Every automaker had some sort of black SUV in their lineup, and a lot of cars had thick grills that looked like the Cheshire Cat.

Penelope heard an engine rev as Jasper sprang to the front living room window, releasing a low growl that sounded more like a lion than a puppy.

"What's wrong, Jasper?"

A black blur flew away from the curb as Penelope peeled back the curtain. She snapped the fabric panels over the window and drew them tightly together. "You've got to be kidding me," she muttered. After checking the locks on the doors and windows, she texted Laurel asking if she was already working at The Tipsy Java.

Penelope did not wait for a reply from her best friend. In under five minutes, she dressed and bolted out the door with Jasper tucked tightly under her arm.

The Tipsy Java was packed from six o'clock in the morning to midnight every day with its cozy interior of lime-washed walls the color of honey and heavy walnut and wrought-iron tables. The coffee bar showed off the latest espresso gadgets and flavorings while the corner pastry cases made customers hungry with delectable aromas that rivaled the stunning presentation. Slate menu boards advertised the latest specials in colorful chalk.

Penelope had an unspoken, permanent reservation on the leather-cushioned stool at the end of the coffee bar. She sank onto the chair and slung her burgundy canvas messenger bag over the backrest. The bag was well-worn from years in the field, but Penelope could not let it go. Her messenger bag had been through some of the toughest terrain and was her trusted companion for carrying maps and rock samples through the mountains and across more than a few streams. It was her safety blanket, of sorts. Penelope waved at Laurel to catch her attention.

Jasper nestled between the chair legs and quickly closed her eyes. Most Husky puppies are hard to train, but Jasper was surprisingly docile unless Midnight was nearby. Laurel shoved a steaming mug of Penelope's favorite drink in front of her. She had spent almost every night in this very spot since Laurel opened The Tipsy Java.

Penelope and Laurel became best friends in sixth grade. It surprised their friends and families when Penelope attended the University of North Carolina at Chapel Hill for college and Laurel stayed closer to home at the local campus in Asheville. But the across-state distance never dulled their friendship, and neither had Penelope's rotten breakup with Laurel's older brother. They were as close in college as they had been in high school and remained inseparable while growing their careers in the hometown they loved.

"You alright?" Laurel asked, leaning over the hand-carved walnut counter. "Are you sure that you saw the black SUV again this morning?"

"I can't be one hundred percent. I just saw a flash of something big, black, and shiny." Penelope wrapped her hands around the thick mug and took a slow sip. The warm liquid always calmed her, and Laurel knew just how to fix her favorite espresso chai vanilla latte.

"Let's go sit away from listening ears and you can tell me everything." Laurel turned toward the young man working the cash register. "Tristan, can you take care of things up here for me for a minute while I go talk to Penelope?"

"Sure thing, Laurel. Hey, Penelope." His short and fluffy dark hair and piercing electric blue eyes enhanced Tristan's youthful appearance and brightened his olive complexion.

Penelope smiled at him as she slid off the stool and made her way to the corner table by the side windows. Tristan had only one semester left in college, but his baby face made him seem much younger and the high school girls in town often flocked around him. Laurel credited much of her before-and-after-school income to Tristan's presence in the coffee shop.

Even on a Sunday, the closest tables to the register were filled with two groups of giggling girls pretending to study for final exams.

"These girls are going to be sad when they realize he has a boyfriend," Laurel whispered as she snatched a plate of pastries from the end of the bar.

"And when they realize that he's almost twenty-three years old!" Penelope snapped her fingers at Jasper, who jumped to attention.

The girls settled into overstuffed dining chairs and spent a few minutes critiquing the cranberry scones, a potentially fresh addition to the menu. Jasper followed the girls to their new spot and settled in beside them, whimpering until Penelope handed her a piece of pastry. The small talk did little to lighten Penelope's mood.

Olivia appeared at the table, removing her apron. She placed a bowl of water and a plate of dog treats next to Jasper.

"These are great," Penelope said.

"Thanks, sis. How are you doing?"

Penelope shrugged. "Hanging in. These scones will sell like crazy. They'd even go great with a glass of red wine at night."

"Ooh, look at my sister coming up with food pairings." Olivia pulled the elastic from her ponytail, letting her hair fall around her shoulders.

"You off?" Laurel asked.

"Yes. The baking is done, and I've briefed Tristan on what he needs to do this afternoon if we run low on anything."

"Do you keep in touch with Jessie Hanlon?" Penelope asked.

Olivia nodded. "Yeah, we see each other now and then. We aren't as close as we were in high school. I tried to call her last night after I heard what happened, but she didn't answer. Why?"

"Just curious." Penelope snagged another scone from the plate in the center of the table and tore it in half. "Thank you for taking Mom antiquing."

"You'd better thank me. When I called her this morning, she was gathering supplies for a love spell for you and Ryan."

"No. Go." Penelope waved her hands and shooed Olivia from the table. "Do not let her do that!"

Penelope closed her eyes and slid further into the chair, resting her head on top of the backrest. After a minute of total silence, Penelope could tell that Laurel wanted to ask her something, so instead of waiting for the inevitable *How are you* question, Penelope jumped in. She opened her eyes. "I'm fine. You don't have to worry about me. I'm not even sure what I saw this morning. I guess I'm just a little spooked after what happened to Tessa and then thinking that the car was following us last night."

"You can say you're fine, but I know you better." Laurel ripped apart the end of a scone and dropped the pieces in front of Jasper, who had already scarfed the dog treats.

"I'm doing the best I can. I would like to figure out why and how she was murdered. It's a little freaky finding one of your friends like that in the middle of a crowded festival and nobody seems to have a clue about what happened." Penelope tossed the rest of her scone onto the plate. She rubbed her temples. "The craziest thing is that Jessie was in the tent next door all day and says that she saw and heard nothing."

"I can believe she was busy with her customers. The side flaps do make it so you can't see into the next tent and the festival can be loud with the bands and people."

Penelope pushed herself up and rested her elbows on her knees. "I guess you may be right. She took off as soon as she hung up with 9-1-1. I wonder if Ryan found her."

"She comes here pretty often."

"Really? I've never noticed her."

"She comes in at slow times, usually like mid-mornings and mid-afternoons. She rarely speaks to anyone and just gets her coffee and a cherry hand pie and leaves."

"Something sure set her off yesterday morning. It's a wonder she has any customers."

"I think she's nice, but super shy and insecure. Or she might just come here to see Tristan." Laurel smirked.

"Oh, speak of the devil." Penelope pointed at the large windows at the front of the cafe just as Jessie zipped past and flung open the door.

"Why don't you talk to her?"

"Hi Jessie, the usual?" Tristan asked.

Jessie nodded as she slipped her debit card into the register. She glanced at Penelope, who beelined for Jessie before she could grab her food and go.

"Hi, Jessie. I was hoping to find you." Penelope positioned herself between Jessie and the door.

"I spent all morning at the police station. I was on my way home and saw a car with The Crystal Cove bumper sticker. I thought it might be yours."

"You came in to find me?" Penelope shifted her weight, ready to move if Jessie tried to scurry past.

"I wanted to apologize for yesterday. I'm not usually that awful." Jessie's shoulders slumped.

"What was going on?"

"This is embarrassing." Jessie fought back tears. "I found out that my boyfriend was cheating on me."

"Oh, no. I'm sorry." Penelope knew how gut-wrenching a breakup could be.

"She's tall and pretty. I found out when he accidentally texted me a picture of her instead of sending it to his friend. She looks a little like Tessa and I guess I just took it out on you guys."

Penelope winced. She knew what it was like to get shocking news over text.

"When I saw Robby's jewelry, I just lost it. I thought that I just lost my boyfriend, and I couldn't lose my business, too." Tears filled Jessie's eyes. "I've been hoping to turn the jewelry into a full-time career."

Penelope reached for her arm. "I think we've all been there at some point." She remembered Andre's break-up text. He had found a new girlfriend at college and no longer had time for someone who was in a different town.

Laurel joined them at the counter. "Hi Jessie, I heard that you and Penelope had a rough time at the festival."

"Hey, Laurel. Yes. Yesterday was not good." She dabbed her eyes with a napkin.

Laurel pointed to a table. "Why don't you two sit? I'll get your food."

Jessie nodded and followed Penelope to the table where Jasper was waiting patiently.

Laurel went to the bar for a quick second and came back with a plate of cranberry scones, muffins, and hand pies. "Tristan will be here in a minute with your coffee." Laurel sat beside Penelope.

"Thank you," Jessie said.

"Try a scone." Penelope pushed the plate toward Jessie and snagged another for herself. "This is my third one. Olivia makes the food for the cafe."

"I know. We've kept in touch a little since high school." Jessie took a small bite. "Wow, they're good." She set the scone on a napkin and glanced around the cafe.

Penelope eyed her with curiosity. Breaking up with her boyfriend would explain her foul mood, but Penelope sensed Jessie was still hiding something. "Are you okay?"

Jessie exhaled quickly. "Yeah, I guess so. Detective Snow tracked me down last night. He wasn't happy that I left the festival. I had to go to the police station this morning and make a statement. I think he might suspect me of killing Tessa. You should have heard his questions."

Penelope watched Jessie as she spoke. Her knee never stopped bouncing under the table as she described Ryan's tone during the questioning. She looked oddly meek compared to her demeanor at the festival just a day before.

"Did the police officially decide that she was murdered? With all those boxes around her, I think she must have been."

Jessie leaned toward the table. "They were acting like she was murdered. I had little to tell him. Just that you were there when I got upset with Tessa in the morning, but after that, I stayed in my tent and tried my best to make every sale that I could. I didn't pay any attention to Tessa."

"You didn't talk with her the rest of the day?"

"No. I mean, there were so many customers, and the bands were so loud. I could barely hear people talking with Tessa. But I certainly never heard shouting or a fight."

Penelope watched Jessie's expressions. She didn't know her well enough to know if she was lying.

"If I wasn't so self-absorbed, Tessa might still be alive."

"What do you mean?" Penelope wished Olivia hadn't left to pick up their mother.

"I lost my boyfriend, my full-time job also stinks, and I was really feeling pressure to make a lot of sales yesterday, but then I just snapped when I saw Tessa's tent and their beautiful merchandise. If I hadn't been so worried about myself, I may have heard if Tessa was fighting with someone. I wonder if I could have done something."

Tristan arrived with Jessie's coffee. "Thank you," she said.

"You're welcome. Um, I hate to eavesdrop, but I just overheard you talking. If Tessa was murdered, I doubt that you would have been able to stop it. In my experience, if a killer wants to commit a crime, they'll find a way to do it."

Laurel rocked back in her chair. "In your experience? What experience might that be?"

"My vast crime show binge-watching. They are more real than you think," Tristan said.

"Ignore him." Penelope waved her hand to shoo him away. "He thinks he knows everything because he watches reruns of Colombo and Perry Mason."

"That is the pot calling the kettle black, missy." Tristan blew a kiss at Penelope as he turned back to the counter.

"Huh?" Jessie asked.

"I *might* be a crime show junkie too. But I'm more into modern shows and he likes the classics."

"I just hope he's right."

Penelope's mind raced, trying to think about who would want to hurt Tessa.

Did they come planning to harm her?

Was it an accident?

Penelope remembered the 'back soon' sign hanging on Tessa's tent. She wondered if Tessa put the sign out or if her killer had.

"What else did Detective Snow ask?"

Jessie stared past Penelope, avoiding eye contact. "He wanted my account of the day. He asked about customers who didn't look like they were shopping. If I heard fighting. That type of thing."

"Hmmm."

Jessie's knee smacked against the underside of the table, causing the coffee mugs to jump. "Oh, sorry," she said, reaching for the napkin dispenser.

"Did you tell Ryan anything that you haven't told us?" Penelope sensed her holding back.

She mopped up the spilled coffee. "No, not really. These biker-type guys were hanging around some."

"Bikers?" Laurel asked. "That is unusual. We don't have too many around here because of the noise ordinances."

Penelope flipped through her memories of the festival. She hadn't noticed bikers near The Crystal Cove tent. It's unusual for people to miss walking through the area where it was staged because it was so close to the entrance. She wondered if Jessie was just making up a story to hide her guilt.

"I need to get going." Jessie jumped up. "The scones are amazing. Please tell Olivia that I'll text her soon. It would be nice to catch up."

"Thank—"

Jessie hurried out of the cafe so quickly that Penelope couldn't finish the sentence before the door flung open and Jessie was gone.

"Odd," Laurel said.

"Oh yes, she is," Penelope agreed. "And I'm not so sure that she is telling the truth, either."

"No?"

"Yesterday when I found Tessa's body, Jessie swore she heard and saw nothing unusual during the day and now she mysteriously remembers bikers at the festival. I didn't see anyone like that."

Laurel picked up the coffee-soaked napkins and dirty dishes. "She could have something to hide."

Penelope slowly tapped her index finger on the tabletop as she stared toward the cafe door. "Yes, I think she does."

***

Penelope spent the afternoon training for her next aquathlon race. As she began the tenth mile of her run, her mind was swimming with questions about Tessa's death. Her gut told her it was murder. Based on her conversation with Jessie, she assumed the cops thought it was murder, too. By the time she finished her twelfth mile and returned to her condominium, Penelope's brain was in overdrive, trying to connect every detail.

"I've got to write all of this down," she muttered to Jasper as she sat on the floor to stretch her legs. Jasper barely opened one eye from her position on the doggy hammock. Penelope threw her sweaty running clothes in the hamper and opted for thick cotton sweatpants, a tank top, and fuzzy slippers after a quick shower.

She planted herself on the couch, opened her notes app, and typed a list of suspects and questions as swiftly as her fingers could move.

Who would want to murder Tessa? Was her murder personal or professional? Was her murder premeditated or an accident? Was it just a robbery?

Penelope had known Tessa for many years and didn't recall her having any enemies. Penelope's mother had spoken the sharpest words about her. She needed to brainstorm with Laurel. Penelope called her friend and put the phone on speaker so she could continue typing.

"Something seems off," Penelope blurted out when Laurel answered.

"Why hello, Penelope."

Penelope stood and shuffled to her kitchen to brew a cup of coffee. "I have a list of questions, and none of the answers seem to fit." After a splash of vanilla creamer and a second of plain oat milk, Penelope was back on the couch. In her absence, Jasper had tiptoed from the dog hammock to the couch and claimed the pre-warmed spot.

"How much Googling have you done since you left the cafe?"

Penelope heard the concern in Laurel's voice. She pulled Jasper onto her lap.

"I haven't been on the computer. I ran twelve miles. That's a lot of thinking time." Penelope patted Jasper's head and scrolled back to the top of her list. "Okay, this is what I have so far for suspects. Jessie. Obviously, she's a suspect. Then, I have a list of all the other store owners along Main Street and the festival vendors, but I don't know why any of them would have a motive. Robby. But he's so sweet, I can't imagine that he would've done anything to Tessa. But on *Murder, She Wrote*, Jessica Fletcher always suspects the spouse." Penelope scratched her head. "Okay, that doesn't seem like too many suspects." Penelope's thoughts were in overdrive. Her sadness for Tessa merged into frantic anger for the killer. *What were the five stages of grief?* she wondered.

"Don't forget the woman who was leaving the store upset when we went in on Friday. She seemed very mad."

"Oh, yes. The mad woman from the candle shop on Friday...added." Penelope realized she had never told Ryan about the woman who came flying out of The Drip Shack. She was clearly upset, and Tessa had been very tight-lipped. She set a reminder on her phone to call Ryan later...maybe.

"Penelope, you're using words like suspects. Now you sound like my brother."

"Do not mention your brother. I'm still annoyed with him and with you, a little, for not warning me sooner."

"He asked me about you again last night."

Penelope rolled her eyes and stuck her tongue out. She was glad Laurel couldn't see her childish antics. "Okay, moving on. Is not knowing who killed Tessa driving you crazy? Our friend is dead. We don't know how, we don't know by who, and what if one of us is next? What if some psychopath killed Tessa to get rid of the candle shop? What if they want to get rid of The Crystal Cove next? I have to think about my mother, too. And you. What if The Tipsy Java is a target?"

"You need to chill out and let Ryan and Andre figure this out. Nothing will happen to your mom or me. If you ask questions and Andre finds out, he might just throw you in jail to keep you safe."

Penelope smiled. "I don't plan on running into your brother or letting him or Ryan find out that I'm investigating. This is a puzzle, and I plan to solve it."

"What if you run into cute Detective Ryan? He sure has improved since high school. Yummy."

"Oh, Laurel. We were just friends."

"Seriously, Penelope, he was in love with you in high school. Ryan followed you around, just like Jasper does now."

"Oh, come on." Penelope fluffed her curls, then pulled them into a ponytail.

"You didn't see it because of Andre. But he was totally into you. And he's good-looking and available. Hmm, just like you."

"I never thought of Ryan that way."

"Well, you should. Your track record is pretty dismal. Perhaps you should let your mom do that love spell."

"My track record? Yours isn't any better." Penelope exclaimed. "And no. No spells."

"Just think about it. And stop trying to figure out who killed Tessa. You have a gala to worry about. Let Andre and Ryan do the police work."

"Oops, you're breaking up...must be a terrible connection." Penelope scratched her fingernails across the phone and abruptly hung up. She squeezed Jasper in a big hug, making the pup yap.

"I'll be okay. I'm getting justice for Tessa."

Clara's Love Spell for Ryan & Penelope

To promote love for yourself, a friend, or a family member, you must open the heart chakra.

Spell Supplies

3 Pink or Red Candles | Magnets | Rose Water | Red Rose Petals | Photos of the people you want to connect or Paper and Pen

Light your candles. You can lay your chakra stones in a heart shape around the candle if you like. Place photos of the people that you want to connect inside the heart. If you do not have photos, you can write their names on two pieces of paper. Place one magnet on each photo and place a few drops of rose water on each.
Sprinkle the rose petals on top of the photos and recite three times:
Positive and negative opposites attract. Draw love and romance together intact. So mote it be!

Chakra Stones for Promoting Love

Use these love stones in your spell for extra benefit. You can also wear jewelry made with these crystals or keep them in your pockets until the love connection is complete.

Pink Tourmaline | Rhodonite | Citrine

Chapter Seven

As Monday morning rolled around, the reality of Penelope's responsibilities came crashing into view. Tessa's death had consumed her for the past two days, and now she needed to focus on work. She had less than two weeks until the museum gala that would unveil her biggest display yet and hopefully bring in enough donations to fully fund the new children's center.

Penelope was still tired from her long run the day before, so she took Jasper on a short loop around the neighborhood to loosen her muscles before heading to the museum. Keeping to her training routine helped her focus during the rest of the day. Huskies were great runners, but Jasper's short puppy legs turned a run into a slow jog for Penelope, which was perfect for today's shake-out.

Penelope thought about her task list for the day. She had one last group of minerals to re-evaluate to make sure that the display was flawless. She had tested the samples three times, but her obsessive tendencies were bursting to the forefront when she carefully lined each sample from Black Top Mountain along the far edge of the worktable on Friday, planning one last examination for this morning.

The Black Top samples were among the first of Penelope's discoveries. These were the minerals and rocks that launched her research into rare mineral deposits around the world. Black Top Mountain sat at the edge of Sierra Springs in Western North Carolina. Penelope still remembered the day when she was out for a hike during her summer break in college and ran across a rock boulder with the most unusual mineral crystals she had ever seen.

She collected a few samples to show her professors when the new school year started in the fall, but she couldn't wait to see what type of minerals they were. Penelope performed the usual tests for minerals like streak color, hardness, the reaction of acid, determination of luster, and an evaluation of the surrounding rocks for clues to the type of crystals that may be in the area. None of her tests matched known minerals. She assumed she wasn't far enough along in her classes to identify the samples, so Penelope stuck them in a box and put them out of her mind.

During a graduate school mineralogy seminar, Penelope remembered the samples and inspected them using new techniques she was learning. She created thin sections of the samples, which were paper-thin sheets of each rock and mineral. Penelope mounted each sliver onto a glass slide and examined it under a microscope using a variety of oil solutions to help her determine the mineral content of the rocks. But the thin section results just left her baffled. The results were similar to known rocks and minerals in the western North Carolina area, but not an exact match. Penelope enlisted a chemistry major to help her create a powder from the samples and analyze them using the machines in the research lab to find the elements that comprised the samples, but even those results didn't help Penelope conclusively pinpoint her findings.

After exhausting her knowledge, Penelope made an appointment with her advisor and showed him her work. She was stunned to find that he agreed with all her findings and offered to help her publish her work, proving the existence of another, previously unknown, mineral. Once Penelope published her findings, the scientific world spent the next several years scrutinizing her results. Other scientists corroborated her findings, and she received word that it was time to name her mineral. Penelope had chosen a name, but the only people who knew were her assistant Lucy, the museum director, and the company that made the plaques for the display cases. They were all sworn to secrecy. The world would learn the name at the gala.

Soon after, the most amazing career opportunities opened. Penelope traveled to exotic places around the world on expeditions where she could hunt for rare minerals. Fellow geologists from every continent sent her samples that they had discovered, hoping she could help verify their findings. Penelope had become known as an expert on rare rocks and minerals despite being not yet thirty years old. This display at the museum was a combination of her discoveries and others that she helped verify and deemed unique enough to warrant a slot in the exhibit. The collection stood behind floor-to-ceiling navy velvet curtains. Penelope had invited everyone to the gala who had sent in a sample or asked her to verify their findings, including her professors and classmates from college. The unveiling would be her biggest accomplishment to date and mark one of the largest collaborations in science.

Jasper was doing well on the shake-out run. Penelope had barely needed to slow her pace. Her favorite band,

Matchbox Twenty, was blaring through her earbuds when her phone rang, interrupting the music.

Penelope inspected the caller's identification on the screen. 'Town Hall.' Her heart jumped. It could be Ryan calling about Tessa. She slowed to a walk and answered, breathlessly.

"Penelope? Are you okay?" a voice on the other end of the phone asked.

"Hi, Johnny. Fine. Just finishing my run with Jasper."

The town's engineer was always at work early. He was nice, and Sierra Springs paid Penelope well to consult on Johnny's projects when they involved blasting into the mountainside. He always said that engineers can build solid roads, but he needed a geologist to consult about the dirt and rock below them.

"Oh, sorry to bother you. But I was just wondering if you could stop by my office on your way to the museum today. We got the drawings done for the new road cut for the scenic lookout and I wanted to get you a copy to review for potential geological issues."

"Sure, no problem." Penelope checked her watch. "I can be there in about forty-five minutes."

"Take your time. I'll be here all morning."

"See you soon," Penelope said as the call ended and music flooded her ears once again.

Just after Penelope accepted the job as a resident geologist at the Natural History Museum, the city called and asked her to consult with the engineering and planning team. Sierra Springs was building a network of scenic roadways that were opening new avenues to explore the area's hidden caves and hiking trails. Penelope loved spelunking. Her favorite college field trips were to the caves around North Carolina and Virginia. Sierra Springs was nestled in the Appalachian Mountain range, which was both beautiful and dangerous, and Penelope loved the technical challenge they presented to her city projects.

Penelope fed Jasper, turned on her coffee pot, pulled a protein bar from the fridge to soften, then jumped in the shower. Over the years, she had perfected a twenty-three-minute routine that let her shower, dress, apply a bit of makeup, and get out of the house quickly. She was blessed with the perfect curly hair that dried quickly and into loose, flowing spirals with only a bit of hair oil to keep it smooth. Penelope filled her coffee mug and tossed a bag of treats for Jasper and the protein bar in her messenger bag. Her purple skirt flowed, skimming just above the floor, touching her black leather ankle boots. A dark green sweater with pale purple flowers complimented her auburn hair.

Penelope dropped Jasper at The Crystal Cove before heading to the engineer's office. Clara was on the phone fighting with a vendor, letting her slip in and out of the store with just a wave of thanks.

Penelope pulled into a parking spot for town employees at the municipal building and checked her makeup in the visor mirror. She hoped to run into Ryan and dreaded running into Andre, but either way, she wanted to look her best. As she climbed the stairs of the city building, a sense of déjà vu hit her. Scenes from Saturday's events flooded her mind. In flashes, like flipping through a photo album, Penelope saw Tessa lying on the grass under her tent, her eyes open, then the ambulance carrying her body away as Robby sobbed uncontrollably.

Penelope felt tears fill her eyes. *No. Not today*, she thought. She tilted her head back to stop herself from crying. Today was not the day to fall apart. She needed to check in with Johnny at the engineering office and get the maps he mentioned. Then she had a full day at the museum to prepare for the gala in less than two weeks. But she could not stop thinking about Tessa. She had to figure out who killed her friend. A quick stop at Ryan's office after seeing Johnny couldn't hurt.

***

"Knock, knock," Penelope stuck her head through the crack in the door to Ryan's office.

"Penelope." Ryan jumped up, sending his chair flying backward, throwing him off balance, and landing him squarely on the floor.

Penelope burst out laughing. "Are you alright, Ryan?"

The detective's face flushed an ombre of red from chin to forehead as he pulled himself to a stand as Penelope slipped through the doorway. He cleared his throat and smiled. "That wasn't embarrassing at all."

"Don't worry, I won't tell anyone. Well, maybe Laurel, or my mom, oh, or Olivia. She likes a funny story." Penelope smiled as she watched Ryan try to regain his composure.

"How did you get back here?"

"Well, if you had bothered to stay in touch with me after high school, you would know that I consult with the city on all their road construction projects. I'm friends, or at least acquaintances, with almost everyone in the building, and I have this badge that lets me get in and out of the doors for meetings." Penelope flashed her city credentials.

"That only gets you into the engineering side of the building, not the police side."

"Okay, I may have told one of those twin officers that I had something for you, and he let me in."

"Hmm. I'll talk with him. Did you come down here to harass me about Tessa?"

Penelope waved the stiff cardboard tube full of maps in front of her nose. "No, I was in the building getting some drawings for the new scenic overlook from Johnny Ellingham, and I thought I'd stop by and see if you have any news."

"That's cool that they ask you to consult."

"Yeah, they're going to have to blast through some of the rock formations and want me to go over the calculations to make sure they can withstand the shock from the blasting without triggering a landslide." Penelope closed the door. "Anything new about Tessa?"

"A little. But there's nothing I can tell you. You're a witness and a civilian. My new boss doesn't want details getting out." Ryan leaned on the corner of his desk.

"Humph, Andre," Penelope grunted, crossing her arms.

"Harboring hard feelings, are we?" Ryan rocked back, scrutinizing her reaction.

"No. No feelings," she said flatly. "I just would rather not think about him being around."

"I get it. I remember high school and I heard how you guys broke up."

The high school gossip train moved far and fast to get to Ryan in Maine, she thought.

"Yes, I remember you being one of my best friends in high school. You know, the kind who share details about their lives and secrets that were just between us." Penelope smiled sweetly, hoping her dimples showed. It was one of the few features she inherited from her father.

"You sure are trying hard." Ryan lowered into his chair, bracing himself with both hands gripping the armrests to stop the impending roll.

"Why didn't you stay in touch? These little things called cell phones make it easy these days." Penelope was hurt when Ryan cut ties. She knew she had upset him when she said she was going to keep dating Andre, but she never expected to lose him as a friend.

"Ah, P, high school was hard. I liked you, but you were with Andre, and I was a third wheel."

Penelope softened. "But you were still one of my best friends and you disappeared."

"I'm sorry. I shouldn't have." Ryan's shoulders relaxed.

Penelope walked around the desk and sat on the edge closest to Ryan. "And now I know nothing about you."

"What's to know? I'm the same person."

"Well, you've been working out more," Penelope teased, poking his biceps.

Ryan cracked a smile.

"Wife?"

"No."

"Girlfriend?"

"No."

"Dog?"

"No."

"Cat?"

"No."

"Was Tessa murdered?"

"Yes."

"Ah ha!"

Ryan rolled his eyes. "Damn it, Penelope. Don't trick me."

"I knew it. How?"

Ryan stood, moving toward the office door. "Nothing official yet. Just a hunch. I saw something similar once in Portland."

Ryan took Penelope's hand and pulled her toward him.

"Hint?" she asked as he turned her around to face the door.

"No. Shouldn't you go review those road plans or do something at the museum? I have work to do."

Penelope ignored his attempt to make her leave. "I have a couple of notes for you, though." Penelope spun from his grasp and snatched a peppermint from Ryan's pencil cup, which was mysteriously devoid of pencils but full of candies.

"Notes, Detective Lake?" Ryan mocked.

"Ha, ha. Not like that. I forgot to tell you about a possible suspect."

"Who?" Ryan pulled his small notebook and pen from his back pocket.

"I'm not sure who she was, but Friday morning, Mom, Olivia, Laurel, and I went to Tessa's shop and as we were about to go in, this woman came running out of the shop and she was upset."

"Description?"

"Thirties or early forties, short dark hair, not tall, very pale, and scowling. She looked mad like she and Tessa had been arguing."

"Did you ask Tessa about her?" Ryan was writing furiously in his notebook.

"I asked, but she wouldn't say anything." She spun the peppermint out of its wrapper and tossed it into her mouth.

"Okay, thanks. I'll look into it." He closed the notebook and shoved it into his shirt pocket.

"I was at Tipsy Java yesterday with Laurel and Jessie Hanlon came in."

"I spoke with her yesterday."

"She told me." Penelope winced at the strength of the peppermint. "Is she a suspect?"

"I can't tell you that. I've already told you too much."

"But we're friends." Penelope elbowed his ribs, frustrated that she could not get him to reveal any details.

"And friends can have secrets. Can you do me a favor, though?"

"What?"

Ryan scooped her hands in his. "Stop talking with potential suspects and witnesses. I would rather you stay in one piece."

"I didn't go looking for her," Penelope protested. She snatched her hands away from his grasp. "She walked into the cafe while I was having breakfast."

"Regardless. I would like you to be safe." Ryan wagged his finger at her. "Promise me. No investigating."

Penelope slipped her hands behind her back. "Okay, okay, I promise I won't go searching for people to talk to about Tessa's murder."

"You just crossed your fingers the way you used to in high school when you claimed you wouldn't do something you weren't supposed to, but you planned on doing it anyway, didn't you?"

"I never did that." Penelope objected. Ryan remembered more about her than she assumed he would.

"Eleventh grade. You stole your dad's car, and we went to get ice cream after you promised him you would study for the chemistry final."

Penelope raised her hands as a mea culpa. "Okay, maybe I did that."

"I was sorry to hear about your dad. He was nice. Did you ever find out what happened?"

Penelope cringed. She didn't want to talk about her father. He disappeared several years earlier, and it almost destroyed her family. "No."

"I can't imagine what you guys went through. Not knowing what happened to him. My mom and your mom are friendly. She told me."

"I know." Penelope didn't want to cry anymore. Very few people knew that Penelope's father disappeared mysteriously on a business trip. The details were sketchy, and the Federal Bureau of Investigation was hesitant to give even close family members details about their agent's assignments. Penelope knew he was out of the country and never returned. The FBI declared him dead shortly after. She always wondered, though, why an FBI agent was out of the country. Usually, they only worked in the States. After he disappeared, Clara rarely mentioned him. Neither did Olivia nor Penelope. She shook her head and took a sharp breath. "I don't want to talk about him. Let's talk about Tessa."

Ryan deftly led Penelope toward the office door. "Murder investigations can get dangerous, Penelope. I don't want anything to happen to you. So you need to let me handle this."

"Fine." Penelope was tired of the conversation.

Ryan opened the door and pulled her through. "I do still need to get your mother's statement. I tried to call her yesterday, but she didn't answer."

"She was pretty shaken up, so Olivia took her to some of those antique shops in Asheville."

"You didn't go?"

Penelope shuddered. "I probably should have, but I hate sifting through old junk, so I ran twelve miles instead."

"Gotcha." Ryan nodded. "Oh. Can you sign your statement from yesterday?" He retrieved a yellow folder and handed it to Penelope with a pen.

Penelope read through the typed statement, then signed the bottom. She looked at her watch. "Oh man, I'm late for the museum. I have so much to do before next Saturday night."

"What's next Saturday night?"

"There is a gala at the museum. I'm unveiling my new exhibit and it's a fundraiser. You should come."

"Maybe I will."

"Bring your checkbook." Penelope's phone chimed. She checked the text. "I have to go."

Chapter Eight

Penelope breezed into her office at the Natural History Museum with a gazelle intensity that she had not felt since her college days when her final exams started in an hour and all she wanted was to get it over with. Her stop at the city building left little work time before lunch, and the urgency of the gala was skyrocketing her stress level. She dropped the tube of engineering maps for the scenic overlook on her office project table and sank onto the plush cushion perched atop her wooden desk chair.

Penelope closed her eyes and slowly inhaled. As she slowly released the air from her lungs, she realized that Ryan's confirmation that Tessa was murdered made her more uptight than she had expected. A quiet tapping on the door caused Penelope to sit up straight.

"Oh, good. You got my text. Sorry if I pulled you away from something important, but I was freaking out a little about how much we have to do before the gala." Lucy Arden stepped through the door. Her long blonde hair bobbed from a high ponytail, accentuating her tall, thin frame. A classic beauty, Lucy was oblivious to her charms on the men of Sierra Springs.

Lucy had been Penelope's assistant since she started working at the museum. The two were more friends than boss and employee. Lucy studied science in college but dropped out after her parents died in a car crash, leaving her to care for her younger brother. She never resented derailing her schooling for a time. Lucy stepped in immediately to care for her sibling.

It was rare to find an assistant who could manage your calendar and research rare rock types, so Penelope had insisted that the museum's owners fund the rest of Lucy's college. Now, she was closing in on finishing her master's degree in geological and environmental education with a minor in business.

"Hey, Lucy. Sorry I'm so late. I was at—"

"City Hall. Johnny left a voice mail here early this morning."

Lucy set a drink can in front of Penelope and took a seat across the desk. "New flavor. Coconut pomegranate."

"Is it good?" Penelope inspected the label and then scrunched her nose. "It doesn't sound good."

"Yes, it's good. As long as I've known you, the only things you drink are coffee, cherry Gatorade, and fizzy blueberry caffeinated water. When a new flavor comes out, you should try it." Lucy cracked open her can and took a sip. "Did you hear about the murder this weekend?"

"First, I told you that you never have to bring me coffee or fizzy water, even if it is a new flavor. Second, not only did I hear about the murder, but I found the body."

Lucy choked on the bubbles.

"Do I need to do the Heimlich?"

Lucy shook her head, trying to control her cough. "You found the body?" Her hand thumped her chest. "That wasn't in the paper."

Penelope nodded. "It's been a stressful weekend. I was just at the festival to help Mom sell her crystals, drum up donations for the museum, and sell a few tickets to the gala. Fun stuff. But it was not fun."

"Details?"

Penelope told Lucy the play-by-play of the past two days. By the time she was done, she felt even more certain that she had to find out what had happened. Lucy stayed silent, but her face registered a mix of horror and concern. Penelope was unsure if Lucy's concern was more for her or Tessa.

When Penelope started working at the museum, it was Tessa who helped her develop the curriculum for the kid's programs. Penelope had never worked with kids, so she asked Tessa to give her some pointers about how to structure the programs and unique ways to use the activities to keep the children busy and entertained.

Penelope needed to refocus and get her mind on the gala. She cracked open the pop top on her drink and took a tentative sip. "You were right." She never wanted Lucy to feel like she was a secretary, so she had been adamant all these years about her not doing meaningless errands. But she was thankful for the fizzy caffeine jolt.

"See. It's good to try new things."

Penelope surveyed her office. Her eyes darted from one corner to another. Stacks of papers teetered precariously on every surface, threatening to topple at the slightest breeze. Cardboard boxes overflowing with rock samples littered the floor, creating an obstacle course between her desk and the worktable. A thick layer of dust coated the neglected blinds, and coffee-stained mugs dotted the landscape like miniature towers.

She sighed, thinking of the neighboring rock laboratory. The floors were filled with more boxes of geological specimens, revealing a scene of equal chaos. Folders and equipment spilled into the hallway, encroaching on her already cramped space.

The display cases delivered on Friday were being installed in the new exhibit room, awaiting their unveiling at the gala. The samples were being prepped in Penelope's office and the rock lab and kept in the storage closets down the hall before placement into the cases. Penelope had been working on this special display since she started at the museum and she was looking forward to her friends, family, and the public seeing the unique samples she had collected.

Lucy and Penelope ran through the list of samples that were stored, undergoing final preparation, and were ready for installation. "I'll keep the installation on track and you finish prepping the remaining samples in the next day or so. Then we'll move on to your speech."

"Ugh. The speech is the only part I dread."

Lucy rose. As she stepped toward the door, Penelope noticed an unmistakable limp in Lucy's gait.

"Lucy, why are you limping? I didn't notice when you came in."

"My brother's baseball game needed a fill-in umpire this weekend. Since I played softball in high school, they stuck me behind home plate. I'm sore from being hunched over for a doubleheader. It's worse after I sit."

Penelope smiled. "Oh, I understand how you feel. My legs feel like that after some of my long runs. You need a heating pad, ibuprofen, and a foam roller to help stretch out those muscles again. I have an extra foam roller in the corner over there. Take it with you."

Lucy hobbled to Penelope's extra stash of running equipment. The running group ran three days a week at six o'clock in the evening, and sometimes Penelope did not have time to go home and change, so she always kept extra workout gear in her office. Lucy took the roller and went to check on the display installation.

Penelope scanned her calendar to see what she had missed that morning and what she still needed to get done. The list of samples that needed to be cataloged, cleaned, and prepared for display seemed to grow daily as Penelope decided that more samples warranted placement in the rare rock and mineral collection. When she focused, Penelope would work through meals, phone calls, and even the occasional date, which was just one reason she was still single, despite her mother's request for grandchildren.

Four hours later, Penelope was covered in rock dust and water spray from her saw that cut the wafer-thin slices of rock she used to make detailed observations of the inside of each rock sample. Printed photos of the colorful, intertwined crystals would accompany each sample in the display cases like a portrait. Regardless of how long she worked and how hard she tried to focus, questions about Tessa kept seeping into Penelope's mind.

What was it that Ryan suspected but wouldn't say? Penelope's thoughts meandered toward Robby, and she wondered how he was doing.

Her phone rang.

"Penelope, it's Johnny."

"Oh, hey Johnny. I haven't had time to look at the drawings yet." She pushed her safety goggles to the top of her head.

"That's not why I'm calling. I was just in the employee lounge, and I overheard some of the police officers talking."

"Do they have more news about how Tessa died?"

"Penelope, they are planning to bring your mom in for questioning. They think she did it."

"I just saw Detective Snow this morning. He didn't say anything to me." Penelope flipped the speaker on and put her phone on the table. She pulled off her apron.

"I heard that they just found something this afternoon. I wanted you to know."

Before she could think, Penelope snatched her bag from her office and raced down the hallway.

***

"Mom!" Penelope yelled as she flung open the door of The Crystal Cove.

"Back here, hon," Clara sang.

Penelope quickly wound her way through the display tables and pushed away the strands of gemstones hanging across the doorway to her mother's workroom in the private area of the shop. The crystals always reminded her of the 1970s doorways she had seen on television show reruns growing up. The strands tinkled and chimed as they bumped into one another. "I don't see any smoke today. That's a move in the right direction." She hugged her mom.

Clara stood at the workbench, unpacking a new shipment of agate bookends. "The day is young. Would you like for me to do another love spell for you and Ryan? Or how about a friendship spell for you and Andre?" Clara laughed.

"No. Listen. Johnny called."

"Johnny the engineer? What did he want?"

"Nothing. It's what he heard. The police think that you may have killed Tessa. They are planning to question you. Formally."

Clara nodded. "Well, honey, I know that I still need to give them my statement. Ryan called a bit ago and said that he would come pick me up."

The hairs on the back of Penelope's neck stood up. "He doesn't want just a statement. He is coming to bring you in for questioning."

"That's just ridiculous Penelope. Why would they think that I would have any reason to kill Tessa?" She threw an empty shipping box to the floor.

"I don't know. Johnny said he heard them say that there was new evidence. We need to call your lawyer."

Clara's brow furrowed. "This is silly."

"Mom, do you have someone you can call?"

Clara set a second box on the table and slit the tape with a box cutter. "I suppose I could call Sandra Phillips, my business attorney. I'm not sure what she knows about criminal matters. I've known Ryan since you guys were kids. He can't seriously suspect me."

"Just call Sandra and tell her what's going on and see what she says. Whatever she tells you to do, do it."

"Okay. I'll call her." Clara elbowed her daughter. "Now, aren't you supposed to be getting back to the museum to work on that fancy display that I'm eager to see at the gala?"

Penelope was surprised at her mother's indifference to hearing that she was a murder suspect. "If Ryan is on his way here, I'm staying." Penelope picked up Clara's phone and handed it to her. "Call your attorney now, please."

The inaudible murmur of Clara's voice drifted from behind the closed office door, punctuated by the occasional tapping of Clara's boot against the floorboards. Penelope's ears perked up at the sound of the agate chimes above the shop's entrance, followed by a familiar voice.

"Ms. Lake? Are you here?"

Penelope slowly parted the crystal beads, emitting a soft tinkling sound. Ryan's eyes widened, and he took a small step back as she emerged.

"Oh, hi, Penelope," he said, his voice dropping to a softer tone. His eyes darted around the shop before settling back on her. He shifted his weight, clutching a small notepad. "I'm looking for your mom. I need to take her statement." His fingers tapped nervously against the pad's spiral binding.

"Don't lie to me. You're here to take her to the station to question her. Do you seriously think that my mother could kill anyone?" Penelope's heart pounded, a mix of anger and disbelief coursing through her veins. How could Ryan, someone she thought she knew, suspect her mother of such a heinous act?

Ryan stepped back. "Penelope stop. Who told you?"

His surprise only fueled her frustration. Did he think she was naïve? Penelope clenched her fists, struggling to keep her voice steady. "I can't believe you."

Ryan dropped his hands to his hips. "No, Penelope, I can't believe you. Someone killed Tessa. It's my job—my first job on this police force—to find out what happened. I can't just ignore facts because we're friends."

His words stung, and Penelope felt a pang of guilt. Of course, he had to do his job, but why did it have to involve her mother? She drew in a deep breath, trying to push aside her emotions and think rationally.

"What facts?" She held her breath, both dreading and needing the answer.

"I'm not talking to you about the case."

Frustration bubbled up inside her. How could he drop such a bombshell and then clam up? Penelope opened her mouth to argue further, but the sound of the crystal beads fluttering open caught her attention.

Clara emerged from the workroom with her purse in hand. "Let's get this over with. I don't like closing the store. I need to be back before my customers decide to shop somewhere else," she said flatly. Clara swung her purse across her shoulder. "Penelope, look after Midnight and Jasper."

Panic gripped Penelope's chest. She couldn't let her mother go alone, not when she was being suspected of murder.

"Mom, wait—"

Clara spun to face Penelope, keeping Ryan at her back. "Take Jasper and Midnight and go back to work. Sandra's sending someone." Clara winked at her daughter.

The wink confused Penelope. How could her mother be so calm? Was there something she wasn't telling her? A mixture of worry and curiosity swirled through her mind.

Determination set in. Whatever was happening, Penelope would not let her mother face it alone. She steeled herself for what was to come, ready to fight for her family if needed. "Oh, no. I'm coming too."

***

Penelope's access badge could only get her so far in the municipal building. She paced the foyer, unable to enter the hallways of the police station. She tried to manipulate the twin officers into letting her back to Ryan's office again, but they had been warned to tighten security.

Penelope paced. On the way to the station, she called The Tipsy Java and promised Olivia and Laurel to text updates since there was no reason for all of them to wear a hole in the marble flooring at the police station. Olivia agreed to check in on Midnight and Jasper. Penelope had been waiting over an hour before she had any update to text.

The doors to the police station opened wide and Clara emerged like a bull storming through the gates of its pen. Her eyes were watery, but her ears were crimson, a clear sign Ryan had made her more angry than worried. A stout, balding man in a sharp navy pinstripe suit followed behind.

"Let's get out of here," Clara said, pointing toward the front doors.

Penelope watched Ryan hustle down the hallway in the opposite direction as the doors began to close. She let him go.

As they stepped out of the municipal building, the afternoon sun glinted off rows of parked cars. Clara squinted against the glare, fishing in her purse for her sunglasses. Penelope led the way, her keys jingling in her hand as she scanned the lot for her Hummer.

Clara touched Penelope's arm to slow her pace. "I'd like you to meet my attorney." She gestured to the man walking beside them. "Penelope, this is Alan Dukat, my new criminal attorney. Alan, my daughter, Penelope."

They paused between two patrol cars, and Alan extended his hand. "Pleasure to meet you, Penelope. Your mother is a force of nature." He reached into his suit jacket, pulled out two business cards, and handed one each to Clara and Penelope.

Penelope accepted the card, her eyebrow arching as she glanced from Alan to her mother. "So, it went well?"

A gust of wind rustled through the lot, carrying the faint scent of exhaust and hot asphalt. Alan smiled, his teeth gleaming in the sunlight. "I rarely enjoy interrogations like that because the police are just fishing to find little tidbits of information to catch you on. But your mom shredded that detective like he was still a rookie."

Penelope's laugh echoed across the parking lot. "Way to go, Mom. So, you're off the hook?"

Clara adjusted her purse strap, her expression neutral. "I think Ryan understands my position."

"What does that mean?" Penelope's gaze darted between her mother and Alan as they resumed walking, their shoes crunching on loose gravel.

Alan cleared his throat. "Clara gave them enough detail to rule her out as a suspect, but, of course, the police will follow up on everything she said so they won't clear her right away." They reached a gleaming steel gray Mercedes, and Alan fished his keys from his briefcase. "But if they contact you again, Clara, or you need anything, call me first. I'm available day or night."

As Alan climbed into his car, Penelope and Clara continued towards the hulking shape of the Hummer at the far end of the lot. The Mercedes' engine purred to life behind them, and they heard tires grinding against the pavement as Alan pulled away.

Penelope unlocked the Hummer with a beep, then paused with her hand on the door handle. "Do you want to stop at Tipsy Java for some food?" she asked her mother.

Clara shook her head, already rounding the vehicle to the passenger side. "No, let's just go to the rock shop." They climbed into the Hummer. The doors closed with solid thuds as Penelope started the engine. The police station soon receded in her rearview mirror, but Penelope's anger with Ryan remained.

"Okay, so spill. How did you shred Ryan, and what did you find out?" Penelope pushed for details as she wound through the streets.

"He asked me a lot of questions about Tessa and our shops, and about the lunch I took her at the festival. I told him I got her a Monte Cristo sandwich from LB's for lunch, and I stopped by for just five or ten minutes so she could eat. We talked about getting together for coffee next week to discuss the new line of gemstone candles. Then I left and got back to work with the customers at our tent."

"What else?"

"He told me that Tessa was poisoned. They don't know how yet, but since I gave her food, it looks suspicious. And he asked me if I've been out of the country lately."

Penelope felt startled at the word poison. Tessa didn't have any obvious wounds when Penelope found her, but hearing that the police had determined that her cause of death was poison somehow made it final and real and even more excruciating.

Out of the country. It must have something to do with the poison. Why else would they ask that?

"Did he ask where out of the country?"

"Columbia, South America. It all made no sense." Clara threw her hands in the air.

Penelope slammed the brake pedal, bringing the car to an abrupt halt. "Wait, Mom. Isn't that where you suspect Dad disappeared six years ago?"

Clara's face paled. "Yes... but how could they possibly know about that?"

Chapter Nine

The air in McCaul's Fine Jewels carried the subtle aroma of jasmine and lavender. Penelope had tossed and turned most of the night and finally gave up and went into the museum at four o'clock. She had over five hours of solid work in by the time she came up for a break. As she worked, questions about Tessa dotted her thoughts. Lucy offered to keep Jasper company while Penelope took a break and got ready for their afternoon of children's programs, so she slipped out to run a few errands and check on Robby.

Penelope scanned the jewelry packed into the glass cases, admiring Robby's artistry. He was the only jeweler in town who created every piece in his shop. The hunter-green carpet was an attractive complement to the deep mahogany cases that lined the walls. Penelope's favorite piece in the shop was one that Robby refused to sell. In the showroom's corner stood a twenty-four-inch globe on a dark cherry wood stand. Polished blue sodalite formed the oceans while thin lines of silver outlined the continents. Colorful minerals cut with precision and polished to the highest shine, locked together perfectly, forming each country. Penelope slowly spun the tilted earth, admiring the time it had taken Robby to create such a masterpiece.

"Good morning, Penelope."

Penelope turned to see her old high school classmate. "I didn't know you worked here, Maggie."

Penelope and Maggie had known each other since eleventh-grade chemistry class. They were paired as lab partners when a Bunsen burner got the better of them and singed Maggie's acrylic nails, almost burning off the fingertips on her left hand. Maggie had not changed at all since high school. She won best-dressed and class clown their senior year, which Penelope always believed was the best combination.

"I got tired of working at my bookkeeping job. Sitting in that tiny cubicle all day made me claustrophobic. I thought I would try a new challenge where I could talk to actual people while I work." Maggie's golden hair spilled over her hair clip and cascaded over her shoulders. Her navy and white polka-dotted A-line dress looked professional and fun. It always amazed Penelope that Maggie could wear long casual dresses and still somehow make her five-foot frame seem taller than anyone in the room.

Penelope smiled. "That sounds like a good idea." Penelope pointed to the doorway to the private area of the business. "Is he here?"

Maggie lowered her voice. "He's back in his workshop. It's so sad. Tessa was nice."

"Yes, she was. I got to know her pretty well after college."

Maggie motioned for Penelope to follow her to the front of the store. "I heard you found her body," she whispered.

"It was awful." Penelope shuddered. "I feel so bad for Robby. He was devastated when he came back to the festival and found out what happened."

"He's locked away in his shop, working on a new line of jewelry that he was going to launch for Tessa's birthday this summer. He's been working on it constantly. I don't even think he's come up for air and certainly not for any food."

Penelope sighed. Her hand moved across the top of a slick glass case. The cozy village of Sierra Springs had jewelry that rivaled New York City, London, and Paris thanks to Robby's store. It would be a shame if Tessa's murder ruined the work he had put into his career. Penelope worried the stress of what had happened would be too much for him.

"Do you mind if I sneak back there to say hello and see how he's doing?"

Statistically, most murders are committed by the spouse. Everyone who watched murder mystery shows knew that, and Penelope listened to her fair share of true crime podcasts, too. She wondered if Robby really could have been part of poisoning his wife. She hoped not, but you could never assume to know everything about everyone. Everybody has secrets.

Maggie nodded to the doorway that separated the showroom from the hallway leading to Robby's studio. "Go ahead. I'm sure he would like to see you. I've been telling the customers that he's out. That new jewelry line is supposed to be featured in a fashion magazine in a couple of months. The editors want the first pieces in a few weeks for photographs."

"I hadn't heard that," Penelope said. "That's quite an honor."

"I hope the magazine doesn't decide to pull the feature because of what happened to Tessa. The preliminary designs are exquisite, and it would be a shame for the world not to see them."

"I'll just stick my head in and check on him. I'll be quick. Thanks, Maggie." Penelope slipped through the curtain and tiptoed along the concrete floor that would lead her to Robby's workshop. As she moved down the hallway, Penelope admired the sparkling gemstones that filled the storage cases along the walls.

Robby liked to experiment with different minerals in rings and necklaces. Diamonds, emeralds, and rubies were common gems that every jewelry store in the world carried. Robby often used lesser-known minerals like green garnets, ametrine, and watermelon tourmaline, which was one of Penelope's personal favorites. He even had a ring made of galena, but since it was too heavy for most people to wear, he kept it on display inside the showroom.

Penelope saw a light on in the workroom and knocked lightly on the steel door frame to announce her arrival but Robby didn't look up. She stepped gingerly into the room, hoping not to spook him, then waved to catch his attention.

"Oh, Penelope, give me just a second." Robby's studio was meticulously organized. His faceting and cabbing machines were staged in the center of the room, flanked by saws, sanders, and ultrasonic drills. Stations were set along the back wall for each step of the designing and crafting process. Buckets of settings, clasps, chains, and raw metals awaited their turn to become a necklace, bracelet, or ring.

Penelope leaned against the doorframe, watching the master jeweler polish a pink rhodonite, revealing the crystal's shimmering luster.

Robby pulled earplugs from deep inside of each ear and laid them on the table. He cut the power, letting the stone sander slowly whirl to a stop. He stood, removing his safety goggles and gloves.

"How are you doing?" Penelope's heart clenched as she took in his appearance. His once-vibrant eyes now seemed dull, his face rounder, as if grief had softened his features.

"It's good to see you, Penelope." Robby embraced her in a brief hug before releasing and backing away.

A wave of pity washed over Penelope. She couldn't imagine the pain he must be going through. And yet...a small, nagging voice in the back of her mind whispered doubts she didn't want to be true.

"I'm so sorry about Tessa." Penelope's eyes filled with tears. Her mind flashed back to the festival. An enormous lump formed in her throat as she pictured Tessa lying amongst the boxes on the floor of her tent, her eyes fixed and lifeless. Penelope hoped she would never see such a horrible sight again. The memory sent a shiver down her spine. She pushed it away, focusing on Robby. "How are you holding up?" Penelope asked, studying his face.

Robby motioned her to a nearby chair and returned to his seat at the lapidary table.

Penelope noticed how his movements seemed slower and heavier, as if the weight of his loss was a physical burden.

"I'm hanging in there. But I'm a little frustrated with the police."

"I agree with you on that one," she said, trying to sound supportive. "It seems like they're taking the easy way out by questioning you, and now they are focusing on my mother. The two people in the world that I know would never hurt Tessa." Even as she said it, Penelope felt a twinge of uncertainty. Did she actually know that for sure? Could some hidden motive have driven Robby to do the unthinkable?

"What do you mean they are focusing on your mother?" Robby's mouth hung wide.

Penelope studied his reaction carefully. She hated these doubts creeping into her mind, but she couldn't shake them entirely. Still, looking at Robby's pain-filled eyes, all she wanted was to comfort him.

"Mom took lunch to Tessa on Saturday, and because she died from poison, they automatically thought that my mother had something to do with it. They questioned her and she explained that she and Tessa had talked about doing some candles together the day before the festival, so there was no reason for her to hurt her."

Robby's head cocked to the side. "What type of candles?"

"We were at the shop on Friday, and she showed us the candles that she made with the gems inside and the wax dripping down the sides." Penelope could see Robby was confused. "They talked about doing a line of candles with all different crystals inside instead of the cut gems she had in the test candles—the ones she called Amethyst Falls." Penelope searched Robby's expression for any sign of acknowledgment. His mind was elsewhere. "Mom was going to supply the rough crystals, and Tessa was going to make the candles, and then they were both going to sell them in each of their shops."

Robby smiled faintly. "Oh, yes. Sorry. Tessa took some stones from the shop that I couldn't use. Crystal candles. They would have been nice."

"It is a great idea, but how the police think my mother would have anything to do with hurting Tessa when they had come up with a brilliant partnership that would only have helped both of their stores is beyond me."

Penelope heard the click of stiletto heels tapping along the concrete hallway outside Robby's workshop. She turned just as Katia sailed into the room, tears streaming down her cheeks. Penelope met Katia three years ago when she first came to Sierra Springs offering to supply Robby's business with gemstones through her family's wholesale supply company in Russia. Robby asked Penelope for her thoughts on the quality of the gemstones. Their interaction was brief and focused on the stones, but Katia was very sweet, and Robby was happy to have a new supplier for exotic crystals.

Katia had moved to the United States to attend Yale. When her fiancée, Tom, got a job as a manager for one of the largest banks in western North Carolina, the couple settled in Sierra Springs. Shortly after they began working together, Robby offered Katia a partnership in the business so that he could focus on designing and creating new jewelry, the part of the business he loved the most. Katia took over sourcing the raw materials, managing the accounts, and marketing.

Katia flew toward Robby with her arms outstretched. Her tall frame equaled his height. She was a striking beauty, with platinum hair cascading down her back. Penelope felt a twinge of unease as she watched Katia approach. There was something about the woman's presence that always made her feel slightly off-balance. Penelope was equally pretty, but Katia had a confidence that she envied.

"Oh Robby, I'm so sorry to hear about Tessa. I just got back in town and heard the news. I came as fast as I could. Why didn't you call me?"

"I've been just so overwhelmed, but I'm glad you're back," Robby said, sinking into her hug. He closed his eyes and inhaled deeply.

The intimacy of their embrace stirred a mix of emotions—sympathy for Robby's need for comfort, yet also strangely protective of Tessa's memory.

Katia's embrace lingered. Penelope cleared her throat, hoping Katia would release her grasp. She felt like an intruder witnessing a private moment.

Katia backed away. "Penelope, hello. What are you doing here?"

Surprise flashed through Penelope. Katia knew she was friends with Robby and Tessa.

"She was the one who found Tessa," Robby said quietly.

Penelope's stomach churned. The image of Tessa's lifeless body flashed in her mind, and she had to take a deep breath to steady herself. She wondered how long her brain would keep showing her those images.

"I just came to see how Robby is doing," Penelope explained.

Katia leaned forward, clasping Penelope's hand between both of hers, and shook vigorously. "Thank you for checking on Robby."

Penelope pulled her hand away, splaying her fingers, then clenching them into a fist and back out again. Katia's grip was deceptively strong.

"I'm just devastated to hear about Tessa. Does anybody know what happened?" Katia's English was good, but her accent thickened the faster she spoke.

Robby shook his head.

"That's what Penelope and I were just discussing. On Saturday, they kept me at the police station for half of the night. They asked me the same questions over and over. They thought that I could have something to do with Tessa's murder. And then Penelope found out that the police are looking at her mother as a suspect."

Penelope's heart clenched at the mention of her mother. Yesterday's fear and anger came rushing back. Clara was confident she would be cleared, but as of now, she was still a suspect.

"Why would the police think that your mother would hurt Tessa?" Katia pulled a chair next to Penelope.

"I have no idea, but I think she explained herself well enough for them to move on to other suspects. I was going to ask you, Robby, how well you knew Jessie Hanlon?" She held her breath, hoping her question didn't seem too pointed. She was walking a fine line between being a friend and an amateur detective.

"Jessie Hanlon?" Katia repeated.

"She was the vendor next to us at the festival. She's very competitive," Robby replied.

"Jessie was next to Tessa all day, and she was really rude in the morning. The police questioned her on Sunday," Penelope said, trying to keep her tone neutral even as her mind whirled with possibilities.

Robby's cell phone rang. "Excuse me." He stepped into the hallway.

Katia watched as he exited, then turned her attention to Penelope. "I hope they find who did this quickly. This Jessie Hanlon seems like a good suspect. Do you know what she told the police?"

Penelope felt a surge of irrational defensiveness. She had her suspicions about Jessie, but she wasn't the only suspect on the list. "I talked to her a couple of days ago and I can't imagine she was involved. She and my sister are old high school friends." Penelope surprised herself by lying. She suspected Jessie. There was no way to rule her out yet. The conflict between her words and thoughts made her feel dishonest, adding to her discomfort.

Katia leaned toward Penelope and lowered her voice. "I hope everything settles down after the funeral. I realize this sounds insensitive, but Robby needs to pull it together fast. He has some national press lined up for the new jewelry collection."

"Maggie mentioned the magazine," Penelope said. "That's wonderful. I hope he can finish the new pieces, but it would certainly be understandable if he needed to take some time." She tried to balance acknowledging the opportunity and respecting Robby's grief.

"Between us, the shop is struggling because our vendors have increased their prices substantially. We need the press for this new line to draw in more customers with bigger wallets," Katia whispered.

Penelope's eyes widened slightly. She never expected the shop to have financial problems. Could that be a motive? She immediately felt guilty entertaining the idea that Robby could care more about money than his wife.

"Oh, I didn't realize. I always thought that the shop made a nice profit. Robby orders a lot of crystals from my mother. I assumed everything was okay." As she spoke, Penelope's mind was working overtime, trying to fit this new piece into the puzzle of Tessa's death. The weight of suspicion and secrets lingered in the air, making her long for the simplicity of her life before the murder.

"I have been trying to keep the business side away from him. But Robby had to meet with our accountant on Saturday while I was out of town, so I assume he knows everything now."

"I had no idea there were problems." Penelope shifted in her seat.

"I hope this doesn't sound inappropriate, but the money from Tessa's life insurance may just save us." Katia spun a black onyx ring around the middle finger of her right hand while a three-carat diamond engagement ring sparkled on her left. The black onyx reminded Penelope of the bracelet Robby gave her at the festival.

Her candor was disturbing. "Life insurance? Did she have a lot?"

"Yeah. The business pays for a two-million-dollar policy each for Robby, Tessa, me, and Tom to ensure the company will survive."

Penelope gulped. "Wow." Two million dollars seemed like a big policy, but Penelope had never been married, so she could be totally off base. She made a mental note to research life insurance.

Katia nodded. "I understand it's crass, but we will need every penny to keep this place going."

Penelope was shocked at how forthcoming Katia was being since they were only casual acquaintances. She wondered if Katia simply needed a friend to talk to. Penelope never saw Katia at a restaurant or shop with anyone. "I didn't—"

"That was the funeral home," Robby said, reentering the workshop.

"Have you decided when the service will be?" Penelope asked.

"Uh, yes. The police released her body today, so the service will be Saturday morning." Robby sat back at the gemstone sander. Penelope sensed he wanted to be alone.

"Do you need any help with the arrangements? I'd be happy to pitch in," Penelope offered.

Robby nodded. "I—"

"I'll help," Katia interrupted. "I mean, Robby is my business partner, so I should be the one to help him organize the service." Katia smiled sweetly, catching Penelope's eye.

"We are all here for you, Robby." Penelope stood. "I'd better get going back to the museum. I have a group of Girl Scouts coming in to earn their geology badges this afternoon."

"I need to run too," Katia said. "I'm vetting a new vendor."

"Oh? You didn't mention this before," Robby said.

"You don't need to worry about it. I've got it all handled." Katia hopped up and strode through the doorway. "It was nice to see you, Penelope. See you later, Robby," she called from halfway down the hall.

Penelope raised her eyebrows. "She has a lot of energy."

Robby let out a slight chuckle. "Yeah, she's never at a loss for words, and she walks as fast as she talks."

"She sure seems to have great connections in the gemstone world, though. Your new pieces are just stunning, Robby. I heard about the magazine spread for the new line."

Robby sighed and leaned back onto his stool. "Instead of a birthday line, it's now a memorial line. I hope to tie them into some of her different candles that she made and use them in the photographs of the jewelry."

"I'm sure whatever you decide to do will be wonderful. She would have loved that you made a special line for her." Penelope squeezed Robby's forearm.

"I'll ask Clara for some ideas on how to coordinate with the candles she and Tessa were planning."

"I'm sure she would love to help you with that." Listening to Robby talk about the candles made Penelope depressed. Sadness seemed to stop time, but with so much to do before the gala, she couldn't let herself sink into the emptiness.

"Listen, Penelope. Please tell Clara how sorry I am that the police would suspect her even for a minute. I was surprised how invasive they were during my questioning, and I feel bad that Clara had to go through that, too."

"What do you mean, invasive?"

"Some questions were things I would expect, but some of it was personal, and some were embarrassing."

Personal and embarrassing. Penelope made a mental note to write that down.

"What did they ask?"

"They asked me about my business, her business, and if our relationship was good. They wanted to know if there was anything stressful that we were dealing with and asked about our finances—how much money we had, and if we had life insurance."

Penelope rocked on her heels, trying to stop herself from prying about the business finances. "Love and money are big motivators for some people."

Robby ran his hands down his face. "I'm shocked anybody could think that I would murder Tessa over money. Both of our shops did okay. We weren't millionaires, but we were certainly comfortable. Maybe they just didn't think that somebody that looked like me could be married to somebody that looked like her if there wasn't money involved."

"Tessa was a beautiful woman, but you're no slouch yourself, Robby." Penelope smiled, but her mind was buzzing. Katia said that the shop was struggling. Something was off. Was Robby lying to her?

"Did Tessa have insurance? I mean. I'm sure it would be helpful to take some pressure off you," she pried timidly.

"Of course. Most married couples do. But we only had insurance to make sure that the other person was okay if something happened. We never really thought that something would happen to one of us, at least not for a long time. But we had always said that we would do our best to keep the other's shop afloat because we both loved what we did so much."

"So, you're going to keep Tessa's candle shop open? That's wonderful. Do you know how to make candles?" Penelope wondered why Katia would keep the financial state of the jewelry business from Robby. Surely, if he met with the shop's accountant on the day of the festival, he would know that the business needed money. But then, Penelope remembered him saying that the accountant was only dropping by to pick up paperwork, so perhaps he was truly unaware of the problems.

Did he really meet with the accountant or simply hand over the paperwork? Was Robby even at the shop on Saturday, or did he go somewhere else and lie to Tessa? Maybe he's just in denial about everything that is happening. It is one of the stages of grief, after all. Penelope's thoughts were spiraling out of control.

"Tessa has an entire book that she calls her candle recipe book. She always told me that if I could make jewelry, I could learn to make candles. But I may have to hire someone to help me learn or just hire someone to make the candles for me. If I can understand and follow the recipes, I can make sure that they make them exactly the way Tessa would have. That will keep her memory alive."

"I think that's wonderful, Robby." Penelope walked to the far side of Robby's project table and scanned the gemstones and metals that Robby had organized in tiny containers along the edge. "I don't know how to make candles but I'm certainly willing to help you figure it out if you need." Penelope gasped. "Olivia could do it. She's a chef, but if making candles is kind of like a recipe, I'm certain that she could help us figure out exactly how Tessa made them. My mother would still love to create the crystal candle line, too." Penelope grinned. She felt good about her small part in keeping Tessa's memory alive.

"That would be fantastic, Penelope." Robby jumped from the stool and engulfed Penelope in a hug.

"No problem. I'll talk to Olivia and Mom the next time I see them. If you can find Tessa's recipe book, I'm sure between us, we can learn." Penelope wrenched herself from Robby's embrace. A glance at her watch made her gasp again. "Oh my gosh, I'd better go. I have to run by my mom's shop and grab some minerals and then get back to the museum before the Girl Scouts show up for their badge meeting."

"You are certainly one of the busiest people I've ever met. You have your jobs at the museum and with the city, and I've even seen you working in your mom's crystal shop from time to time. I certainly hope you have time for fun."

Penelope shrugged. "Sometimes. I'm training for an aquathlon, so plenty of running and swimming to do. I should get going. I'll call you after I talk to Olivia and Mom, okay?"

"Yes, that would be fantastic. Thank you so much for stopping by. It made me feel better. I think I'll sketch a few more ideas this afternoon for Tessa's line."

Penelope said goodbye and hustled down the hallway to the front of the jewelry store.

"Bye, Maggie," she hollered, whizzing through the front door of the shop on her way to The Crystal Cove to gather a few last things she needed for her afternoon visit from the scouts.

Penelope hopped into her Hummer and pushed the start button, running the conversations with Katia and Robby through her mind as she put the car in gear.

Money was a popular motive for murder, according to the television shows she watched. Penelope felt a piercing pain in her stomach when she pressed her foot on the brake pedal and slipped the car into neutral. She opened the notes application on her phone and wrote, "Suspect: Robby, Motive: Life Insurance."

Chapter Ten

Penelope pushed the door to the shop, but it wouldn't budge. *Early lunch, huh, Mom?* Penelope searched for the shop key on her thick ring. As she unlocked the front door, Penelope could smell the burning herbs, which meant Clara was in the back of the shop hard at work in front of her mini table-top cauldron she purchased at an antique store in Salem, Massachusetts. The agate door chimes announced her arrival. Penelope was never sure if Clara believed she was a genuine witch, but she certainly liked to try to convince people she was one.

If it wasn't always so smelly it would be endearing, Penelope thought as an herbal wave assaulted her olfactory system. Before Clara could put away the spell ingredients, Penelope burst through the hanging crystal bead curtain.

"Ha! Caught you red-handed this time. Please don't blow anything up like you did before. I don't have time to help you clean the ash from every surface of the shop today."

Clara jumped back, clutching her heart with her right hand, leaving her left to steady herself against the cabinet. A smoldering pot sat on the counter behind her. "Goodness Penelope, you scared me. What are you doing here? Did you hear anything new from the police?"

"No. I went to see Robby this morning." Penelope peered into the cauldron.

Clara swatted her away. "Oh, how is he doing? Poor thing must be devastated."

Penelope pressed her lips together and nodded solemnly. "He's like a hermit in his workroom. Maggie Flynn works there now. She said that he hasn't seen or talked to anyone since Tessa's death."

"Oh, Maggie is such a nice girl. Were you able to see him?"

"Yes, we spoke for a few minutes, then Katia came in."

Clara turned to stir the contents in her pot. "Oh, good. I'm glad she's back. She's such a sweetheart. I'm sure it will help Robby to have her around."

"She came whizzing into the workshop while I was talking to Robby. She said that she just got back into town and heard about Tessa."

"I wonder why Robby didn't tell her?" Clara tossed a handful of dried herbs in her mortar and pestle and ground them into small pieces.

"He isn't thinking straight. How could you? Maggie said he has barely come out of his studio." Penelope surveyed the workbench, trying to figure out what her mother was brewing. She didn't want to ask. It might encourage her. "I mentioned the diamonds in the candles, and he hardly remembered."

"I'll check in on him later." Clara added dried rose petals to the herb mix. "Katia is good with the business. I heard her give a talk once at a chamber meeting about how she finds new vendors and she is very skilled for as young as she is."

"I thought her family was in the gemstone business already."

"Yes, but she has grown way beyond her family's connections. She flies all over the world. Robby has access to some of the rarest stones, thanks to her."

"You know a lot about their business."

Clara handed Penelope a long-handled metal spoon. "Stir. I make it a point to keep up with the other businesses in town. Plus, Katia sometimes passes along names of vendors she thinks I may like."

"Oh, that reminds me. Robby is planning to keep the candle shop going, and I told him I would ask you and Olivia to help decipher Tessa's candle recipes."

Clara turned and threw a handful of the crushed herbs and petals and two citrine crystals into her boiling pot. "I'd be happy to help, and I'm sure Olivia will, too."

"I'll try to call her later, but if you see her, ask her for me, okay?"

Clara nodded, watching the liquid boil. She took the spoon from Penelope and kept stirring. A distinctive stench permeated the air, forcing Penelope to wave her hand in front of her nose.

"Ugh, Mom, that is awful. Why are you back here making stinky spells rather than having the rock shop open for business?" Penelope clamped a hand over her nose and mouth.

"It's lunch. This is a wonderful time for me to practice my craft."

Penelope gagged. "Or it's an even better time for people on their lunch breaks to go shopping. Besides, how many times do I have to tell you that you are not a witch?"

"And how many times do I have to tell you, Penelope, that I am constantly evolving?"

"Well, I'll agree with that." Penelope hugged her mother and patted her shoulder. "What is that spell for, anyway?"

Clara winked. "You'll find out soon enough."

"On second thought, I don't want to know." Penelope backed away.

Clara sighed. "Why are you here, dear, if you have no news?"

"I need some mineral samples for the Girl Scout troop this afternoon."

"Just the typical amethyst, quartz, hematite, sulfur, and Iceland Spar?"

"Yep. Same speech and experiments. Just a different troop." Penelope backed through the crystal bead curtain. Midnight lay curled up on his bed, fast asleep. Penelope wondered if he couldn't smell Clara's potions or if the feline was just used to the stench.

"Top cabinet by the register. I just got a new shipment in a few days ago and hid the best samples for you."

Penelope retrieved the box of mineral samples labeled with her name. She glimpsed a flame at the opposite end of the shop. "Oh, you're burning Tessa's Amethyst Falls candle she gave you?"

"Not exactly." Clara hollered as the brew in her cauldron reached a roaring boil, its sound reverberating through the shop.

"What do you mean, not exactly?"

"That's the candle that I sort of stole from the crime scene the other day. The one Tessa gave me is behind it on the shelf."

"What do you mean, the one you stole?" she asked, unsure if she wanted to hear the answer.

"Do you remember the candle that Tessa was displaying at the festival but wasn't selling?"

Penelope pictured the tent filled with jewelry and candles. She remembered Tessa had the matching Amethyst Falls at the festival. "Yes."

"I didn't want Tessa's candle locked up in some police station, so when the cops weren't looking, I swiped it," Clara admitted. Penelope walked back to the workroom so she and her mother could stop shouting.

"Mom!" Penelope was both shocked and impressed by her mother's tenacity. "How could you?"

"It was easy. The officers packing up the evidence weren't looking too closely at me, and you and Ryan were focused on Robby. When they told me I shouldn't be in the tent, I just wrapped my sweater around it and hustled out of there." Clara turned off the burner. "Need to let it rest now," she said, tapping the lip of the pot.

"Tessa gave you one the day before. I still don't understand why you took the other one."

Clara sailed into the showroom with Penelope close behind. She flipped the shop sign to 'open,' and checked that the door was unlocked. "Because these candles were special to Tessa and me. They were the prototype for the line we were going to create together. I wanted to keep the police from getting their hands on it. Who knows what would happen to that beautiful candle then?"

"You better hope the police don't find out what you did. It was evidence."

"Oh, please. It's a candle," Clara retorted.

Penelope looked closely at the Amethyst Falls burning on the shelf. It had different speckles near the bottom than the one Tessa had given her mother. "Mom, did you notice these little flecks near the bottom? And the crystals are bigger."

Clara took a deep inhale. "Perhaps the flecks are for extra fragrance. This candle smells stronger than the other one."

Penelope nodded. "Hopefully, when we find her recipes, we can figure out what she was doing."

"This lavender scent will work great with a lot of my spells." Clara winked at Penelope.

Penelope shook open a sales bag and filled it with a dozen crystals of each mineral from the box for the scouts, then stuffed them into her messenger bag.

"Take the whole box, honey." Clara grabbed a cloth and began dusting the mineral spheres that lined the shelves.

"My office and workroom are overflowing with samples and maps for the new collection. I just need enough for the troop today. I'll get the rest later if that's okay." Penelope gave her mother a quick hug and kiss and left the shop, thinking about the two candles her mom had from Tessa's collection. They were different, but similar. Tessa was most likely experimenting with different recipes. She hoped they could look at Tessa's recipe book soon to get some answers. Certainly, no one would kill Tessa over a candle. But in the show *Murdoch Mysteries*, people would kill for less.

The day was sunny and clear, with a hint of a chill in the air. Penelope watched window shoppers glide down Main Street as she unlocked her car. She gazed across the road toward The Drip Shack, which sat forgotten after the weekend's chaos.

A shadow flitted across the window. Penelope blinked hard, but the shadow remained. Someone was in Tessa's candle shop.

Penelope pushed the door to The Crystal Cove open without taking her eyes off the shop across the street. "Mom, come here. Someone is in Tessa's shop!" She wrapped her sweater tightly around her sides, protecting herself from the crisp spring breeze.

Clara was at Penelope's side in a flash. "Who could it be?"

"I don't know, but we need to find out. Come on."

Penelope and Clara sprinted across the street to the candle store. A closed sign hung tilted in the window and the lights were out. Penelope shook the door, but it was locked. She peered through the window and knocked on the glass, but didn't see any movement.

Penelope searched the sidewalk in front of Tessa's store, looking for something to pick the lock. Her auburn curls bobbed around her face while she meandered along the sidewalk. Laurel had taught Penelope how to pick a door lock after she left her keys inside her dorm room more than once. She had become quite skilled at opening different locks over the years when she forgot or lost her keys. Penelope picked up a discarded toothpick near the road gutter. "Yes! Now I just need a paperclip or something." She rooted through her messenger bag and found a stray bobby pin. Penelope rarely wore them, but she was grateful that she never cleaned out her bag. "This will work."

Penelope grabbed the bobby pin and folded it like the letter "L."

"Oh, geez, Penelope. Why are you touching a used toothpick? Gross," Clara complained.

"Shush." The trick to picking a lock was a couple of good picks, a little patience, and concentration. In less than thirty seconds flat, Penelope and Clara were inside the candle store.

Penelope pulled her cell phone from the pocket of her cardigan and flipped on the flashlight. She did not dare turn on the store lights in case someone outside was looking in. Tessa's murder was in all the television news reports and newspapers. There could not possibly be anyone in town who hadn't heard what happened at the festival. Penelope tiptoed around the inside of the candle shop, making sure her boots did not make the normal clapping sound. Clara was silent on her heels.

She was unsure why she was trying to be so quiet, but it just seemed like what you do in the dark when you're chasing a shadow. Penelope wandered the store in a circle, inspected the candle displays, and looked inside the empty register. Most store owners emptied their cash boxes in the evenings using the after-hours deposit slot at the bank. Tessa would only have money in the store if she'd come back on Saturday after the festival. Which she didn't. Because she was dead.

Clara hurried to the back door of the shop, leaving Penelope alone in the darkness.

Penelope circled back to the display near the front window. The store was empty. Had her eyes played tricks on her? Was there a shadow in the candle shop earlier, or was that just Penelope's overactive imagination at play?

"I checked the back. I don't see anything," Clara whispered through the darkness. The only light, other than from Penelope's phone, came from the front windows.

"Me either," Penelope said, moving toward Tessa's workroom. Her candle-making shop was meticulous, like an assembly line with base ingredients like waxes and containers on one end, then wicks, fragrances, and colors along the length of the tables. The setup reminded her of Robby's workshop at the jewelry store. Baskets of clear, purple, and golden crystals were perched near the middle of the table for adding to the freshly poured wax. "We should probably get back to your store before someone sees us in here and grows suspicious."

"I agree. I would rather not have that cute Ryan arrest you for breaking and entering," Clara paused. "Or maybe I do..."

"Mom. Give it a rest. He's just a friend from high school and have you already forgotten that he thinks that you may have killed Tessa with a Monte Cristo sandwich?"

Clara chuckled. "Oh honey, if I were going to murder someone, I would just use a spell." She winked, making Penelope cringe.

"Please don't say things like that around other people. The last thing we need is the police thinking that you are a lunatic who believes in witches and spells and magic."

"But I do believe in witches and spells and magic."

Penelope followed Clara to the front of the store and turned off her flashlight. She picked up two of the drip candles and held them up to the window. Penelope spun the candles, inspecting them closely. "Mom, I love you, but some people, like the police, will think that you are a little off your rocker and use that against you. Remember, Andre is the chief now, and he is a by-the-book kind of guy. They need to solve this murder, so why not pin it on this eccentric crystal shop owner who does spells in her back room? Certainly, she could poison a sandwich."

"Oh honey, I would never poison a Monte Cristo. They're just too delicious!" Clara cackled so loud it made Penelope burst out laughing. "Plus, Andre knows me."

"Hmm."

"Have you talked to him since he's been back in town?"

"No. Avoiding him is easier."

Penelope set the drip candles back on the stand when the sunlight caught a gleam of the tiny crystals. Looking closer, she could see purple crystals inside the candles. They were not as bright as the diamonds in the candle that Tessa had given to Clara on Friday. *This must be one of the first ones she tried with the real amethysts that didn't work as well,* she thought. Penelope took her fingernail and scratched the edge, trying to loosen the gemstone, when suddenly the overhead lights flooded the inside of the shop.

"What are you doing here?" a voice demanded.

Penelope's heart thumped while her eyes adjusted to the sudden brightness. She whipped around to see Robby standing in front of her. "I'm so sorry, Robby. We saw a shadow through the windows, and I was worried someone had broken into the store."

"That's okay, Penelope. Hi Clara. I didn't realize it was you two when I came in through the back door." Robby's face softened. "After we spoke, Penelope, I decided to look for the candle recipes. How did you get in here, anyway?"

Penelope shrugged. "I can sort of pick locks. Sorry."

"I was thinking of taking some candles to my shop to sell and then some I'm going to keep at home. I need to hire someone to run her shop, but at least I can sell them in my store for the time being." Tears flooded his eyes, spilling over his cheeks.

Penelope moved toward Robby. "I'd be happy to go through her candles and pack them up. If you tell me which ones you want to keep and which you want to go to your store, I'll take care of it for you. This must be hard on you."

He welcomed her hug. "I'm so sorry. I didn't mean to blubber all over you. I don't think I've been able to really cry yet. I've just been in shock about what happened. Everybody just loved Tessa. I can't imagine why she was murdered. I'm having a hard time believing this is all real."

"That's what friends are for. Were you able to get in touch with Tessa's family?" Clara asked. "She never talked about her family."

"Tessa didn't have much. Her parents passed away years ago, and she has one sister. They aren't close."

"That's too bad, but at least she had you."

"That's true."

"You guys were one of the happiest couples I've ever met," Clara said.

Robby started crying again.

"Oh, my goodness," Clara hugged Robby. "Did I say something wrong?"

"No," Robby sniffed. "Tessa was acting weird and distant the last few days. I was worried that she was unhappy with me."

Penelope felt surprised. Robby never mentioned Tessa being unhappy earlier this morning.

"Sweetie, don't you think that for a second." Clara pulled a stool from behind the counter and directed him to sit.

Robby wiped his tears with a handkerchief and cleared his throat. "I can't think of anyone who would want to hurt her, and I feel helpless."

"Robby, when we were here on Friday, there was a woman that came out of the shop while we were crossing the street, and she was very upset. Tessa said it was a former employee. Did she tell you about that?" Penelope asked.

Robby rocked backward on the stool. "No, she didn't."

"She had short, dark hair and was not very tall. I would guess late thirties," Clara said.

Robby shook his head. "I don't know. The only people who worked in the shop were high schoolers. I wonder why Tessa didn't tell me. The only thing I can think of is there was one day last week Tessa came home fuming mad. I first thought she was mad at me about something, but then she said that somebody had come into the shop and challenged the Amethyst Falls candle design. They claimed she stole the design and was violating their patent. But then she never mentioned it again, so I figured it was resolved or not a big deal."

"Did you tell the police?"

Robby nodded. "They said that they would look into it."

Penelope took a mental note. She planned to investigate and find out who that mystery woman was and if she was involved with the patent claim. "I didn't realize you could patent a candle."

Robby smiled. "That's what Tessa said. It had something to do with the fact that she had a scented core, but the outside of the candle had a different scent than the inside."

"It was about the fragrance? Not the diamonds inside?" Clara asked.

"Diamonds?" Robby shook his head.

"The little ones inside the purple candles?" Penelope pressed. She wondered if Robby should see a doctor. He was struggling mentally and physically. He didn't seem to remember details about the candles, and his movements seemed labored.

"Oh, yeah. I doubt it. I've never heard of anyone else using diamonds in candles and those were just little junk diamonds that I had in the shop that were too small to use in any of the jewelry. They were worthless." Robby stood up and rubbed his forehead. "I've got to go. I can't be here anymore today."

"We understand. Why don't you give us your key, and we will come back and choose some candles to bring to your shop," Clara offered.

"Thank you." Robby spun a key from his ring and handed it to Clara.

Penelope helped Clara lock up the candle shop, then drove to the museum, replaying their conversation. Each time she talked with him, Robby dropped more information that made her question everything surrounding Tessa's murder. The suspects were mounting, and Penelope was determined to make sure that the police headed their investigation in the right direction, away from her mother.

Chapter Eleven

Penelope tossed her cell phone into her messenger bag and slung it onto the couch in her office, giving Jasper a head scratch as she lay sleeping beside the desk. With a bag of minerals in hand, she meandered from her office, down the echoing hallway, around the corner by the dinosaur displays, through the rock showroom, and to the front of the museum to greet twelve anxious and excited Girl Scouts.

"Hi, Miss Penelope!"

"Hi, Charlie," Penelope raised her hand, and the young troop leader smacked it with a painful high-five. "Wow, girl, that's got some sting on it." Penelope laughed. She shook her hand in the air, hoping to make the tingling stop. Charlie and her mother had been coming to the museum since she was a toddler, so Penelope was excited to entertain her Girl Scout troop, finally. "Where's your Den Mom?"

"She went to the gift shop. She'll be back." Charlie took charge and counted the girls. Penelope wasn't surprised that the scouts voted for Charlie as their youth leader. "We're all here. We can start."

"Are you ladies ready to earn your geology badges today?" Penelope asked. Charlie and her friends clapped and cheered. Penelope loved it when groups of kids were so enthusiastic about the museum. Showing students the wonders of science was Penelope's favorite part of the job. Most kids love rocks, minerals, and fossils, and the museum was the ideal place for fun school field trips and overnight lock-ins for youth groups and scouts.

Penelope enjoyed so many aspects of science that instructing the kids, researching rock samples and formations from around the world, and working with the city gave her a balance that kept her happy and excited to get up and go to work each day. She could spend the morning explaining the difference between quartz and fluorite to a group of kids and showing them how to do all the different mineral tests to determine the sample's name. Then, in the afternoon, she could help the city engineers figure out how to stop the latest sinkhole that was about to engulf a bridge crossing near the Sierra Springs Lake, or catalog and study the latest shipment of rocks from exotic locations. Every day held something new.

By four o'clock, the scouts from Troop 901 left the museum with geology badges in hand and a bag full of new treasures, so Penelope inspected the display cases and organized the load-in process for the next few days for the new samples that would be unveiled at the gala. For the first time in the past few weeks, Penelope felt that preparations for the gala were on track.

Penelope returned to The Crystal Cove to help her mother pick some candles to take to Robby's shop. Jasper was happy to join Midnight for some evening playtime. Laurel texted Penelope to see if she wanted to drop by the cafe for dinner, but when Penelope mentioned she was helping Robby, Laurel and Olivia showed up at Clara's store with dinner in hand.

The evening sun filtered through the windows of The Crystal Cove, casting rainbow prisms across the polished wooden floor. The scent of lavender incense filled the air inside. Wind chimes hung in the shop corners, tinkling in the breeze from the ceiling fan. Shelves lined with an array of colorful crystals, geodes, and healing stones stretched from floor to ceiling, creating a labyrinth of mystical treasures.

Clara recounted her and Penelope's conversation with Robby while they ate. Penelope was hunched over the counter, her fingers flying across Clara's laptop keyboard as she delved deep into an internet search on candle patents. The soft glow of the screen illuminated her concentrated face.

Suddenly, a handmade orange creamsicle appeared under Penelope's nose, the condensation already forming on its surface. Laurel stood there, a playful smile on her face, holding out the treat.

"Thanks, Laurel." Penelope's eyes darted to the nearby stack of napkins on the counter, her hand instinctively reaching for one.

"No! Take it." Laurel insisted, waving the creamsicle enticingly.

"Napkin," Penelope countered, her fingers already grasping the edge of a paper napkin.

"Take the stick, Penelope." Laurel's voice held a note of exasperation as she continued to hold out the frozen treat.

Penelope eyed the creamsicle. Her hand hovered uncertainly between the dessert and the napkins. Finally, unable to resist any longer, she grabbed a napkin and, in one fluid motion, spun it around the wooden stick, snatching the creamsicle from Laurel's fingers.

"You are so strange." Laurel laughed, shaking her head as she set the cooler bag of remaining treats on the counter.

Penelope's cheeks flushed slightly as she defended herself. "No, I'm not. You know I hate the feel of wooden popsicle sticks. They are so dry and gross." She shuddered dramatically for effect.

Olivia's voice chimed in from below the counter, "And wooden cooking spoons and cutting boards. Weirdo." She sat on the floor feeding small pieces of turkey to Jasper and Midnight.

"Am not," Penelope retorted, taking a defiant bite of the dessert.

"Now you three, stop fighting. Honestly," Clara admonished, though her tone was more amused than stern. "I may have to do a friendship spell on the three of you." Clara laughed, pulling a stack of tarot cards from beneath the counter.

"Olivia, you have outdone yourself with this batch," Penelope admitted.

"They are fantastic," Laurel commented, leaning against the counter, and twirling a strand of hair around her finger.

Olivia beamed with pride. "I'm working on some new flavors, too."

Clara perched on the stool next to her oldest daughter, the wooden seat creaking slightly under her weight. "Olivia gets that creativity from me. I've blessed her gifts." She winked at Penelope, who responded with an eye roll.

"I'm pretty sure Olivia learned how to be a chef at culinary school, not from your spells."

Clara grunted. "You could benefit from some of my spells too, young lady. I have a love potion ready to go for you and Ryan. Well, unless he throws me in jail."

"Oh, Mom. Stop."

Laurel laughed. "She could be on to something, Penelope. If you date him, he wouldn't dare throw your mom in prison."

"Let's change the subject." Penelope stared at the computer screen. "Like, how do you prove a patent on a candle design?" She finished the creamsicle, launching the stick into the trash can.

Clara waved the key to Tessa's shop in the air. "Why don't we go see what we can find out? I'll get some boxes from my workroom to take over."

With the dinner trash put away, the women hustled across Main Street to the darkened candle shop. A flick of the light switch brought back memories of just a few short days ago when the foursome visited Tessa to investigate the fancy candles that Clara spied in the window display.

"I can't believe Robby caught you breaking into Tessa's candle shop," Laurel laughed.

"We weren't breaking in. We were trying to protect the store," Clara exclaimed. "Like neighborhood watch."

"We're just lucky it was Robby, and he is still in shock, so he didn't seem to care that we picked the lock," Penelope said.

"Thank you, ladies, for helping pack up some candles. I couldn't bring myself to watch him sort through all of this by himself," Clara said, setting the boxes on the floor.

"I'm glad he plans to keep the store open," Olivia commented. "I like the idea of trying to learn how to recreate her candles. If I can figure out her wax and fragrance recipes, we can teach his new employees how to do it."

"That would be wonderful," Clara said. "I'm sure he'd appreciate that."

"You can use the one Mom stole from the crime scene and reverse-engineer how Tessa constructed the candles."

Olivia raised her eyebrows and stared at Clara. "Mom, you didn't," she exclaimed.

Penelope nodded wildly. "Mmm, hmm. You know, Mom, you may end up in jail after all...for theft."

"Stop it, Penelope." Clara brushed off her daughter's teasing. "I'll pick some nice candles for Robby's shop."

"And I'm going to go through her files and see if I can find anything about this patent dispute," Penelope said.

Olivia looked at Laurel. "I guess that leaves us to look for her recipe book."

"I wonder if he would mind if I take some to Tipsy Java. We could sell them, take that money, and match it, and make a donation to Tessa's favorite charity," Laurel said.

Olivia moved the nicer candles to an empty table in the corner. "That's a great idea. I'm also going to spread the word that Robby is looking for a manager. I have a few friends who may want the job."

In just a few scant hours, their favorite candles were boxed up for transport to McCaul's Fine Jewels and The Tipsy Java. Clara rearranged the leftover inventory and found more in the storeroom to fill out the shelves. When Robby was ready to reopen, all he would need was a couple of employees, because the store was ready.

Laurel and Olivia found Tessa's candle list and details of how to mix, pour, and set the wax into molds.

"These look pretty similar to food recipes, but learning how to re-create the look of the more intricate ones, like the Amethyst Falls, will take a little time," Olivia said.

"I'm sure you can figure it out." Laurel hopped onto a stool by the register.

"I'll also have to figure out how you get the wick to stay straight and in the center of the candle." Olivia flipped through Tessa's candle recipe book.

"Hey Penelope, did you find anything about the patent lawsuit?" Laurel asked, peering over the counter.

Penelope sat on the floor with dozens of files around her. She had barely said a word as the others packed candles and rearranged the shop. She nodded.

"Boy, did I." She looked up. "It's all here. I'm going to take these with me."

"You should turn it over to Robby or the police," Clara said.

"A candle company called Wicked Thyme Candles, spelled like the herb, filed a lawsuit against Tessa about the fragrance cores. The lawsuit says that she stole their design, and they not only wanted her to stop, but they were asking for over three million dollars in damages." Penelope stood up, clutching the documents.

Oh my gosh, Tessa, Penelope thought, her heart pounded. Three million? That's... that's insane! Her hands trembled slightly as she held the papers, the weight of the situation settling heavily on her shoulders. Could someone from Wicked Thyme Candles have murdered Tessa because of the lawsuit?

"Wow, that's awful," Olivia said.

Awful doesn't even begin to cover it, Penelope thought. "This would have ruined Tessa if she lost." Penelope wondered if the lawsuit was the reason that Tessa seemed distant to Robby. This lawsuit could certainly have preoccupied her.

"Wicked Thyme Candles sounds familiar," Clara commented. "I'm not sure why, though."

"They sound familiar to me, too. Was there an article in the business journal?" Laurel pulled her phone from her pocket and began typing.

Penelope set a reminder on her phone to investigate Wicked Thyme Candles when she got home to her computer. She thumbed through the papers, her eyes scanning rapidly. "Tessa was countersuing. She had tons of research on candle making, fragrances, and the different industry-accepted methods of candle production." As she spoke, Penelope's admiration for her friend grew. Tessa was not letting her company and creativity go down without a fight. Penelope wondered if this determination cost Tessa her life.

"I'm glad she was going to fight back," Clara said.

"Her counterclaim was asking for five million dollars. She uses the same business attorney that you do, Mom." Penelope wondered if Sandra would talk with her. Even though Tessa was dead, Robby was keeping the company alive, meaning the lawsuit could continue, she assumed.

"A countersuit like that would certainly give someone motive to kill her," Olivia said.

"Got it," Laurel exclaimed. "That's why we recognize them. Wicked Thyme Candles is owned by Marlene Black."

"Louis Black's sister," Clara said. "Of course. There was a write-up about her in the business journal, but I think her shop is only online."

"Wait. Louis Black of LB's Deli is her brother?" Olivia asked.

Penelope sank onto a nearby stool. "The same LB's Deli who sold you the Monte Cristo sandwich for Tessa at the festival."

Chapter Twelve

The gray clouds hung heavy in the sky while the locals filed into the Sierra Springs Methodist church to mourn the untimely passing of Tessa McCaul. The shops along Main Street were closed on Saturday morning to give the owners time to grieve one of their own.

Penelope slipped into the back pew just before the minister stepped to the podium. She timed her late arrival so that she could inconspicuously choose a spot that would give her the best vantage point to observe the attendees. She heard on a true crime podcast that killers sometimes attended their victim's funerals. So far, her suspect list was growing, but she still had no answers. Penelope scrutinized the mourners. She couldn't help but notice the undercurrent of sadness and tension among them.

Tessa had been a member of the Chamber of Commerce, and town officials filled the front pews. One by one, friends stood and remarked about her warm heart, her love of candles and gardening, and her unbreakable bond with her husband Robby. His eulogy was sweet and touching. Nearly every person in the church was reaching for tissues. Behind the tears, a dark secret lingered among them, hidden beneath the cries and condolences. Penelope was certain a killer was present.

Her eyes swept over the pews, taking in the faces of friends and family who had come to say their last good-byes. Penelope looked for clues, like someone at the funeral who wasn't sad enough or appeared to be faking their sorrow. Her mother and sister invited her to sit with them near the front, but she preferred the view from the back row.

Penelope saw Ryan and Andre out of her peripheral vision. The police maintained a presence inside and outside of the church sanctuary. She was still unsettled seeing Andre. She had worked hard to keep him out of her mind, but even after all these years, butterflies filled her stomach when she saw him. Penelope could feel him and Ryan glancing in her direction. She focused on the crowd.

After the ceremony, the minister announced that the family would receive visitors immediately after the private burial. Penelope was relieved that she was not expected to go to the cemetery. While the mourners huddled together in the pews before leaving the church, Penelope quietly took photographs of the crowd by holding the phone to her ear and using her thumb to take photo bursts while she slowly spun in a circle.

She followed the crowd out of the church and into the cold. The weather matched Penelope's mood. Sunlight hid behind thick gray clouds while a soft drizzle of spring rain coated her hair. She snapped one more set of photos of the mourners searching for their cars in the crowded lot.

"Who are you talking to?"

Penelope twirled around to see Andre standing before her.

"Nobody. Why are you here? You weren't friends with Tessa or Robby." Penelope turned and moved toward her car.

"Just paying my respects." He fell in lockstep with her.

"You mean looking for suspects?" Penelope slid her phone into her coat pocket so he wouldn't see the photos on her screen.

"We aren't talking about the investigation. I saw you and just wanted to say hello." Andre shoved his hands into the pockets of his trench coat. Penelope always loved him in a suit.

"Yeah, well. I'm still getting used to the idea of you being back in town." Penelope's auburn curls swirled in a gust of wind.

Andre touched her arm, freezing her mid-step. "Listen, can we talk sometime? Even though it has been a while, I feel like we need to clear the air."

Penelope spun and looked him in the eyes. "No, Andre. I would rather not talk about how you broke up with me by text from sixteen hundred miles away." Penelope wrapped her raincoat around her waist, knotting the belt.

"I can't tell you how sorry I am for that." Andre shuffled his feet. "If I could go back in time, I would never do that to you. I was young and stupid, well, mainly stupid."

"Stop." Penelope raised her hand. "It's okay. We were far apart and had completely different lives. I'm over it." Penelope tried to smile. "Sort of."

Andre looked relieved. "You look good."

Penelope shrugged. "You too. You could have at least come back ugly. That would have made it easier."

Andre chuckled softly.

"Andre, we need to get going," Ryan interrupted their reunion. "Something's come up."

"Is there news about the investigation?" Penelope asked.

Ryan put his hand on hers. "Go home, Penelope."

Penelope audibly sighed.

Andre and Ryan leaped into a police car and swiftly sped away from the parking lot. The rain had stopped, but the wind was whipping. Penelope hustled through the parking lot toward her mother's car where Clara, Olivia, and Laurel were waiting.

"You could have sat with us," Clara remarked.

"I wanted to watch the crowd."

"We saw you talking with Andre," Laurel said. "Did you guys make nice?"

Penelope seesawed her hand. "Uh...as much as possible."

Olivia grinned. "You still like him. I knew it."

"Shush, Olivia. We're at a funeral, for crying out loud," Penelope chastised her sister. She wasn't as concerned that they were at the funeral, but that she wanted to stop the conversation about Andre.

"There were a lot of people at the service. Tessa was well-loved," Clara commented, watching the cars slowly exit the parking lot.

"Do you guys want to go to Robby's?" Laurel asked.

"Yes, let's," Clara said. "I said a blessing spell for Tessa, and I'd like to say a blessing over Robby's home, too. I did a spell to help him heal emotionally before the service. I hope it finds him some comfort."

Penelope was unsure how to respond when her mother talked about casting spells that she was sure helped nothing, but to Clara meant everything. "I have my car, so I am going to swing by the condo to walk Jasper, and then I'll meet you guys there."

"See you in a bit, then," Clara said.

Before Penelope left the parking lot, she scrolled through her photos of the crowd. She recognized most of the people in the photos from town, including Louis Black, with a woman she assumed was his sister Marlene. But the last photo had one person who Penelope recognized but didn't know—the woman who ran out of Tessa's shop on Friday morning.

***

"I'm so sorry, Robby." Penelope embraced her friend.

"Thank you for coming. Your mom is here, and you won't believe how much food Laurel and Olivia brought with them. I really appreciate it." Robby stood up straight. His house was lovely. She had never been there before, but Penelope felt Tessa's presence. The Elgar cello concerto played softly in the background as visitors slowly mingled after paying respects to their unfortunate host.

Wandering through the home, Penelope could see the combination of Robby and Tessa's creativity in the décor. The cozy home was warm and inviting, even on a cold, sad day. Oak bookshelves lined the mossy green walls of the living room and hallways. Each shelf was filled with books and candles of all shapes, sizes, and colors. Large mineral samples sat atop display pedestals between the books.

"I'm going to see if I can help Laurel and Olivia." Penelope squeezed Robby's hands, then slipped through the living room. She spotted her mother's business attorney on the screened porch talking on the phone. Penelope waited for her to hang up. "Excuse me, Sandra?" Penelope removed her raincoat, turned it inside out, and draped it over a chaise lounge.

Sandra Phillips was a tall woman who reminded Penelope of Lily Munster from the 1960s television show. "Penelope, hello."

"Hi, Sandra. I'm glad that I ran into you."

The attorney tucked her phone into her purse. "Is your mom here? That was Alan. He wanted me to tell her the police have officially cleared her."

"Oh, that's wonderful. Yes, she's here somewhere." Penelope looked around to ensure no one was close enough to overhear. "I can't thank you enough for sending Alan when the police questioned her."

"My pleasure. Clara is one of my favorite clients."

Penelope cleared her throat. "I wanted to ask you about another client. Tessa."

Sandra shifted her weight. "I can't talk about her, Penelope."

"I heard you were representing her on the patent lawsuit," Penelope pressed.

Sandra seemed surprised even though she registered little expression. "How do you know that? We hadn't filed the countersuit yet. That information is privileged."

"Robby mentioned that someone was trying to sue Tessa over a candle patent, and I found some of her research and a draft of your countersuit when we were helping organize the candle shop for him. I'm just trying to help." Penelope opened the camera on her phone and showed Sandra a photo. "Is this Marlene Black? The person behind Wicked Thyme Candles?"

Sandra nodded. She leaned toward Penelope, ensuring their conversation was private. "People love Louis, but his sister is vile. She is insisting on proceeding with the lawsuit, and now she is trying to attach it to Robby since they were married." Sandra's anger was palpable.

"You are kidding."

"I wish," Sandra replied. "I'm going to do my best to squash it, but this could ruin Robby."

Penelope stood in stunned silence.

Sandra's eyes widened. "I shouldn't be telling you this, so please keep it quiet. I want to get this settled quickly and quietly, for Robby's sake."

Penelope nodded. "Sure. No problem."

Sandra excused herself to refill her snack plate.

Penelope never understood why the family of the deceased had to host everyone in their house. The mountain of dirty dishes would take days to clean. Penelope did her best to follow the guests, gather discarded cups and plates, and take them to the kitchen. Moving about the house, she monitored the front door and the visitors who doubled as suspects.

"Thank you for helping, Penelope." Katia brought a fresh stack of dirty plates to the sink. Penelope had loaded the dishwasher with silverware, plates, and mugs. She was cleaning stemware by hand.

"No problem. How's he doing, Katia?"

"He's still burying himself in his work." Katia picked up a rag and began to dry the cleaned wine glasses. "The magazine agreed to wait as long as possible to photograph the new line so that they could get it in their jewelry spectacular for the holidays."

Penelope smiled. "That's fantastic."

"There are a lot of people here that I don't know," Katia commented.

"You've lived here for several years. You should try to meet more people."

"I travel so much for work and my fiancée is busy, so we are still working on the social part of life," Katia said. "He's even out of town now."

"Oh, hi Penelope," Jessie greeted, adding her coffee cup to the growing pile.

"Hi. Oh, Jessie, have you met Katia Lazofsky? She's Robby's business partner."

Jessie extended her hand. "No, it's nice to meet you, Katia. I had the booth next to Tessa at the festival."

Katia stiffened, ignoring the gesture. "You as well, Jessie," she said.

"It's so sad being here. I feel awful that I wasn't any help to the police." Jessie sniffed.

"If you were next to Tessa all day, how could you not see or hear anything?" Katia asked. "You were so close."

Jessie shook her head. "I wish I had but, everything is just a blur. Nothing. Nothing helpful, at least. I could just hear customers coming and going, but no one specific."

"It's okay. I'm sure the police will figure it out," Penelope said. She wanted to believe that the police were close to an arrest, but after a week, there was no new information about the case.

"Well, I better go. It was nice to see you both."

As Jessie exited the room, Katia leaned backward against the sink next to Penelope, who was elbow-deep in washing suds.

"I think she's guilty," Katia said.

"I'm not sure if she is guilty, but I think she knows something that she isn't saying," Penelope remarked, handing Katia a champagne glass. "Her story keeps changing a little, too."

"How?"

"She told me at the festival that she never heard Tessa talking with anyone because it was too loud, then she told the police that she saw a group of bikers at the tent."

"Hmm. That is strange," Katia replied. "Just now she said she could hear customers coming and going."

The afternoon moved slowly. Penelope and Katia washed dishes while Laurel and Olivia kept the food and drinks flowing, and Clara helped Robby herd the guests in and out of his home.

When most of the dishes were cleaned and the crowd was thinning, Penelope sat in the living room welcoming a quick break. As Clara joined her daughter on the sofa, Friday's mystery woman appeared in the doorway and hugged Robby. Penelope elbowed her mother's side. "Look."

Clara gasped. "It's the woman from the candle shop."

"Go find out who that is." Penelope pushed her mother up from her seat.

In a flash, Clara was by Robby's side, introducing herself to the mystery woman. Penelope watched her mother work her magic. She was great at talking to strangers, which was one reason the rock shop was so successful. The mystery woman glanced at the couch. Penelope could feel herself shrinking to avoid eye contact. She worried the woman might remember her from the morning at the candle shop.

A few short minutes later, Clara was back on the couch with the details. "Her name is Betsy Peterson. She was Tessa's bookkeeper."

"Really?" Penelope was surprised. Tessa had never mentioned using a bookkeeper, but Penelope realized that there was a lot about Tessa's business that she didn't know.

"She just stood there and told Robby that she hadn't talked to Tessa since last month." Clara raised her eyebrows, shaking her head slowly.

"Well...liar, liar, pants on fire." Penelope stared at Betsy. The cozy town of Sierra Springs, once a haven of tranquility, was now a place of mystery and suspicion, and ripe with people lying.

What are you hiding? she wondered.

Emotional Healing Spell

To promote blessings and healing for yourself, your family, and friends who are recovering from a profound and emotional loss.

Spell Supplies

Rose Quartz Crystals | Blue Candles | White Candles
Form a circle with the candles and place the rose quartz crystals in the center. Light the candles.
Close your eyes, focus on the loss, and recite:
Healing magic, grant peace and calm for [name] like a soothing balm. Release their grief. Let blessings flow. All day long may comfort grow. So mote it be!

Chakra Stones for Promoting Emotional Healing

Use these healing stones in your spell for extra benefit. You can also wear jewelry made with these crystals or keep them in your pockets until the healing process is unfolding.
Rose Quartz | Rhodonite | Lepidolite

Chapter Thirteen

After the funeral, Penelope spent a restless Sunday at the museum trying to catch up on her work. A cloud of sadness hung in the air as she triple-checked the display cases and made a list of everything left to do before the gala in a short six days. By dinner time, Penelope needed a break and went for a swim at the recreation department pool. The cool water and methodical rhythm of her strokes always helped her think. Her body was exhausted after a week of relentless work on the exhibit, tracking down clues in the murder investigation, and saying a last goodbye to her friend.

She was the only swimmer, earning the lifeguard's full attention. Penelope's favorite easy swim was alternating lengths of freestyle and backstroke with slow, controlled flip turns at each end. Backstroke was her favorite, but freestyle was the stroke of choice for aquathlons. It was the fastest stroke and let you raise your head to see your location in open water.

Two miles of backstroke and freestyle gave Penelope plenty of time to sort her thoughts. The museum display was almost done, and she only had to attend to the last details and prepare her presentation. The investigation into

Tessa's murder was not as tidy. She had added Marlene Black to the suspect list but couldn't eliminate anyone else.

Penelope finished her swim and wrapped herself in sweatpants and a thick t-shirt. She traipsed through the parking lot in well-worn flip-flops, opened the door to her Hummer, and threw her swim bag into the passenger seat. She climbed in, noticing a piece of paper clamped between her windshield and the wiper. Penelope looked around the parking lot, but the setting sun quickly swallowed her surroundings.

Penelope opened the door and stood on the running board. She snatched the paper and returned to her seat, quickly locking the doors. She opened the note and read: *"YOU'RE LOOKING IN THE WRONG DIREC-TION."*

***

Penelope shoved the handwritten note across the table and yawned. "What do you think this means?" She took a sip of her latte and sunk into the padded walnut chair, leaving her sunglasses covering her eyes. Penelope hadn't slept well. She tossed and turned all night, trying to let her mind make sense of the note. The storm in the middle of the night kept Jasper awake as well. The pup now lay sleeping in Penelope's lap, wrapped in her favorite pink sweater. Penelope was waiting for Laurel when she arrived to open the café, her usual work clothes replaced with sweatpants and a running shirt, with her normally bouncy curls trapped in a topknot.

Laurel was staring at the letter when Tristan arrived with a plate of blueberry breakfast tarts and hopped into an open chair.

"So, what are we talking about, ladies?"

Penelope groaned. "You know what happened at the festival to Tessa."

"The candle woman. I loved her. I can't believe she was murdered." Tristan craned his neck for a quick look around the room, shrank his shoulders, and then whispered, "I heard that someone poisoned her at the festival because she was in witness protection and hiding from the Mexican drug cartels."

"Where did you hear that? That's ridiculous." Penelope couldn't believe the gossip that flew through her small town. Drug cartels? In Sierra Springs? Absurd.

Tristan shrugged. "I'm cute and easy to talk to. People like to gossip with me, especially when they come at night, and I feed them sugar and alcohol."

"Penelope's been sticking her nose in it ever since she found the body. Look at this." Laurel slipped the note to Tristan.

His eyes grew wide as he examined the crayon handwriting. Tristan gasped. "What have you gotten yourself into, girl? Why don't you let the police handle this?" Tristan tilted his head. "Wait, Laurel, you should send this to your Chief Brother." His glance darted from Laurel to Penelope.

"Chief Brother?" Laurel looked ruefully at Penelope. "Andre and Ryan really should know about this."

Penelope grimaced and slid backward in her chair, propping her chin on her fists. "I know. I just really don't want to show it to them."

Laurel broke an oversized breakfast tart in half. She took a quick bite, holding the crumbs to Jasper. The pup licked her hand clean. "Penelope, eat something." Laurel pushed the other half across the table.

"I helped Olivia make them," Tristan declared.

"Really?" Laurel raised her eyebrows.

"She called me her pastry assistant-in-training."

Penelope took a tiny bite, hoping the sugar would lift her mood. "So, what do I do about this note?"

"You didn't see who left it?" Tristan asked.

"It was on the car when I got out of the pool. I was there a long time." Penelope was delaying the inevitable. She needed to turn the note over to Ryan, but she didn't want to admit that she had been snooping around about the murder.

"They tracked you to the pool," Laurel said.

"Creepy." Tristan picked up the note again and read aloud, "You're looking in the wrong direction." He fell silent for a moment. "That's kind of ominous. But it doesn't mean it's from the killer."

"What's going on?" Olivia slipped into the chair beside her sister. "You look like hell, Penelope."

Laurel popped another piece of tart into her mouth. "That's true. I didn't want to say anything," she said, letting crumbs fly through her lips.

"Gross, Laurel. Jasper woke me up at four thirty this morning, scared of the storm. I'm a little tired, thank you very much."

"I don't think Jasper is the cause of your, shall we say, disheveled look today." Tristan handed Olivia the note. "We're trying to convince your stubborn sister to take this to the police."

"What is this?" Olivia read the note.

Penelope shrugged. "Someone left this on my car last night when I was swimming."

"You need to show this to Ryan. Why are you not there already?" Olivia asked.

"Because it's early. I needed coffee, and I want to do a little digging on my own."

"You're going to get yourself hurt," Olivia said. "Don't make me tell Mom on you."

"I'll be fine. We don't know that this is about Tessa."

"Seriously?" Laurel admonished. "There's no way it isn't."

"What else could it be about?" Tristan questioned.

Penelope shrugged. "A rival geologist who thinks that I picked the wrong samples for my new display?"

Olivia laughed. "Ridiculous. That's not a thing. I'm pretty sure there is no rivalry with you rock-nerds."

"Hey." Penelope tossed a wadded napkin at her sister. "Rude."

Olivia stood. "Well, the first thing you are going to do is let me feed you some proper breakfast. I've got a great Croque Monsieur mini quiche in back."

Penelope's stomach growled like a lion. "Croque Monsieur quiches? Is that a thing?"

Tristan hopped up beside Olivia, ready to help again as her assistant-in-training. "It sure is. And then the second thing you're going to do is take that letter right to the police." Tristan wagged his finger at Penelope.

"I will. Later."

The cafe door burst open. A group of high schoolers breezed into the restaurant. Laurel's shoulders sank. She inhaled sharply, stood, and straightened her apron. "Penelope, just take the note to Ryan. You don't have to talk to Andre."

"Why not talk to Andre?" Olivia smirked.

Penelope stared at her. "Weren't you getting me some mini-quiches, little sister?"

Olivia scrunched her nose. "Let's go, Tristan."

The two sped off to the kitchen.

"I'll be right there to help," Laurel hollered. She grabbed Penelope's phone.

"Wait, what are you doing?" Penelope demanded.

"What do you think I'm doing? I'm texting Ryan and telling him about the note." Jasper yipped as Penelope lunged for the phone, but Laurel held tight.

Olivia returned and tossed a bag of food at her sister. "These are to eat on your way to the police station. Call me after you talk to Ryan. I've got to get back," she called over her shoulder, hustling to the kitchen.

Penelope was thankful for the food. She hated cooking. Some days, it was all Penelope could do to crack open a can of dog food and scoop some dry chicken crunchies for Jasper before she dug into cold, left-over pizza.

Penelope's phone chimed. "Oh good," Laurel said, reading the text. "Ryan said to come by the station on your way to the museum this morning so that he can see the note."

"Whoever sent me this just wants me to know something. I doubt they would hurt me." Penelope peeked in the food bag. A comforting aroma of ham and cheese wafted from within.

Laurel leaned on the table and lowered her voice. "You don't know that. They could be crazy. They could be trying to scare you. They could be the killer."

"You're right. I'll take the note to him later." Penelope stood and stretched. "I better get to the museum. We are doing the final installations today.

"Okay, call me if you want me to go by the police station with you."

"Thanks, but I'll be fine." Penelope shifted Jasper under her left arm.

"Then text me after you speak to Ryan."

"Okay. Thanks, Laurel." Penelope slung her messenger bag across her shoulder and gave her friend a quick hug before slipping into the crisp morning air with Jasper clamped to her side.

***

Penelope arrived at the police station at precisely five o'clock when the afternoon rush hour was picking up. The morning thunderstorms had returned with a vengeance. In Sierra Springs, rush hour was more like a slow drip of cars meandering through town, but the rain made maneuvering the hilly curves moderately treacherous even in a Hummer. Penelope was hoping Ryan had left for the day but found him waiting in his office when one of the twin officers escorted her through the building. She promised herself that one day she would figure out the names of the two twins. One twin was Joe, and the other was Jim, but Penelope hadn't figured out a way to tell them apart.

"You texted this morning saying that you would come right by."

"Technically, Laurel sent that text." The rain dripped from Penelope's hood onto her jeans.

"Where have you been?"

"I had to drop Jasper with my mother and then work. In case you haven't heard, there is this huge gala this weekend, and I get to unveil an enormous rock exhibition that I've spent years putting together. So, I'm kind of busy." Penelope removed her raincoat and hung it on the rack next to the door. Rainy days were typically a favorite of hers after finding the perfect raincoat in a little shop in Brevard. The coat was the sweetest shade of lavender, with tiny white flowers that made a dreary day more cheerful. Penelope had stopped at home to change into jeans and a lightweight teal sweater with ribbons woven through the wrists. She didn't want to show up at the police station in sweatpants and luckily her hair had calmed since the morning.

"Umbrellas are amazing inventions. You should try one."

"Ha. Funny. Not." Penelope crinkled her nose.

"Let me see it." Ryan held out his hand.

Penelope made herself comfortable in the chair opposite the detective's desk. She dug into her messenger bag and retrieved the note. Ryan motioned for her to place it on his desk while he donned rubber gloves and retrieved an evidence bag from the top desk drawer.

"Are you coming?"

"Huh?" Ryan looked up from the note.

"To the gala. You'll need a tux." Penelope watched him as he examined the note.

"Oh, so you are hoping I'll be there?" Ryan smiled.

"I hope your cash will be there." Penelope grinned, knowing that her comment would irritate him. Ryan was from a wealthy family. He never spoke about his financial situation because he didn't want to be treated differently. Penelope knew Ryan worked as a cop because he wanted to, not because he needed a job.

Ryan cleared his throat. "How many people have touched this?"

"Why?"

Ryan stared. "Seriously. How many people did you show this to?"

"Laurel. Tristan. Olivia." Penelope counted on her fingers.

Ryan rolled his eyes. "Great. Now I need comparison prints for all of them."

"Oh, sorry. I wasn't thinking you might want to look for fingerprints on the note."

Ryan grimaced. "It will make it harder because the more prints there are, the more difficult it will be to find the first set, which likely belongs to the person who left it on your car."

"Sorry." Penelope leaned back in the chair, rubbing her temples. "I'm tired."

"So, someone left this on your car while you were swimming?" Ryan listed the details in his notebook.

"Yeah. I was at the recreation department."

"I wonder if they have cameras," Ryan said.

"It won't matter. It was getting dark out and my car was under a tree." Penelope studied his face, trying to get a sense of what he was thinking. But Ryan was more difficult to read than he was in high school. "What do you think? You're acting very serious. What happened to my fun-loving friend?"

Ryan glanced at Penelope, then immediately back to the note. "He became a cop whose not-serious-enough friend is being targeted by a killer."

"I'm not being targeted."

"Oh, no? You were snooping around about Tessa's murder and then someone who knows what you are doing took the risk of leaving this note on your car. I'm concerned about you, P."

"I'm fine."

"Who have you talked to about Tessa's murder?"

"Not many people. Just family and friends. Robby, obviously. But other than that, no one." Penelope did not feel like recounting every conversation with him.

"You still talk a lot, just like you did in high school."

"Hey." Penelope cracked the knuckles on her right hand. "I can't help it if people find me easy to communicate with. Did you get any results from the autopsy yet?" Penelope watched as Ryan snapped a few pictures of the note with his phone camera, emailed them to himself, and then carefully sealed the note in the evidence bag.

"Uh. No." Ryan shot a glance at a red file in the corner of his desk.

"You're lying." Penelope followed his eyes to the file. "I hope you don't gamble because you are a terrible poker player. Surely you know something by now."

"No. Autopsies take weeks, Penelope. This isn't television."

Penelope reached toward the note, only to have her hand swatted away. Ryan was studying the letter through the clear baggie. "It's interesting that it was written in crayon."

Penelope tilted her head. "Maybe it is someone with kids or who is around kids."

"Or someone who just didn't want you to recognize their handwriting. Crayon doesn't exactly make hand-writing analysis easy."

"It could be anyone. I need to make a list."

"No, you don't. I'll work on who sent this note. You go to the museum and do your geology stuff." Ryan moved around the desk and pulled Penelope from her chair.

"My geology stuff?"

"You know what I mean. You're the geologist. I'm the cop. I trust you to do your job, and you must trust me to do mine." Ryan retrieved Penelope's coat from the rack and shook off the remaining droplets. "Penelope, you are one of my oldest friends. I won't let anything happen to you. But help me out with that by not doing anything stupid, please. Someone is upset that you've been asking around about Tessa, and I don't want you to put yourself at risk anymore."

Ryan subtly pushed Penelope toward his office door. The autopsy file was getting further from her grasp. "Wait, hey Ryan. Can you do me a favor? I'm cold from the rain. Do you mind getting me a cup of coffee to take with me?"

Ryan nodded. "Sure thing. Stay here for a second. Real cream and sugar, like high school, or have you matured to black coffee?"

"No maturing with my hot beverages," Penelope replied. Ryan disappeared into the break room. When he was out of sight, Penelope grabbed the red folder. "Just a few snaps," she whispered as she snuck a photo of each page in the folder and then put it back in place. She had just a split second to pick up her phone and shove it to her ear before Ryan sauntered into the office with two to-go cups.

"Okay, Mom. I'll be right over." Penelope shoved the phone into her bag. "I need to run and get Jasper."

That was close, she thought. Penelope smiled and thanked Ryan for the coffee.

"Do you have your running group tonight?"

"No, the weather is too gross, and we were supposed to run part of the 10K racecourse that goes up through the road cuts. A dry day would be better for that."

Ryan nodded. "Makes sense." He took her elbow, guiding her to the door.

"I'm going to hit the pool at the gym for some cross-training. You should come with me sometime."

"If I have time. I'm a little more concerned with the fact that someone is after you."

Penelope put a hand on his shoulder. "I appreciate that, but the fourth of July 10K will be here before you know it and you don't want to be last," Penelope teased.

"I won't be last. I run almost every day before I come to work."

"Sure, you do." Penelope winked at the detective and slipped through the door. "Have a good night, Ryan!"

"You too, Penelope."

Penelope scampered down the hallway with the likely illegal pictures on her phone. She sprinted out of the police station through the pounding raindrops. Less than ten minutes later, she was back in her office at the museum, printing full-sized photos of the autopsy report.

Chapter Fourteen

Penelope was bursting with news by the time she arrived at The Crystal Cove just before noon. She'd spent the past hour poring over the details of Tessa's preliminary autopsy results she photographed in Ryan's office and wanted to tell someone what she discovered. Ryan had only the initial narrative from the medical examiner. Penelope was thankful that there were no graphic pictures. She could barely watch television shows based on hospitals and those scenes were fake. Laurel and Olivia would be swamped with lunch customers at The Tipsy Java, so Penelope headed to her next confidant, her mother.

Clara was setting up a beautiful set of cracked amethyst geode bookends when Penelope popped into the store, passing delighted customers as they exited with their newly discovered crystals.

"Hi dear. Hi Jasper." Clara picked up two bags of herbs and headed to her workroom.

Jasper ran straight past Clara toward Midnight and landed on the adjoining bed with a thud.

"Hi, Mom! You won't believe what I found out about Tessa's murder."

"Did you find out who wrote the note?" The alarm on Clara's face almost made Penelope laugh.

"No. I haven't heard from Ryan," Penelope said, waving her hand through the fragrant air of the gem shop. "But while I was at the police station yesterday. I caught a glimpse, or rather a few pictures, of Tessa's preliminary autopsy report." She followed her mother through the store.

Clara stopped short of the crystal bead curtain and spun on her heels, nearly causing Penelope to slam into her. The toe-tapping began, and Penelope sensed she was in trouble. She immediately felt six years old.

"Did Ryan voluntarily show you the autopsy report?" Tap. Tap. Tap.

Penelope hunched her shoulders. "Not exactly. When I asked him if he had the results, I could tell that he lied to me."

"Honestly, Penelope. How? No. Wait. I don't want to know."

"I...I asked him to get me some coffee and snuck a little peek around his desk."

"And, by sneaking a peek, you meant, took out your phone and photographed it?"

Penelope nodded and winced.

"Penelope Jade Lake. Honestly. I raised you better." Three more loud toe taps rang through the shop, and then Clara disappeared through the crystal curtain. Penelope could hear the tapping continue.

She followed. "Mom, seriously. Ryan has known me for a long time. Don't you think he might have guessed that I would look around?"

Clara reemerged into the showroom and patted Penelope's nose with a slender index finger. "No, Penelope. He told you he had nothing and probably trusted that you believed him."

Penelope raised her hands. "It doesn't matter how I found out. Do you want to know what I know?"

"I don't. You're not a cop. You are a geologist, who, if I'm not mistaken, should be at the museum getting your rock display ready for the unveiling at the gala. There are only a few days left." Clara picked up a dusting cloth to wipe down the counters.

"I was there all morning and I'm going right back." Penelope perched herself on a stool behind the check-out counter. A group of tourists sauntered into the store. Penelope watched her mother help the customers find the perfect crystal for their current ailment, then followed with the upsell for her more expensive samples that were so big that they were a conversation starter. She was a gifted saleswoman.

Clara thanked her customers, waited for the door to clamp shut, then laid her arms onto the counter opposite Penelope and leaned close. "I can guess what you found."

"Yeah?" Penelope grinned. She knew her mother was interested in the details.

"You found that I'm no longer a suspect."

She stared at her mother. "No. Sandra told me that at the funeral. You know that."

Clara smiled. "Ryan also called me earlier. He thanked me for answering their questions and apologized for having to question me. He also asked me to keep you from trying to find out who left that note on your car."

"Hmm. I bet that is the real reason he called you. Can I show you what I found now?"

"Honestly, Penelope. Where did this stubborn streak come from?"

"I think you could look in the mirror for that answer." Penelope pulled her phone from her bag and navigated to the autopsy notes in the camera. "There isn't much information, but it says that Tessa didn't have any marks on her at all except for a few scratches on the back of her right triceps."

"So, she didn't have any other bruises or cuts at all on her body?" Clara stuck her nose over Penelope's phone and read.

"That seems weird, right?" Penelope flipped through the images of the report. "If Tessa was physically attacked, it seems like she would try to fight back."

"Not if she didn't see it coming. Does it say what the poison was?"

"Yes, it lists the name, but I haven't had time to look it up. I came over to tell you that the notes say that nothing she ate contained poisons," Penelope said. "So, how else was she poisoned that she didn't see coming?"

The shop door opened with the tinkling of the wind chimes and another group of tourists filed into The Crystal Cove. Clara smiled and greeted her customers before turning back to Penelope's images of the autopsy report.

"What does it say the poison was?" she whispered.

Penelope flipped through the images looking for the information when the gem shop door flew open again. Olivia ran through the door carrying three large white bags and a big smile. "Guess what I have?" She waved the bags in the air like Usain Bolt crossing the finish line.

"Food?" Clara asked. "But that's just a guess, Chef Olivia."

"It is lunchtime," Penelope added. "So, I hope it's food."

Olivia's face deflated. "You guys are no fun. You're supposed to guess what I brought. Laurel wants to try a new special out tomorrow. We've been super slammed at the cafe, but I had just enough time to bring you some to try."

"How did you know I was here?" Penelope asked.

Olivia tossed Penelope and her mother each a white bag, then hopped up on the countertop and opened her own. "You're always here."

"No, I'm always at the museum."

Olivia rolled her eyes. "I looked at your location on the phone app Mom made us get. For safety," she said, complete with air quotes.

"It is for safety," Clara defended herself. "I'm not trying to keep tabs on you girls."

"Uh, huh." Penelope opened her bag. "Oh my gosh, it smells so good. What is this?"

"You're terrible at this 'guess what I brought' game," Olivia teased.

"It smells amazing, Olivia," Clara chimed in.

"It's a salmon burger with kale and mango on top. For dessert, I made personal chocolate torts."

Clara rang up purchases from the tourists and locked the door behind them, turning the door sign from 'open' to 'out for lunch.'

As they dug into the burgers, Clara asked Penelope to read the name of the poison from the autopsy report.

Olivia's eyebrows perked up. "Autopsy report? Did Ryan or Andre give you a copy?"

Penelope almost choked on her burger. "Not exactly."

"Don't ask," Clara remarked. "Your sister is going to end up in jail if she keeps nosing into police business."

"I am not," Penelope protested.

"That's why I'm so thankful that you're a chef, dear. At least I don't have to worry about one of my daughters." Clara tossed a handful of treats onto the floor for Midnight and Jasper. The furry pair were inching closer to the burgers as the scent of salmon filled the shop.

"Hey, what do I do that is so dangerous? I collect rocks and teach kids and consult with the city to make sure that the pretty scenic overlooks don't slide down the mountains."

"You fib to the police and take pictures of their reports." Clara tossed a second handful of treats to Jasper and Midnight.

"And you sneak into candle shops and get killers to write you letters telling you to back off," Olivia smirked. "On the other hand, maybe Penelope *wants* to be handcuffed by Andre or Ryan."

"Olivia!" Penelope exclaimed.

"I'll see if I can find a spell to help you pick between the two," Clara offered.

"Ahhh," Penelope shook her shoulders like she was trying to wake up from a bad dream. "Ya'll are awful. Look, here is the name of the poison that they say killed Tessa." Penelope handed her phone to Clara, desperate to change the subject. Olivia leaned over her mother's shoulder to see the screen.

"Batrachotoxin," Clara slowly read aloud, then set the phone on the counter. Her complexion turned ghostly.

The horror in her mother's expression made Penelope's stomach flip. "You know what that is, Mom?"

Clara nodded. "I've heard of it."

"I haven't," Olivia said, scanning the information on Penelope's phone.

"If it is what I think, this poison is incredibly deadly." Clara trotted to her private office. She returned through the crystal curtain with an old book in hand. Clara blew the dust off the top and spine and laid it on the counter.

"What is that book?" Penelope asked.

Clara turned to the glossary. "It's called *The Witches Guide to Herbs, Potions, and Poisons.*"

Penelope choked as particles of dust swirled through the air. "You better keep that book hidden, or the police will put you back on the suspect list."

"Oh, Penelope, don't be ridiculous. There is so much old dirt on this book, it's obvious that I haven't read it in a while. But that poison name, Batrachotoxin, always stood out to me. It comes from the poison dart frog, I believe." Clara gently opened the heavy cover and found the table of contents.

"Does that big, dirty book have a love potion for Penelope?" Olivia teased.

"Ooh," Clara cooed. "Good idea."

"What does the book say about the poison?" Penelope asked, to refocus the conversation away from her tepid love life. Since she turned twenty-nine a few months earlier, Clara's requests for grandchildren were getting louder and more frequent. Penelope had no interest in finding a date at the moment. She only wanted to find the killer.

"Here we go." Clara read aloud. "Yes, the poison comes from the poison dart frog in South America."

"I've never heard of that frog," Olivia said.

"It's a tiny frog that secretes the poison when it gets scared. Even the smallest amount of the liquid can kill a person in less than two minutes." Clara slowly turned the page. "They're cute frogs. They're usually red, yellow, or blue with spots. But very deadly."

"Two minutes. Tessa didn't stand a chance," Penelope remarked.

"I wonder how the killer gave her the poison without Tessa knowing?" Olivia asked.

"The report says that there were scratches on the back of Tessa's arm." Penelope finished her burger and opened the tort.

"The books say that it works quickest when directly injected into the bloodstream," Clara read.

"The scratches could be from an injection. Someone may have come up behind her with a needle," Olivia speculated.

"They would have to be fast for her not to see a syringe. But they could have knocked her down and then injected her," Penelope said. "That would explain why she didn't fight back. But how could the killer do that with no witnesses?"

"What if someone else gave her poisoned food? If it has a mild taste, then you could theoretically put it in anything and mask it," Olivia said.

"No, they tested everything in her stomach," Clara said.

"That's how they ruled Mom out," Penelope explained.

Olivia hugged her mother's shoulders. "I'm happy about that."

"I wonder if Ryan has any theories about how she was poisoned?" Penelope asked.

"You wonder a lot," Olivia commented.

"It's my scientific mind trying to solve a murder. It's like solving a puzzle," Penelope retorted. "The autopsy says she didn't have any obvious wounds other than the scratches on her triceps, but if someone injected her with a needle, couldn't the scratches hide where the needle went in?"

Penelope sat motionless as her mother read off more horrifying symptoms that Tessa must have felt from the effects of the poison. "I don't think I'm too hungry anymore. I think I'll save the tort for later if that's okay, Olivia?"

Olivia closed the Styrofoam over the chocolate desserts and nodded. "I think that's a good idea. It's scary to think of what Tessa must have gone through and what she could have been thinking. I wonder if she realized what was happening?"

Clara put her arm around her youngest daughter and squeezed. "Well, the one good thing about Batrachotoxin is that it is fast-acting. She probably only suffered for a minute or two before she died."

"The fact that I found her with boxes on top of her body means that whoever killed her stood there and watched her die and somehow shielded her from everyone at the park." Penelope recalled the moment she discovered Tessa on the ground. "That takes a lot of guts."

How did no one at the festival see Tessa being murdered? If someone injected her with poison, the killer had to be clever and quick.

"It took pure evil." Olivia shivered. "Do you think zoos around here have those frogs?"

"Why?" Penelope secured her phone inside her messenger bag.

"This may be nothing, but Jessie's brother works at the state zoo."

"If they have poison dart frogs, that could give her access. I'll look into it." Penelope added investigating the zoo to her mental to-do list.

"Did the autopsy say what time she died?" Clara closed the substantial book and slid it onto the shelf beneath the register.

"It said between three and four o'clock in the afternoon. The killer could have walked right by us."

Clara flipped the sign, unlocked the door, and sighed. "We all better get back to work."

Penelope and Olivia were cleaning up the lunch containers as a customer swung through the door of the gem shop.

"How can I help you today?" Clara asked, turning around. "Oh, hi, Katia."

"Hello." Katia wore jeans and a short-sleeved cashmere sweater, an unusually casual look.

"Can we help you find something?" Penelope asked.

"Robby said that you offered to help pack up some candles from Tessa's shop so that we can sell them at the jewelry store." Katia admired the agate bookends and crystal obelisks in the display by the register.

"Yes. He seemed a little overwhelmed being in the shop," Clara said.

"Do you still have a key to the candle store?" Katia asked, a Jaguar key spun anxiously around her finger. "I thought since I was around here shopping that I could grab the boxes and take them back to the jewelry store, but after I parked behind the shop, I realized I forgot to get an extra key."

"That would be great," Penelope said. "We finished very late the other night, so we left them stacked up by the back door. I was going to get them later."

"I'm happy to take them." Katia spied the candles on the shelf by the amethyst spheres behind the register. "You have a nice selection, Clara."

"Thank you," she said, watching Katia's eyes fixed on the shelves behind her. "Is there something you need? Some crystals, perhaps?" Clara removed the key to the candle shop from her chain.

Katia shook her head as if waking from a deep distraction. "Oh no, thank you." She looked toward the register. "You have some of Tessa's candles," she said, pointing at the Amethyst Falls on the shelf.

Clara smiled. "Yes, she and I were going to team up on this new line of candles. We were going to put my crystals inside her candles, and we were both going to sell them." She handed the key to Katia.

"That is a lovely idea," Katia said. "Too bad it can't happen now."

"I've been looking at Tessa's recipes. I might be able to create the type of candle she was planning," Olivia said.

"Oh, that's wonderful." Katia smiled and handed Olivia her business card. "When you do, call me. I'll be your first customer."

As Katia exited the store, Penelope turned to her mother and sister. "I'm so glad that Robby has her to keep the business going." Penelope walked to the front of the store and watched through the window as lights brightened the candle shop. She sighed, thinking about Tessa. Even without the murder, the gala was only a few short days away, and the pressure was increasing exponentially. She knew she needed to focus on the museum. But her brain just could not let go of the search for Tessa's killer. Finding her body made Penelope feel responsible.

The clues were stacking up but not fitting together. As Penelope stared across the road, she could see Katia milling about the store, gathering the boxes of candles to take to Robby, and she knew instantly what she must do.

Chapter Fifteen

P enelope spent a busy afternoon triple-checking the rare mineral specimens that would be included in the gala display, but her mind kept going back to the mysterious note she had given to Ryan. *Could Katia be the person who sent the cryptic note? Or Marlene? Jessie? Robby? Perhaps it was Betsy.*

Is someone trying to tell me if there's something else going on that I need to know about, or are they just trying to scare me?

The preparations for the gala were intensifying. Penelope and Lucy were spending more time in the lab with each passing day. Penelope had been working on the new collection on and off for the last five years and the realization that the collection was complete and ready to show to the public was hard to comprehend. The countless field trips to remote locations, the collection and mapping of every mineral and rock type, and the cutting and preparation of thin sections for microscopic review and analysis all led to a unique collection.

The exhibit was going to be perfect. Plaques for each of the samples were being engraved by a local crafter and the display cases were ready. The final loading of the samples, checking the details of each plaque, and carefully placing each pad of velvet and lighted stand was more tedious than Penelope would have liked. She was determined to focus on the gala and, after it was over, she could focus on Tessa's murder. Penelope knew Tessa would want her to make the most of the gala.

As the day faded, she sent Lucy home and prepared to close the rock lab. Penelope locked the most valuable samples in the laboratory safe. For security, she would install the mineral, which she would name at the ceremony, the day before the unveiling. Penelope cleaned the floors and the countertops and flicked off the lights. The rock lab and her office were finally neat and organized after sending the extra sample boxes to the warehouse area for storage. Penelope appreciated a cleaner, less cluttered workspace. It helped her think.

After a short drive to the recreation department, Penelope was dragging her swim bag, flippers, snorkel, kickboard, and pull buoy from the back seat of her Hummer. She loved swimming even more than running. The pool was therapeutic, and Penelope's heartbeat calmed with the mere smell of humidity and chlorine. The quiet that surrounded her when she swam lap after lap with her face submerged gave her time to meditate without distractions. Usually, she was thinking about her work or her friends or family. But today, every thought that didn't concern the museum exhibit focused on Tessa.

After changing into her favorite racing suit, Penelope sat on the bleachers and braided her hair, waiting for the rest of the swimmers to arrive. She inhaled deeply and smiled. Salt-water pools were all the rage in local neighborhoods, but Penelope loved the potent smell of chlorine at the recreation center. It smelled like home.

Penelope tucked her hair neatly inside a silicone cap to keep it from tangling. Like most swimmers, she had a vast collection of caps. Today's was midnight blue to match the spiral pattern on her swimsuit with a large fish outlined in yellow and a slogan that read "Eat my Bubbles," her favorite motto from age-group meets as a child. In the summer, she and her teammates would sit at evening competitions with thick black markers writing on each other's backs. Clara called her an amateur tattoo artist, but Penelope thought it was just a great way to drive her parents crazy when the marker refused to wash off for days after the meet.

Penelope dove into the icy water, letting the chill wash over her skin. She hadn't been part of a formal swim team since she was young, but when Penelope discovered aquathlons, she decided that a master's team would help her get in shape for her next event. Many people ran road races or challenged themselves with triathlons, but Penelope hated biking, and a simple five-kilometer run was becoming boring after years of road racing. Aquathlons were the perfect challenge. Run—Swim—Run. Or sometimes, just Swim—Run. These endurance races took running and swimming to a new level, with varying distances for each leg, depending on who was hosting the event. Her next aquathlon was in Sierra Springs in just a few short months. With all of her work getting ready for the gala, Penelope was worried she was falling behind in her training.

When she first tried an aquathlons, Penelope was amazed at how quickly the strokes had come back to her. Today's practice was no different. She dove into the pool and muscle memory took over. Her feet began to flutter kick just before her right arm pulled strongly beneath her body, sending her to the surface, letting her left arm begin its turn, propelling her forward. She never turned for a breath until after she broke the surface of the water and had taken three uninterrupted strokes, a rule her youth coach drilled into her. As Penelope approached the wall for her fourth flip-turn, she saw someone pushing off the wall in the adjacent lane through the purple tint of her goggles. She knew immediately who had joined the practice.

Andre.

She would know his stroke anywhere and Andre was the only person in Sierra Springs who had colorful, intertwined Olympic rings on his shoulder blade. Andre got the tattoo the month after he qualified for Team USA during his freshman year of college.

Penelope swam across the twenty-five-yard pool thirty times for her warm-up before stopping. She glided into the wall and spun around, letting her backrest against the tile. Penelope grabbed the gutter with her fingertips, allowing her feet to float to the surface. She slid her body to the side so the other swimmers in her lane could make their turns. Even in the sanctuary of the pool, images of Tessa's body invaded her mind. She wished it would stop. Penelope tried to figure out the best way to ask Andre if the police determined how Tessa was poisoned. She didn't expect him to tell her, but she had to try.

Penelope pulled her feet back to the bottom and took a sip from her water bottle as Andre coasted into the wall.

"What are you doing here?"

"I thought I'd join the team," Andre said, moving his goggles from his eyes to his forehead. "I was swimming master's meets in Charlotte for the past few years."

"I should have known." Penelope set her water bottle on the side of the pool next to her equipment bag.

Andre dove his six-foot frame under the lane line. "If it bothers you, I can go to the morning workouts."

"No. It's fine. I can handle you being here, but you have to get back in your lane."

"Why?" Andre asked.

"Because I don't need my swimming compared to an Olympian."

"Ex-Olympian." Andre laughed. "That was a long time ago."

"You still look pretty good to me," Penelope commented.

Andre's eyes widened. "Oh, really?"

"I mean your stroke. Get back in your lane." Penelope splashed water at Andre. "The workout is about to start." Penelope was surprised that she felt comfortable around him. *Maybe I am over him*, she thought as she waited for the other swimmers to finish their warmups and the coach to explain the first set.

"All right guys, we're going to start the workout with a ten-minute kick with the board. One minute hard, then one minute easy, and repeat. Go on the top," Coach Lee called loudly so swimmers could all hear him from the side of the pool deck. Greg Lee was a veteran coach in Sierra Springs and had touched the lives of every swimmer in the area during his career. Coach Lee was Penelope's age group coach when she was young and became the head coach at Sierra Springs High School, but by then, Penelope had left the pool for the track.

Penelope and Andre retrieved their kickboards from their fabric fish net equipment bags and waited for the tip of the arm on the pace clock to reach zero. Andre pushed off quickly and sprinted down the lane using a flutter kick. Penelope used a stronger butterfly kick, trying to catch up. The first minute seemed like an eternity, with Andre inching further and further away while they glided down the pool. Penelope's leg muscles burned. The clock arm reached zero again. Coach Lee blew his whistle, signaling the team to slow down for the one-minute recovery to rest and get ready for the next sprint. Penelope did not slow down until she and Andre were side-by-side with the kickboards outstretched in front of their bodies, floating on the water's surface. The blue and white lane line divided their space in the pool.

"Hey Andre, how's the investigation going?"

"What investigation?"

"Don't play dumb. Tessa."

"No. You will not get any information out of me."

Coach Lee blew his whistle, and Andre took off. He was so strong that Penelope quickly fell behind. If she slowed down a little, Andre would catch back up to her by the time the minute was over. Coach Lee blew his whistle again.

Penelope held the top of the kickboard with her right hand, using her arm to balance the rest of her body while she turned backward toward Andre, who was right on her heels.

"Just a hint? Look, Ryan told my mom that Tessa was poisoned when he questioned her. Do you know how?"

"I'm not telling you anything about Tessa's investigation."

"Just tell me how. She didn't fight back. The Tessa I was friends with was a fighter."

Andre sprinted away as Coach Lee blew the whistle, signaling the next minute of sprints.

Penelope did her best to catch up, but she could tell her questions annoyed Andre and sent him flying down the pool. When the coach whistled again for a minute of recovery to begin, Penelope and Andre were passing each other in opposite directions.

Penelope stopped and turned around so they were kicking side-by-side toward the starting blocks. She tried to apologize. "I'm sorry. I shouldn't have asked. It's just that I've known Tessa since I was in high school, and I feel this need to help."

"We've got this, Penelope, and we're making progress."

"So, you have suspects?"

"Penelope, at this point, everybody is a suspect. Even you, because you were at the tent to see Tessa and Robby in the morning."

"You don't seriously think that I killed Tessa? I'm really a suspect?"

"No. But that just goes to show what type of murder we have on her hands. A dangerous poison and too many suspects. You need to stay out of it and stay away from Ryan."

"Ryan is my friend."

"He's my detective. And I know about the note someone left on your car. Stay out of this."

"Okay, fine. I'll drop it." Penelope hoped Andre didn't see her ears twitch, a side effect of her lying.

"Good." Coach Lee blew the whistle again. "Now kick." Andre took off, speeding down the lane.

Penelope finished the workout and then drove home, frustrated she didn't get any new details. Andre said that the poison was dangerous and that there could be a lot of suspects. She needed to make a murder board like the police did on television. It was going to be a long night.

Chapter Sixteen

Jasper lay on her dog bed in the living room. Her piercing blue eyes followed Penelope as she paced the room. She was still in her sweatpants and University of North Carolina sweatshirt when she heard a knock at the door. Penelope gasped. It was before six o'clock in the morning and she had avoided mirrors since her body had been evading sleep all night. Penelope turned to Jasper. "Stay."

Smoothing her hair, Penelope hurried to the door in her padded thick socks and peeked through the eyehole. She sighed, relieved, as she swung the door open to greet her best friend. "Hi! Come in quick. I'm not exactly people-ready." Penelope turned and hurried back to the kitchen. Laurel closed the door and trailed behind.

"I was going to ask you what happened between you and Andre at practice last night. He was grumpy and tight-lipped when he stopped by the cafe. But now I'm kind of wondering what's going on here." Laurel looked over at the kitchen counters. She tiptoed through the maze of pictures and mementos that were strewn about. Penelope had taken every picture, note, and recipe off her large corkboard and scattered them around the kitchen. A bowl of thumbtacks sat on the table. A half-eaten bagel lay face-down, raspberry preserves coating the tabletop.

Penelope watched her friend scan the scene. When her brain wouldn't allow her to sleep, Penelope put the overnight hours to good use. She dismantled her kitchen board to make it a murder board. She was failing in the gala-first promise she made herself.

"You look like hell," Laurel exclaimed, dropping her bags on a chair and peeling the sticky bagel from the table. "And your kitchen is a health hazard."

"Be nice. Andre wouldn't tell me anything at practice last night, but he let it slip that there were a lot of suspects still. I realized on the way home that I have a pretty big suspect list too and I need to organize them and start asking questions. So, voilà!"

"So, you took your frustrations out on your poor kitchen?"

"Well, I—" Penelope looked around at the disaster she created. "No. I'm making a murder board like they do on TV cop shows." Penelope motioned for Laurel to follow her to the living room. "See. I'm putting pictures of my suspects on my corkboard, just like the TV detectives do," she said, lifting the board onto her couch.

Laurel studied the board and saw Tessa's handwritten name on a neon pink index card pinned to the top. Below her name was a color-coded investigation matrix. Blue cards contained evidence notes, including details about the Batrachotoxin poison and the empty cash box. Yellow index cards listed questions and observations like Jessie's changing story details, Betsy lying to Robby about not seeing Tessa for a month, and the cryptic note someone left on Penelope's car. Bright green index cards held the names of suspects, and orange index cards listed motives in bold, black letters. Purple cards hung at the bottom waiting for the proof Penelope hoped would point to the killer.

"First, you watch too much television, my friend."

"That may be true, but this murder board is going to help us figure out who killed Tessa." Penelope wrapped her hair into a ponytail.

Laurel nodded. "I want to help. That is a lot of blank purple cards. We have suspects and questions, but no proof."

Penelope was using thumbtacks and string to connect suspects with motives, evidence, and observations. "The suspects I have so far are Robby, of course, because they always suspect the husband. Katia because she said they needed money for the shop, although she was out of town. Then, Marlene Black from Wicked Thyme Candles over the patent infringement lawsuit, but that seems more a motive for money than murder, and Betsy, the woman we saw coming out of the candle shop on Friday."

"You also have Jessie who fought with Tessa at the festival over customers, but then claims that she saw nothing during the day."

"Absolutely." Penelope raised her eyebrows. "So far, Jessie seems most likely, especially since her brother works at a zoo."

"You've put a lot of thought into this," Laurel commented, admiring Penelope's work. "But didn't Andre and Ryan both tell you to leave it alone? They don't want you to get hurt. Andre was pretty freaked out when I first told him about someone leaving the note on your car. He must have asked me a dozen times if you were okay."

Penelope smiled slightly. "Well, that's nice of him, but he probably doesn't care anymore. I annoyed him pretty good at practice."

"What did you say?" Laurel picked up Jasper and ruffled her fur.

"I asked him how Tessa was poisoned like five times and then argued with him when he wouldn't tell me."

Laurel giggled as Jasper licked her cheek. "No wonder he was snippy at the café." She set the puppy on the couch.

The doorbell rang. Only her mother rang the doorbell. The button sat beneath an aluminum dog head that concealed the button, and most people didn't know it was there.

"Come in, Mom!" Penelope yelled. "What is she doing here so early?" Penelope whispered to Laurel.

Clara slowly opened the front door and carried a stack of three donut boxes through the opening. "Penelope, how many times have I told you not to leave your front door unlocked?" she chastised.

"Sorry, Mom. Laurel is here."

"I honestly don't understand how you think you're taking good care of yourself when you don't even bother to lock the door." Clara sat the donut boxes on the coffee table. "Take these to your friends at the museum." Jasper hopped up from her comfortable position on the couch and smelled each of the boxes, touching the top one with her nose to see if she could get it open.

Clara scooped up the puppy and rubbed her nose. "Those aren't for you, little one, but I have something special instead." Clara pulled a huge dog bone from her coat pocket. Jasper's eyes gleamed. She understood exactly what was going to be her breakfast treat.

"I thought you would like that." Clara held the bone so Jasper could take it from her before scampering away to the bedroom.

"What are you two up to so early?"

Penelope and Laurel stood side-by-side trying to hide the corkboard.

"How's the murder board coming?" Clara placed three Boston cream donuts on paper napkins.

"How did you—"

"Penelope Jade. I'm your mother, and I know how your brain works. Plus, you watch all of those cop shows on television." She handed each of them a donut.

"Well, I have suspects, but not enough information on motives yet," Penelope admitted, moving the corkboard to the floor.

Clara sat on the couch. "Good. Keep it that way," she said. "You need to stop playing amateur police, or I'm going to tell Ryan on you."

"Oh, Mom. I'm just trying to find out what happened." Penelope sat crisscross applesauce on her end chair.

"I'll tell you what happened. Our friend was murdered with a fast-acting poison in the middle of an enormous crowd, and no one noticed. You need to stay out of it, Penelope." Clara pointed a finger at her.

"Mom—"

"Don't mom me. That poison is incredibly dangerous, and I won't have you putting yourself at risk. Let Andre and Ryan handle things. Have you seen Ryan lately?" Clara winked at Penelope, her tone softening.

"Stop. He's just a friend and don't you dare try any more of your love spells on us."

"Too late. Come on Jasper. Let's go to the shop," Clara sang, fetching her purse and swinging open Penelope's front door. "Ta, Ta ladies." As quickly as she had breezed in, Clara was off with Jasper in tow. The young husky knew when Clara said it was time to leave that playtime with Midnight was only a brief car ride away.

Laurel plopped into the closest chair and stared at the murder board. She took a bite of her donut. "Your mom is a force of nature."

Penelope laughed. "Yes, she is. But she reminded me of something."

"What?" Laurel asked.

"The love spell."

"Huh?"

"There are only two reasons people murder, according to the TV shows. Love and money."

"And Jessie, Marlene, and Robby would have the motive of money."

"So, what if someone had the motive of love?"

Chapter Seventeen

By nine o'clock, Penelope had pulled herself together and sat in her office in the Natural History Museum. Her fingernails, painted a deep maroon, tapped lightly on the keyboard while she searched for information. Penelope realized after talking with Laurel and Clara that she needed to investigate more about the poison. It was rare, and she assumed, not available to purchase easily. How did the killer get it?

She had learned a lot in her years as a geologist, but unfortunately today, details of specific poisons were not on the list. She set a timer on her computer for thirty minutes to research before getting back to work on the gala. The search results returned in a split second and Penelope scanned the first page of results, then stopped briefly on the highlighted word 'fast-acting.'

Penelope clicked on the link, which took her to a page that reminded her of her mother's spell book, only dark and more sinister. *Paige's House of Poisons* was a website full of detailed analyses of various poisons and their uses. Some of them were deadly, and some were not as harmful depending on the amount ingested, inhaled, or absorbed through the skin. Penelope scrolled quickly through the list and found Batrachotoxin. *How could a tiny frog be so deadly,* she wondered. The website had mostly the same information as Clara's book, but reading it again made Penelope's stomach churn. She couldn't imagine the agony that Tessa felt.

Her eyes quickly scanned left to right and back again. Batrachotoxin was deadly to the largest humans and biggest animals. Poison dart frogs secrete the neurotoxin to protect themselves from predators and it turned out to be one of the most lethal poisons in the world. Unfortunately for Tessa, the poison is easily extracted from the frog and a single drop will attack your central nervous system in less than a minute, leaving you paralyzed before you die a minute or two later. Penelope shuddered.

She wondered if there was any way for the murderer to have given Tessa the poison and somehow caused a delayed reaction. Penelope submitted another search on her computer.

"Batrachotoxin plus slow acting," she said aloud. Her fingers tapped quickly, revealing her words across the screen. "Enter," she muttered.

Penelope scanned each website on the first three pages of the results. She found little evidence suggesting that the poison's effects could be slowed and there was no cure. She pulled a new green *Rain Writer* geologist's field book and a purple gel pen from her desk drawer and filled the first five waterproof pages with details on Batrachotoxin.

Who would want Tessa to die in such an excruciating way? She jotted down the names from her murder board. *If Jessie's brother had access to the frogs, did that mean he could easily collect the poison? Or can you buy the poison on the dark web from someone in South America giving every suspect access?*

She stared at the computer screen, strumming her right fingernails across her cherry wood desk. Her chin rested in her left palm. Penelope reread the field notebook that should be filled with details about the latest rock and mineral samples donated to the museum, but instead, was filled with notes on poisons and questions about who wanted to kill her friend. She would add these additional details to her murder board when she got home.

This was one instance where her scientific research skills were coming in handy for something besides geology. Penelope replayed the festival day over in her mind. By the time she had gone to see Tessa, she was dead for at least an hour and no one at the festival admitted to seeing anything. "How is that possible?" she wrote at the bottom of the page, simultaneously saying the words aloud.

The phone rang, and Penelope sprang backward in her chair. She fumbled to answer as the loud ringing startled her again.

"Penelope, are you there?"

"Hi, Lucy, sorry I was doing some research. I wasn't expecting the phone to ring. What's up?"

"I'm stuck in the lobby with your guests. Get up here."

Penelope looked at her watch and jumped from her seat, knocking her pencil cup, and throwing two dozen colorful pens flying across her desk. "Oh my gosh, I'm late for my class," Penelope said, staring at her watch. "The kindergarteners. I promised to take them on a tour of the museum and then do a couple of experiments."

"Yes, you did. Hurry! I'm not good with large groups of little people," Lucy pleaded.

Penelope struggled to jam the pens back into the black metal woven cup.

"Okay, I'll be there in a minute. I can't believe that I agreed to let a school class tour during the week before the gala."

"Get these kids in and out and we'll get back to it."

***

After spending an hour showing five-year-olds how to make calcite crystals bubble when you plop them into cups of lemon juice, Penelope spent most of the late morning and afternoon in her rock lab. A large shipment of sedimentary rocks had arrived from a quarry dug in the South Dakota wilderness. The geologist working on-site thought the rocks and minerals would make a unique display for the museum because fossils lay hidden between the layers.

Intrigued by the description from the local geologist, Penelope opened the boxes and scanned the rocks. They looked interesting, but the fossils simply wouldn't fit with the mineral theme of the new exhibit. Sometimes the shipments that Penelope received from locations around the world were fascinating discoveries, while others were full of nothing but common rocks that you can find on any decent nature hike, which she promptly sent back to the owner.

She didn't have time for an in-depth study of each sample that came in from South Dakota because all her attention needed to focus on the remaining samples she needed to install in the display room. Since the fossils could be interesting for future exhibits, Penelope opted to store the rocks until she could properly examine them in a few weeks. She quickly re-packed the boxes.

"Lucy, can you ask the warehouse to store the boxes, please?"

"No problem, Penelope. Let me get the tape gun and I'll close them up." Lucy stepped out of the lab.

"Oh hello. She's in there," Lucy said from the hallway.

Penelope's ear perked. Who was Lucy talking to? She didn't have time for idle chitchat with the rest of the staff. She was almost finished with the display details, then needed to turn her attention toward writing and practicing her speech. The day of the gala was rushing at her and Penelope felt increasingly unprepared in this final push toward the finish line.

She was securing the last of the South Dakota samples in boxes when she heard a slight tapping on the lab door.

"Penelope?"

Penelope spun around. "Katia, what are you doing here?" She stacked the three boxes on the floor near the worktable.

"I hope you don't mind me coming by. I was buying tickets to the gala and thought I would drop in to see you."

Penelope tilted her head and eyed Katia slowly stepping through the doorway of the lab. "How did you get back here? This is a secure area."

"I know. Sorry. I might have fibbed a little to the security guard."

"Fibbed?"

"Okay, I flirted with him." Katia forced a laugh as she gazed around the lab.

Penelope would need to remind the security officer never to let anyone back in the restricted area without clearing it with her first, no matter how pretty the visitor is. "Huh, he usually texts me if somebody needs to see me." Penelope picked up her phone. No texts. "Is there something that I can help you with?"

"I just…I'm worried about Robby and I know how close you two are. He locks himself in the lab all day and half of the night. He isn't sleeping and barely eating. I hoped we could keep in touch more to make sure he is okay."

Penelope felt uneasy with Katia's unexpected visit when she had so little time to chat. But she was reaching out, and Penelope was very concerned about Robby. "Absolutely. I've been worried about him, too." Penelope motioned for her to take a seat.

Katia scanned the room, then eased onto one of the high-back stools.

Penelope took a seat opposite her. The stool teetered beneath her weight.

"You have an interesting laboratory with all of your rocks and minerals and maps."

"Thank you." The laboratory was impressive. Although Penelope spent so much time there that the uniqueness of her work often became mundane.

"I'm excited about the party."

"Will your fiancée be there? I've never met him."

"Yes, he will actually be in town for once. I look forward to introducing you."

Penelope was growing anxious. She needed to get back to work, but worried that shuffling Katia out of her office would be unreasonably rude. "Can we get together for coffee or lunch after the gala is over and talk about some ways we can help Robby?" Penelope stood, hoping that Katia would, too.

The Russian beauty laid her hands on her lap. "Yes, that would be nice."

"Um, did you have any trouble getting the boxes of candles to the jewelry store?"

Katia nodded. "Oh, yes. No problems."

"That's wonderful. I'm sure Maggie made a nice display." Penelope slid back into her seat.

"Did Tessa give you any candles?" Katia sat cemented on the stool.

"No. She just gave one to my mother. Two actually," Penelope said quickly, unwilling to expose her mother's evidence theft from the festival.

"They are very nice. Tessa was talented."

"She said that she made the candles with some diamonds from the jewelry shop." Penelope felt her toe tap the floor, a sure sign she was her mother's anxious daughter.

"Oh, yes?" Katia seemed surprised.

The metal stool squeaked as Penelope shifted her position. "I guess just little ones that Robby couldn't use. He said that you had been a big help in getting a lot of good-quality stones since you two became partners. You must have great connections."

"I do. Is that a problem?" Katia asked.

"No. I didn't mean anything by it. He mentioned those diamonds that you found are the ones that Tessa used. Right?"

"Yes, we got a big shipment from a new supplier just a few weeks ago. They're from Brazil. We also got some emeralds and rubies."

"Wow, that's unusual. Brazilian diamonds are rare. There is mostly amethyst and tourmaline from that region. I saw in a journal that they recently found a few moissanite samples there, too."

Katia smiled. "Moissanite would be very rare, too. I've only seen moissanite created in a laboratory. Like yours."

Penelope smiled. "This lab isn't sophisticated enough to grow crystals. I'd love to try one day, though. Robby could make me a ring if I was successful."

"Robby won't make jewelry from lab-grown crystals." Katia shook her head. "I asked him to."

"No? Why not?" Penelope could understand Robby only wanting to use natural stones, but moissanites were becoming very popular. They are only found naturally in a few rocks like kimberlites and meteorites, but are easily grown in a lab and look almost identical to diamonds at a fraction of the price.

"They're not good enough for his customers, he says."

"I can see him saying that." Penelope knew Robby was protective of the jewelry's quality.

"If you do ever create a lab-grown moissanite or any other crystal, please convince him to make jewelry from it. I would love to offer a lower-priced line to our customers."

Penelope chuckled. "I will do that. I get it. Sometimes you just want to feel pretty without a big price tag. Katia, I hate to be rude, but I really must get back to work." Penelope stood once again. This time, Katia did as well.

"Oh, no problem. I'm sorry to just drop in on you like this."

"No worries. I'd love to get together next week," Penelope offered again. "It's just that if I don't start writing my speech for Saturday, my assistant is going to lock me in a closet until I do."

Penelope gave Katia directions back to the lobby of the museum but felt guilty for hurrying her out of the lab. After Robby's business partner left, Penelope dashed to her laptop and entered 'Katia Lazovsky' into the search bar. If she had Instagram or Facebook, she could send her a friend request. *Huh, that's odd,* Penelope thought. Katia had no social media.

Chapter Eighteen

Penelope wandered through the door of The Tipsy Java, her eyes still half-closed from lack of sleep. She and Lucy stayed at the museum until midnight, working to finish the display and outlining her speech. With everything in place, Penelope needed to spend the next two days perfecting her talk for the unveiling. Public speaking was her least favorite class in college. She always hoped that she would learn to calm her nerves, but even a course through Toastmasters hadn't helped. Penelope was perfectly comfortable crouching beside a stream with muddy-kneed students or showing them how to break a galena cube into perfect tiny squares, but formal presentations sent her insides into violent gymnastics routines, leaving her lightheaded.

She flopped onto her favorite high-back chair at the bar as Laurel pushed a warm latte across the counter.

"Where's Jasper?"

"Mom's going to pick him up at my place and take him to the shop."

"You look awful. Again. Long night?" Laurel asked.

"Yup." Penelope's head leaned into her right hand while her left hand reached for the warm caffeine. She took a slow sip and closed her eyes, hoping the morning brew would wake her up more quickly than usual.

"Did you learn anything helpful?"

"About rocks?" She smiled. "I already know a lot."

"No, about Tessa."

"Nothing new about the poison. I'm not sure how you get a hold of Poison Dart Frog venom. I promised myself that I would focus on the gala and not think about Tessa until after it was over."

"Can you just buy a frog?" Laurel pushed.

"I'm not sure, but you would have to know how to get the poison out of or off the frog. It all seems very dangerous because you can die just from picking one up." Penelope sat back and her eyes opened wider. She scanned the glass pastry container to her right. "Looks like Olivia has been busy."

"Yeah, she's made some great new pastries for us to sell, and they've been going like hotcakes. What do you want?"

"One of everything, please. I'm going to need as much sugar and caffeine as I can get these next two days. I should take some extras for everyone at the museum who has been helping."

Laurel opened the backside of the glass case and pulled the bottom tray toward her. She reached deep with the tongs and pulled out a raspberry Danish topped with chopped nuts, pineapple bits, and marshmallow chunks. She handed a plate to Penelope and watched for her reaction.

Penelope's eyes grew wide with recognition. "Oh my gosh, this looks just like my great grandma's cranberry salad from Thanksgiving," Penelope exclaimed, staring at the plate.

"She's been working on that one for a month now, trying to get it perfect. Although I don't think it qualifies as a salad with whipped cream, grapes, pineapples, and marshmallows. Try it."

Penelope took a generous bite. The flavor transported her back to her childhood on Thanksgiving Day at her great-grandmother's house. Cranberry salad was her favorite part of the meal, which was just candy disguised as a side dish.

Laurel filled a takeaway box with two of each pastry from the case plus a single donut. "The bear claw is for Lucy's brother," Laurel explained, taping the box closed and then filling a second.

"Thanks. Tell Olivia I approve."

"So, who is left on your suspect list?" Laurel asked, wiping the counter.

"Everyone. Jessie, Betsy, Marlene, Katia, and Robby. I haven't found proof to rule anyone out for sure, just my gut instincts. Katia came by my office and asked to get together next week for coffee or lunch. She's worried about Robby."

"Poor guy. Have you found anything out about Betsy?"

"Betsy is a mystery. She worked for Tessa, but I assume only part time," Penelope said, forgetting the promise she made to herself to shelve the investigation until after the gala. Penelope dug her phone out of her bag and searched the internet for Betsy's name.

"Anything?" Laurel asked.

"Wow. You won't believe this. She is a professor at the community college."

"What does she teach?"

"Accounting." Penelope looked at her watch. "I have just enough time to run by the school before I get to the museum for speech rehearsal with Lucy." Penelope stood and gathered her bag.

"How is your speech coming?"

"Awful. Lucy made me promise to block out ten to five o'clock today to practice. She's even bringing lunch in."

"That's probably not a bad idea."

Penelope groaned at the thought of her speech. When she was in graduate school, her professor made her finish her project three weeks early so she could devote the final days to writing and practicing for her dissertation defense. He was right to make her practice. She wasn't a natural in front of a crowd, but with enough thought and planning and a little memorization, she could pull it off. Penelope just wished that she would become more comfortable one day in front of a group of strangers. The butterflies in her stomach hinted that it would not be this week.

Laurel handed her an extra-large latte and a bag filled with the pastry boxes. "For the road. Call me later."

Penelope thanked her friend and waved goodbye to Tristan. She pushed the cafe door open with her foot and launched herself into the chilly morning. Everyone on the street was gearing up for another busy workday and the tourists appeared to be out in force. Tourism was important for Sierra Springs because it drove people to shops like The Crystal Cove and to visit local landmarks like the Natural History Museum.

Penelope strode to her car. She climbed behind the wheel of her deep purple Hummer and revved the engine to life. Penelope thought through a list of the questions that she wanted to ask Betsy.

Penelope pulled out of the parking space, easing her car between the white and cream sport utility vehicles lining the streets. She always wondered why so many people bought white and cream-colored cars and there they were, all in rows along Main Street. A couple of black cars and a pink Cadillac that Caitlin Sparks drove around town to advertise her bridal shop were the only vehicles that broke up the lines of similar sport utility vehicles. Penelope did a double take when her eye caught sight of an ominous black SUV with a big, wide, smiling grill parked up the road. It was empty.

***

Penelope trotted through the parking lot toward the liberal arts building. She had been a guest speaker for the geology department a few times over the years. Sierra Springs Community College's campus was nestled in the foothills on the southern edge of town.

The college was getting ready for the summer session, so only a few students were strolling about while professors prepared for a shortened teaching schedule. The spring sun was rising and warming the air by the minute.

As Penelope approached the building, she saw Betsy walking toward her wearing gray linen pants and an oversized cream blouse, sunglasses, and three-inch heeled riding boots.

Well, she can't run away from me in those boots, Penelope thought.

"Hi, excuse me. Are you Betsy Peterson?"

Betsy looked warily at Penelope.

"I'm Penelope Lake."

"Have we met before?"

Penelope shook her head. "No. But I saw you at Robby McCaul's house after Tessa's funeral."

Betsy shifted on her heels. "Yes. So sad."

"How did you know Tessa?"

"Why is that your business?"

Penelope shrugged. "Oh, it isn't. I'm sorry. I'm just trying to find out what happened to Tessa. She was a friend. When I saw you at the funeral reception, I asked who you were."

"Oh. I hadn't seen Robby in a long time. I wanted to pay my respects."

"Didn't I see you coming out of The Drip Shack the other day?" Penelope faced her back to the sun so she could see Betsy's face without squinting.

Betsy stared blankly at Penelope.

"My mother owns The Crystal Cove. The shop is right across the street from the candle store. We were going to talk to Tessa the other morning, and I thought I saw you coming out of the shop." Penelope watched for any change in expression, but Betsy was difficult to read.

She shifted uncomfortably. "Tessa and I had a business relationship."

"What kind of business relationship?"

"Why are you being nosey?" Betsy snapped.

Penelope's thoughts whirled like a pinwheel. "I... I don't mean to pry. Like I said, Tessa and I were friends." Penelope tried to sound friendlier to get Betsy to open up, although she was disliking her more and more by the second. Betsy was annoyingly defensive.

"Look, I was Tessa's business accountant. I was there the other day because she called and asked me to drop by, and then she accused me of stealing money from The Drip Shack. I told her that wasn't true, but she said that she was planning to report me to the state licensing board and call the cops if I didn't pay her back." Betsy's tone escalated while she spoke, making each passerby glance their way.

"Why would she think you were stealing from her if you didn't?"

Betsy's back stiffened as her head snapped toward Penelope. "I don't know, but we got into an argument, and I left. I was planning to meet with her this week to show her the books and prove I did nothing wrong, but then I heard she was killed."

"Hmm." Penelope stared at Betsy. If she was telling the truth, then someone else must have been taking money from The Drip Shack. Who else could that have been? Robby? Certainly not. At least, she hoped not. On the other hand, if Betsy was lying, she had the perfect motive for murder.

"Are you trying to accuse me of killing her? Who are you anyway? You're not police."

"No, I'm not police." Penelope put her hands up. "I'm the one who found Tessa after she was killed, so I feel obligated to help find out what happened. That's all."

"Because you saw me come out of her candle shop, you are trying to lay the blame on me. You're accusing someone that you have never met of the murder." Betsy's voice climbed as she spoke, ending in a yell that attracted the attention of the students passing by.

Penelope's eyes snapped open. "I'm not accusing you of anything. I'm just trying to see if you know anything that could help me figure out what happened. Were you at the festival on Saturday?"

"No, I was not at the festival. I was at my—. Never mind. I don't have to answer any questions for you." Betsy slung her pocketbook over her shoulder. "Never come near me again. I had nothing to do with her murder, although I can't say that I'm sorry." Betsy spun on her heels and flung open the door to the classroom building, quickly disappearing inside.

Penelope wasn't sure what she expected Betsy to say, but that was certainly not it. She never dreamed that anybody could be happy that someone was murdered. Penelope planned to look further into Betsy's background after the weekend. Perhaps another visit to the jewelry store to ask Robby about The Drip Shack accounts was in order.

"Well, that was ugly," Penelope muttered under her breath.

"You should stay away from her. She's a bit off her rocker."

Penelope turned to see Dr. Miller from the geology department standing behind her. Gary Miller was a few years older than Penelope. They overlapped one year at the University of North Carolina during their undergraduate studies. Gary had gone on to Auburn for his doctorate while Penelope stayed in Chapel Hill. When Professor Miller heard of Penelope's return to Sierra Springs, he asked her to visit with his students to give them insight into career opportunities that were available to geologists. Penelope was more comfortable talking with students in a question-and-answer session. She wished her speech at the gala would be so relaxed.

"I noticed. I didn't mean to upset her so much."

"Everything sets her off. She is the grumpiest person I've ever met. I hate it when we are in meetings together."

"How does she teach?"

"The only people she is nice to are her students."

Dr. Miller stepped closer to Penelope. "The rumor is that she has been seeing a therapist for years. The school can't get rid of her because she has a 'medical condition'," he said with air quotes. "She even goes out of the country for treatments, but I think she is just taking extra vacation."

"Oh, gotcha." Penelope turned. "Well, I need to run back to the museum. We are prepping for the gala this Saturday. Are you coming?"

Dr. Miller winked. "I wouldn't miss it. I hear your new exhibit is amazing."

Penelope drove towards the museum, replaying her conversation with Betsy in her mind. Figuring out who killed Tessa was like a life-sized jigsaw puzzle and Betsy's revelations certainly gave her the motive piece—money.

By the time she pulled into her parking space, Penelope was feeling more confident that the puzzle would soon reveal the face of a killer, although, at this moment, the picture was still blurry.

Chapter Nineteen

"Come in," Penelope hollered from the kitchen while she poured the last of her favorite wine into two oversized goblets.

"I have the goodies," Laurel called out. She breezed through the unlocked door and then bumped it closed with her hip.

"Awesome. Thanks for bringing the food for another dinner and murder board night." Penelope set the wine on the coffee table and helped Laurel unload four bags of food from The Tipsy Java's cafe. "It's a good thing that you and Olivia feed me. The only food I have in the house, other than sports drinks and energy bars, is puppy food."

"If she ever leaves The Tipsy Java, I'm in trouble."

"She loves working with you, Laurel. You know that."

"I do. But I don't want to be one of those business owners who just assumes that my employees will stay with me if they are doing the same thing every day. I have a few ideas in mind that may be good for her and the cafe."

"Like what?" Penelope grabbed a stack of napkins and two plates from the kitchen and set them on the coffee table amongst the containers of food.

"I'm not going to say just yet. I'm still rolling everything around in my mind." Laurel plopped onto the couch.

"Alright. But don't keep me in suspense too long."

"I won't." Laurel took a sip of her wine. "How did your speech prep go?"

"Uh—" Penelope took a sharp breath. "It was useful."

"Useful? Hmm, okay. Sounds like you need more practice."

"I do. But I need a break tonight. I'm practicing all day tomorrow again."

Laurel set her wineglass down and clapped twice. "Alright, let's see the murder board."

Penelope slid the board from behind her television stand and propped it on the end of the coffee table with two purple agate bookends clamping it in place.

They sat in silence for a few minutes, eating their burgers and handmade dill potato chips, and staring at the murder board. Penelope's attention to detail was on display, with an intricate web of suspects, motives, and opportunities to commit the murder.

"Colorful," Laurel commented between swallows.

"Colorful?" Penelope threw a wadded napkin at her friend, hitting her squarely in the nose. "Is that all this tells you?" Penelope was struggling to make connections too, although she did not want to admit that she was as baffled by the board as Laurel.

"I still don't know who did it." Laurel arched her back, making the cracking sound travel down her spine.

"Ah, stop. That sounds terrible." Penelope clamped her hands over her ears to be dramatic. "You could have at least said the board is thoughtful...insightful...detailed," she said once the spine cracking ended.

"It's all of those things," Laurel agreed. "You have six suspects. Robby. Betsy. Jessie. Katia. Marlene. Clara. You listed your mother?"

Penelope tensed. "I had to put her down just so I could cross her off. So, five suspects."

"By the way, I scolded Andre for taking her in for questioning."

Penelope smiled. "Yeah? What did he say?"

"Police business. Leave him alone. Blah, blah...I hope Penelope isn't mad at me," Laurel scoffed. "Typical guy stuff."

Penelope had been thinking about Andre more since his return. She felt comfortable with him at the pool, which surprised her. Penelope wanted to stay mad at him, but her brain and heart were fighting to find a balance.

"You ruled out Katia and Robby, right? Should we cross them off?"

Penelope leaned back in her seat. "Yeah, I don't think they did it. Katia was out of town and Robby was meeting with a vendor and then the accountant. She said they needed money for the store, but I just can't imagine they would kill Tessa for it. Katia and her fiancée are obviously wealthy. Plus, the jewelry magazine is doing an entire article on the new line. They had to believe that it would be good for sales."

Laurel marked an 'X' through Robby and Katia with a thick marker that hung from a string on the corkboard. "That leaves Jessie, Marlene, and Betsy."

"Jessie. I hope she is the one. She seems so phony. Although Olivia says she's a good person." Penelope popped a dill potato chip into her mouth as Jasper wobbled into the room, waking from a nap.

"Betsy is no peach either, based on what you told me." Laurel picked up Jasper and flopped the pup onto her lap.

"Agreed."

"What about Marlene? Do you think Louis knew about the lawsuit? What if he slipped something in the Monte Cristo?" Laurel stroked Jasper's head as the pup's blue eyes slowly closed.

"The police ruled out all food and drinks."

Laurel gently slid Jasper from her lap into the dog bed. "Did Marlene exhibit at the festival?"

Penelope shrugged. "I'm still trying to track down a list of vendors. Even if she didn't exhibit, she could have been there."

"Which has the stronger motive?" Laurel sipped her wine.

Penelope drew in a deep breath and held it while she pondered. "Jessie was battling with Tessa and Robby for customers at the festival. It doesn't sound like they ever got along. Plus, Jessie's brother works at the zoo and they have poison dart frogs there. I checked."

"But Betsy was being accused of stealing from The Drip Shack and Tessa threatened to file a complaint with the police and the state licensing board," Laurel said.

"And Marlene was going to be countersued for five million dollars over the candle patents."

"I thought Sandra said they hadn't filed the countersuit yet." Laurel finished her burger and crumpled the wrapper.

"That's what she told me at the funeral reception, but Tessa could have told Marlene that it was coming, just like she warned Betsy that she was going to call the licensing board. I need to track her down and ask."

"Jessie's motive is money and a fear of a failing business." Penelope refilled their wine glasses.

"Betsy's motive is money, her teaching career, and possible jail, and Marlene's motive is money. Lots of it," Laurel said.

"Money. Career. Fear. Jealousy. Those are all good motives." Penelope raised her glass and clinked hers against Laurel's.

"Hmm. Do you think that there could be anyone else? Did Tessa have any employees or people from her past that gave her trouble?"

"Not that I could find. She just had a couple of local high school kids helping her in the store, and Tessa was not originally from around here. Robby said that her parents were dead, and I don't think her sister even came to the funeral." Penelope gathered the dinner plates and sat them in the kitchen sink.

"There could be someone from her past who didn't like her, and they were visiting town and ran into her at the festival." Laurel followed behind with the trash.

Penelope filled Jasper's bowl with dinner and topped off her water. "And they just randomly had a syringe full of Batrachotoxin in their bag, ready to murder her on the off chance that they found her one day?"

"Okay, probably not." Laurel agreed. "Any idea who left the note on your car?"

"Not yet." Penelope returned to the living room. "What did you bring for dessert?"

Laurel picked up a white pastry bag and tossed it to her. "See for yourself."

Penelope opened the bag and frowned.

"What? You don't like chocolate eclairs?"

"Not when they are in the shape of plain bagels." Penelope held the bag open so Laurel could see inside.

"Oh no! I must have grabbed the wrong bag. I guess there is a customer out here equally sad that they have our eclairs rather than homemade bagels."

"I may have some candy in the pantry from Halloween."

"Ew. You want to eat six-month-old candy? Gross."

"You're spoiled to have Olivia's fresh-baked goodies at your fingertips all day, every day."

"I know. Come on. Let's run to the cafe and get some." Laurel grabbed her purse.

Penelope grinned and rolled off the couch. "You don't have to twist my arm."

"Bring Jasper. I have some chopped chicken at the cafe she can have."

Penelope scooped up the sleeping pup. "You hear that? You get fresh chopped chicken and not from a can either."

Jasper let out the husky 'awoo,' making Penelope wonder if her furry friend understood English.

Penelope hopped into Laurel's car and held Jasper in her lap.

Laurel revved the engine and pulled out of Penelope's driveway. As they eased to the first stop sign, a black car settled behind, uncomfortably close to their bumper. "Ugh, is that the SUV again?" Penelope asked.

"What one?"

"That black one with the fat grill. It looks like it's smiling at me. I think it was the one that followed us the other day and then was outside my place, remember? You haven't seen it around town?" Penelope rubbed Jasper's head.

"Not lately. There are too many big, black cars around." Laurel guided the car along Brookhaven Road, then turned onto Oakmont Avenue. The SUV made the same turn, pulling close behind.

"Why are you going this way?" Penelope asked, watching the side mirror.

"There is a house for sale over on Tremont that I wanted to show you. I'm thinking of getting out of my apartment," Laurel said.

"That's great. What does it look like?"

"It's a little Tudor with a wrap-around porch."

"I can't wait to see it."

Laurel turned left onto Snowflake Drive and then took a quick right onto Devon Lane. Her eyes glanced between the road ahead and the rearview mirror.

"I thought you said it was on Tremont?"

"I did."

"Then you are going the wrong way."

Laurel shook her head. "I think that SUV *is* following us again."

Chapter Twenty

Laurel zigzagged through the streets of Sierra Springs as the women tried to determine if the SUV was indeed following them or if overactive imaginations fueled their paranoia. As the seconds ticked into minutes, Penelope became certain the SUV was following them. Laurel's quick turns through the city streets never lost the menacing vehicle for long.

"Let's try to lose them in the alley behind Mom's house."

The thick, grinning grill dissolved seamlessly into glowing headlights that tracked Laurel's car with the precision of a stalking panther. With shaking hands, she guided her car toward Clara's home, just two blocks away. An alley ran lengthwise behind the bungalow houses, flanked by deep stormwater ditches leading to a community pond where the residents would fish as soon as the weather warmed.

Laurel eased the car to a rolling stop directly behind Clara's house, beneath the overgrown rhododendrons, providing modest cover. Penelope's eyes locked onto the rearview mirror. "I don't see it anymore. I think you lost it."

Cars line the edge of the alley. Penelope saw a ring of dotted light from the lanterns posted beside the night fishers.

"Let's back out and park in front of her house. I don't want to get blocked in back here," Penelope said.

"Okay." Laurel placed the car in reverse. "Oh, no."

"What?" Penelope's pulse quickened.

"What do we do?" Laurel looked frantically from one side of the car to the other. The SUV sat parked at the end of the alley, two houses down from Clara's backyard, leaving them no escape.

"I say we make a run for it." Penelope's breath felt labored. "I don't know who that is, and I'm not sure I want to find out."

"What if they chase us?" Laurel's voice sounded frantic.

Penelope tried to stay calm, betrayed by her frayed nerves. "The only other option is to turn around and confront them, find out who they are, and what they want." She tightened her squeeze on Jasper.

"Why are they just sitting there?"

Penelope and Laurel scooched down in the front seat, hoping it looked like the car was empty. But the SUV sat still, waiting for them to emerge.

"Okay, here's the plan. I'm going to count to three and we're both going to jump out of the car and sprint to your mom's back door and get inside as fast as we can." Laurel strained her neck to look into the rear-view mirror.

The SUV sat motionless.

"Good idea." Penelope pulled her cell phone from her back pocket and sent her mom a short text.

Penelope: Quick. Unlock your back door for me and Laurel.

Laurel rolled her head, stretching her neck toward the side mirror. "That's not ominous at all, Penelope," she admonished.

Penelope clamped her arms around the squirming pup and tilted her head toward Laurel. They kept their eyes fixed on the rearview mirrors, making sure that their friend in the SUV was still inside.

Penelope's cell phone vibrated. She took a quick peek at the message. "The back door is unlocked, but I think Mom is confused. Ready?"

Laurel nodded.

They each took a deep breath.

"One. Two. Three!"

Penelope and Laurel leaped through the front doors of the car and took off running at full speed through Clara's backyard.

Penelope lunged at the back door, twisting the knob in stride. As the door gave way, they tumbled through, landing in a heap on the gray slate floor, with a frightened Jasper clamped between Penelope's arms. Clara quickly closed the door and locked it, then stood over Penelope and Laurel, her arms crossed, and an irritated expression coating her face.

"Would you two ladies like to tell me what's going on?" Clara tapped her toe.

Penelope knew her mother's tone of voice—she and Laurel were in trouble.

"Were you being chased by a lion?"

Penelope gasped. "No. Of course not." Penelope released her grip, and Jasper immediately ran off to find Midnight.

"Then what has gotten into you two?"

Penelope and Laurel pulled themselves off the floor and smoothed out their clothing. Clara tapped her foot again, slowly at first and then quicker as the seconds ticked away, with no explanation.

Penelope felt like she was in high school when Clara called them ladies. "We were going to The Tipsy Java, but—"

"Penelope said somebody was following us, so I drove zigzag through the streets. We thought we could hide behind your house, but when I pulled into the alley, the SUV pulled in behind us and blocked us in," Laurel blurted.

"Following you. Who?"

"We don't know," Penelope said. "That's when I texted you and said to unlock the back door. Then we jumped out of the car and ran."

Penelope walked to the kitchen window and peered into the backyard through the pots of herbs growing along the windowsill. She moved to the right side, trying to see the far-left edge of the backyard. If the person in the SUV was following, they would come from that direction. Nobody was there.

"I'm calling Ryan," Clara said. "Sit." She pointed the girls to the antique oak kitchen table. The intricate carvings on the legs dated the table at over one hundred years old. A marble vase overflowing with pink peonies filled the center.

"No. I don't want to bug him." Penelope was worried about who may be following her, but equally worried about Ryan and Andre finding out that she was still poking around Tessa's murder enough to make someone want to follow her.

Clara folded her arms. "You two are so convinced that someone followed you around town that you came running into my house like a rabbit in a lion's cage and you don't want to tell the police?"

"No, Mom—" Penelope's gut was fighting a battle with her logic. She very well could be in danger. But she hoped she was just being paranoid.

"Laurel, what about you?" Clara asked. Penelope could see her friend shrinking in the wake of her mother's scrutiny.

"I think someone is definitely trying to scare you, Penelope."

"I don't like it." Clara filled the floral-painted steel tea kettle with filtered water and set it on the stove.

Penelope tried to change the subject. "Mom, there are easier ways to make tea than that old-fashioned teapot you insist on using."

"Yes, but it tastes better from my tea kettle." Clara picked up her phone and began dialing. "I like to boil the water in the tea kettle and listen to the whistle. That's when you know you're making great tea," she said as she put the phone to her ear. "Stop trying to distract me. You are not getting out of this, Penelope."

Penelope always loved hanging out at her mom's house with Laurel. The color-drenched walls were coated in deep shades of purple and green. The inside of her home looked similar to the store, with crystals hanging in the doorways and covering the bookshelves. When they were kids, Penelope and Laurel would run from one house to another. But back in those days, there wasn't anyone chasing them down the street, and none of their friends were murdered.

Laurel's parents lived only a few blocks away, and the girls spent almost every minute together.

Clara hung up the phone as the tea kettle whistled. She placed three mugs on the table. "Ryan didn't answer. Which tea would you like?"

"Cinnamon oolong, please," Penelope and Laurel said in unison.

One benefit of Clara thinking she was a witch was that she always played with herbs, which often ended up in a variety of innovative tea blends. Clara dropped sachets in the mugs and filled each with hot boiling water. The girls gratefully inhaled the steam, breathing in the familiar cinnamon sent.

"Laurel, honey, why don't you call your brother?" Clara suggested.

"Yes, Ms. Clara," Laurel said. "I'll text him right now." She turned to Penelope. "Your Mom is right. We have to tell Andre."

Midnight and Jasper wandered into the kitchen and hopped onto the table while the three women drank their tea in silence. Penelope could see the bottom of her mug when Laurel's phone chimed.

"Andre is on his way over." Laurel pulled Midnight onto her lap.

The women had barely refilled their tea mugs when Penelope heard a knock on the front door.

"Hello Andre," Clara greeted the new arrival. "They are in the kitchen."

"Ladies," he said, entering the room. "Are you okay?"

Laurel rose to hug her brother. "We are. Just a little shaken up."

"I checked the alley, and it's empty." Andre stared at Penelope.

"Let's sit in the living room, shall we?" Clara offered. "Tea, Andre?"

"No, thank you, Ms. Lake." Andre nodded at Penelope.

Clara's living room eschewed mundane furniture with patchwork quilt-covered overstuffed poufs instead of couches or chairs. A low table sat in the center of the room with trays of partially burned candles and tarot cards. Antique mirrors flanked the walls on opposite sides of the room with an ornate floral tapestry hung opposite the bay window overlooking the front yard.

Andre sat awkwardly on a pouf next to Laurel and Penelope, peppering them with questions about the mysterious SUV. They recounted every detail of the car—its tinted windows and menacing grill, the times it followed them to Penelope's house and now to Clara's. Andre's jaw tightened as he listened, making detailed notes, his fingers white-knuckled around the pen. Penelope recognized the fury burning below his cool exterior. She wondered if his anger would aim for her or the SUV's driver.

"Give me a few minutes," he grumbled, stepping into the kitchen to make a phone call.

Penelope, Laurel, and Clara sat silently, trying to eavesdrop on Andre's half of the conversation.

Ten minutes later, he reentered the living room. "Okay, one of my officers ran some searches. There are a lot of black SUVs, but the grill you described most likely belongs to an older, high-end vehicle like a Bently, Jag, Lexus, or Astin Martin. I'm leaning toward Lexus based on your description."

"Are there some of those SUVs around?" Penelope asked.

"There are too many of those cars around, so without a license plate, we can't run it down."

"I'll keep an eye open," Penelope said, rising and stretching her back.

Andre put his hand up. "No, you won't. I'm taking you both home. There will be squad cars outside of your homes tonight. And Penelope, if you ask one more question to anyone about Tessa's murder, I will personally put you in jail."

Chapter Twenty-One

Friday morning, Penelope was hard at work on her speech. She paced the floor, quietly reciting the words with only a few prompts from her index cards. She was improving. The unveiling at the gala was only thirty-six hours away and Penelope was feeling a crushing pressure to make sure everything was flawless. Reactions from colleagues around the globe had been pouring in over the past few weeks, skyrocketing Penelope's nervousness. She wondered if her efforts were enough to impress some of the greatest scientists in the field.

"Good morning," Lucy sang out. She handed Penelope a paper travel cup from The Tipsy Java.

"Thanks, Lucy." Penelope took a quick sip, then set it on the worktable next to the dropper bottle filled with hydrochloric acid. "Hey, the lock on the lab door is acting up. Can you ask maintenance to take a look?"

"Sure, no problem." Lucy looked around the lab. "How long have you been here?" she asked, pointing to and silently counting the empty coffee cups huddled on Penelope's desk.

"Uh, not long." Penelope looked up for a split second. Her eyes followed Lucy's to the desk that gave away her lie.

"Uh-huh." Lucy hopped onto the stool next to the table, looking over a line of cut samples. "Were you seriously testing the Black Top Mountain samples again? You verified those. About twenty other geologists verified those. Stop."

"What if I made a mistake? Everyone will find out." Penelope's eyes never left the samples.

"You didn't make any mistakes. The samples are perfect. The research is perfect. The displays are perfect." Lucy waved her hand in front of Penelope's nose.

Penelope looked at her assistant, her face crinkled. "I'm not sure."

Lucy grabbed Penelope's hand. "Come on."

"Where are we going?" Penelope demanded as Lucy dragged her down the hallway and into the museum. "Lucy, I need to get back to work."

Lucy steered Penelope behind the curtains and into the new exhibit room, halting when they reached the center of the floor.

"Look." Lucy stood behind Penelope, grabbed her shoulders from behind, and slowly turned her in a circle.

"Look at what? Is something wrong?"

"No, silly. You did this. You created the biggest, most beautiful display of rare rocks and minerals that the world has ever seen."

"I had help."

"Of course you did. Everyone needs help. But you started all of this with a single hike across Black Top Mountain. You noticed one unusual mineral stuck in a boulder. You went on over a dozen trips and found most of the samples in this room by yourself. The samples you didn't find are from people who want to ride your coattails. But *you* chose and verified every unique sample that came through that door. And *you* are the only person who has ever had the imagination to create something this special."

"But—" Penelope protested.

"Stop talking and look," Lucy commanded.

Penelope's eyes swept across the room. The cherry wood and glass display cabinets were polished to a high shine. The nameplates sparkled in the light. Tiny spotlights inside each case deftly highlighted the intricate details and the beauty of each mineral. Penelope sighed, realizing that Lucy was correct. The display was fabulous, and it was ready. "Thank you."

"You're welcome." Lucy rubbed her friend's arm. "Let's go get the Black Top samples and remount them on the display. Then we'll work on your speech, because that also needs to be perfect."

"Ugh." Penelope's head flopped forward. "I would much rather play with rocks."

Lucy laughed. "People are coming to the gala to see you just as much as to see this display. Plus, you need to knock their socks off so we can get lots of donations."

Penelope smiled and cringed simultaneously. "I know," she croaked. "Fundraising sucks. Although it would be nice to get enough money in one night to build the children's wing."

"Come on." Lucy smiled and pulled Penelope by the wrist back toward the rock lab.

By the time they reached the offices, Penelope's nerves had calmed, only to have them ramp up again when she saw Detective Snow sitting in the rock lab with his feet propped up on the corner of the worktable.

Penelope stopped in the doorway. "I have got to talk with our security guards about unwanted guests."

"I have a badge." Ryan smiled.

"Ryan. Hi. Was I expecting you?" Penelope began organizing the Black Top samples along the lip of the worktable.

"You should have been." He swung his feet to the floor and smiled at Lucy.

"Oh, I'm Lucy Arden. I work with Penelope." Lucy's gaze shot between Penelope and Ryan. "Did you say badge?"

"Detective Ryan Snow." Ryan shook Lucy's hand, then turned his attention squarely on Penelope. "Why didn't you tell me you and Laurel were chased last night?"

"Chased?" Lucy gasped.

"It was nothing, Lucy." Penelope flicked her hand, trying to downplay Ryan's words.

"Not according to the Chief." Ryan's cheeks turned a slight shade of crimson, as a frown blanketed his face.

Penelope smiled at Lucy. "Could you give the detective and me a moment?"

"Sure, I'll take these samples back to the exhibit." Lucy quickly gathered the Black Top samples and cradled them in her arms. She turned to glance at Ryan, then left, closing the door softly behind.

Penelope sat on the opposite stool. Ryan pulled a notebook from his back pocket.

"How did you find out?"

"Your mother and Andre called me early this morning. Why didn't you call me last night?" The scowl never left his face.

Penelope felt chastised. "Because my mother called you last night, and you didn't answer. And because Laurel called Andre. And because nothing happened."

"Nothing?" Ryan said, leaning against the table close to Penelope.

"Well. Not much." Penelope resented his tone. He made her feel like a naughty child.

"Not much. Okay." Ryan opened his notebook and flipped to the last page with writing. "According to your mother, 'Penelope and Laurel showed up at my house panicked after being chased through the streets by a big black SUV.'"

"She exaggerates." Penelope swiped her hand through the air.

"Really? I talked to Laurel, too. She said, 'A black SUV was sitting outside Penelope's house, and it followed us. I sped up, and it chased us through the neighborhood until we finally got away at Clara's house.'"

"Her too."

"No, Penelope. They are not exaggerating and you are in danger. I can't believe that you didn't keep calling me until I answered."

Penelope's frustration grew as Ryan chastised her actions. Her Garmin wristwatch vibrated, showing that her stress level was increasing, and she needed to calm down. "I have so much on my mind with the gala tomorrow night," Penelope asserted. "I just don't have time to worry about some SUV that followed us. Nothing happened to us. Andre came over and handled everything. Two officers sat outside my house all night. Why are you so bent out of shape?"

"Because it's you, Penelope." Ryan jumped from the stool and folded his notebook. He paced the edge of the room.

"So, what do you need from me?" Penelope was quickly becoming exasperated with Ryan's presence in her office.

"A statement about last night."

Penelope sighed. "Ryan, I already gave it to Andre, and I need to get ready for the gala tomorrow. You talked with my mother and Laurel. Why do you need me?" Penelope grabbed a tub of disinfecting cloths and began wiping down the worktable.

Ryan spun around. His pen incessantly tapped his notebook. "You are a hard person at times. It's a good thing that you are my friend." He smacked his notebook onto the table, landing it with a thud on top of the cloth. "Read their statements and just tell me if they left anything out," Ryan snapped.

Penelope quickly scanned Ryan's notes and nodded. "Looks good to me."

Ryan tilted his head. "You didn't read it closely."

"Your handwriting is sloppy." She pushed the notebook toward him.

"No, it isn't." Ryan snatched the notebook and began writing.

"What are you putting in there?"

"That you refuse to cooperate with a full statement but corroborated the initial witnesses."

"Now you're being difficult."

Ryan threw his hands into the air. "You're the difficult one. I care about you and if someone is following you, that is a very bad thing. There is a murderer out there, Penelope, and we haven't found them yet, but they seem to have found you."

"I have a lot of work to do. Are we done?" Penelope stared at Ryan. Her anger grew. She did not have time or the emotional space for a fight.

A soft knocking sounded through the heavy wood door. Lucy pushed slightly and peered through the crack.

"Come in, Lucy," Penelope called.

Lucy glanced at the detective and then at Penelope, raising her eyebrows.

"Do you need something?" Penelope asked, hoping to get out of the conversation with the nosy detective.

"There is a problem with the display. We need you." Lucy smiled slightly, then ducked out of the doorway.

"Oops. Gotta go." Penelope picked up her binder that held details about the display.

"I wasn't done with you."

"Duty calls." Penelope shrugged, spinning on her heels. "I'll trust you can see yourself out."

Penelope yanked the door open and trotted down the hallway, trying to disappear into the display area before Ryan could follow.

As she jumped through the curtain, she could see Lucy laughing.

"There's no problem?" Penelope asked, smiling.

"No. I could hear you arguing through the door and I figured you needed to get out of there. I was just coming to see what you wanted for lunch."

Penelope gave Lucy a high-five and plucked her phone from the back pocket of her jeans. Laurel answered her call quickly.

"Why didn't you warn me that Ryan knew about last night?"

"I texted you," Laurel said. "Didn't you get the messages?"

Penelope pulled the phone from her ear and quickly scrolled through her messages, finally seeing the text from Laurel that came in during her anxiety-filled morning.

"Sorry, I didn't see them. He just showed up at the museum, but he's gone now."

"Are you ready for some huge news?"

"What?"

"Betsy Peterson came in for coffee this morning."

"Really? Did you talk to her?"

"Uh-huh. Sort of."

"What does that mean?"

"After she drank her coffee, she got up to leave and ran right into another customer. She dropped her purse and everything, including a bunch of business cards, fell out. I helped her pick everything up."

"How is that huge news?"

"Because one of the business cards she had was Doctor Nate Sorensen."

Penelope's jaw fell. "You mean anger management psychiatrist Nate Sorensen, who used to ask me out constantly in college?"

"That's the one."

Penelope smiled. She knew exactly how to find out Betsy's secrets. She would invite her old school buddy, Nate Sorensen, to lunch.

Chapter Twenty-Two

The evening of the gala arrived quickly. Penelope assumed she would have more time to find the right dress and shoes and get her nails done at a salon rather than slapping on a coat of deep red Revlon Vixen in her bathroom. But all that was cast aside when she fell into a murder investigation. She stared at an old gown she had left over from a college soiree and hoped it wasn't obviously out of date. Penelope was sitting in a towel on the edge of her bed, cooling off from her shower, when she heard a knock at the front door.

Penelope fastened a robe around her waist, mashed her feet into the nearest pair of fuzzy slippers, and padded to the living room. Just as her hand touched the knob on the front door, she realized her hair was still wet and wrapped in a towel over her head. She stopped turning the knob, trying to decide the best course of action.

Knock, knock, knock. "Penelope, open up!"

Relieved, Penelope whipped the door open as Lucy sauntered into the condominium dressed in a red sequin ball gown, three-inch heels, and an updo to make any pageant queen quake with envy. "What is that?" She was carrying a huge garment bag.

"Just put this on. You'll thank me." Lucy gently laid the fabric wardrobe bag out on Penelope's couch and set a shoebox on her coffee table.

Penelope smiled. "You got me a dress? I was just going to wear my yellow party dress."

"I figured you would." Lucy shook her head. "Tonight is much too special for that party dress. So, I *borrowed* you a dress. Caitlin at the bridal store sent a dress for you and this one that I'm wearing, but we have to make sure and tell everybody at the gala where we got them."

Penelope's mouth hung open. She couldn't believe that Lucy went to the trouble of finding them special dresses, even if it was just borrowed for the evening. "This is so generous," she said, admiring Lucy's gown.

Lucy squealed and clapped. "If you think the gown I'm wearing is pretty, wait until you see the one she sent for you. And there's a little pouch with jewelry at the bottom as well. I feel like a celebrity."

"You look beautiful."

Lucy picked up the wardrobe bag and handed it to Penelope. "And you look like someone who just stepped out of the shower. Go get dressed. We've got to get to the gala early to make sure that everything's set and run through your speech one more time."

Penelope hung her head. "I can't wait until that part is over."

"Just think of everyone at the party as a Girl Scout. You're great with Girl Scouts."

Lucy gently sat on the edge of Penelope's couch so that she didn't wrinkle her dress. Penelope disappeared into the bedroom to get changed for the evening. When she unraveled her hair, she found the extra time wrapped in the towel did it some good. Her auburn curls cascaded down her back. A quick spritz of setting oil to make sure her curls didn't fly away in the evening humidity and Penelope was on to makeup.

Her routine was normally simple. She didn't need foundation, so a little concealer dabbed here and there, and some setting powder gave her a nice clean face. But this evening was special, so Penelope went all out. A thin veil of ivory foundation made her skin look like a porcelain doll. A light touch of shadow to highlight her eyes, a little bronzer on her cheekbones, and deep red lipstick completed the look.

Penelope slipped into the black sequin ball gown. Tiny crystals adorned the silky fabric along the bodice. Thin spaghetti straps accentuated her figure as the skirt kissed the floor as it fell and swirled about her ankles, making her look even taller than her five foot eight inches.

In the bottom of the bag, Penelope found a velvet case of diamond and emerald teardrop earrings with a necklace and a hair comb to match. She swept the left side of her curls back and secured them with the gemstone-encrusted hair accessory, giving her an Audrey Hepburn look from the 1950s. The last touch was a pair of black strappy satin heels with a curtain of crystals draping from her ankle across the top of her foot. Penelope stepped back and scrutinized herself in the full-length mirror on the back of her bedroom door. She was pleased with what she saw. Never in a million years would she have spent her money to buy a dress this expensive. Most of her extra funds went to buy rocks and books about rocks. Penelope admired herself in the mirror and wondered if she should start re-prioritizing her wardrobe.

Penelope emerged from her bedroom to see Jasper waiting on the couch with Lucy.

"How do I look?"

"Beautiful."

"We both look pretty awesome," Penelope said with a twirl.

***

Penelope and Lucy reached the museum an hour before the guests were scheduled to arrive. The design crew had gone overboard decorating each of the halls with a different theme that matched the exhibits. While the gala was designed for adults, the funds were being raised for children's education, so a special room for kids offered a space where they could explore different sciences during the party. There were interactive displays and games for the children to play and dinosaur cookies for snacks.

As they walked the halls, Penelope felt in awe of the work that went into transforming the museum from an everyday fascinating educational space to a magical moment in time where the vital role of science was on display in the most beautiful setting that she had ever witnessed.

"This is amazing," Lucy commented.

They wandered from room to room admiring the displays adorned with twinkling lights and elegant signs which told the story of how each display originated and why it was beneficial for kids and adults alike to understand and enjoy. Penelope's eyes teared as she read the descriptions in the hall of rock and minerals because so much of her work was on display that evening.

"Every day when I come to work here, I know what I do helps teach how important and amazing our earth is, but when you see some of these displays and the comments from people who have visited, it is so, so—. It's truly hard to explain how it makes me feel."

"I think the tears ruining your makeup right now say it all." Lucy chuckled. "You better stop crying or you're going to end up looking like Frankenstein's bride."

Penelope stifled her tears and quickly drew a tissue from her black silk handbag. She dabbed at her face, trying to make the mess of her eye makeup less noticeable. She squinted at her reflection in one of the large fish tanks that lined the entrance foyer.

"Are you ready for your speech?" Lucy asked.

Penelope smiled, pondering the moment later in the evening when she would tug the satin rope that would release the curtain, unveiling the new rare rock and mineral exhibit she had spent the last five years curating. "Let's hope so."

The soft notes of the string quartet wafted through the hallways, telling Penelope that it was almost time for the gala to receive its first guests. She and Lucy spent the final few minutes dashing from room to room, talking with the decorators, Olivia's catering staff, and their colleagues at the museum to make sure everything was perfect. The museum relied heavily on donations and grant money to keep the doors open.

The new children's museum would have interactive displays where kids and their parents and school groups could visit and perform hands-on science experiments that they could not do at home or school. There would be experiments and activities for toddlers through high schoolers.

The night she had agonized over for months had finally arrived. Anxiety wedged its way through the excitement. Penelope controlled her breathing like she was readying herself for battle. Tonight, the battle was separating donors from their cash.

After inspecting every display and sampling every appetizer, Penelope positioned herself in the grand foyer, leaning against the wall awaiting the first guest.

"You did it," Lucy said, handing Penelope a glass of champagne.

"No. *We* did it. All these years you've worked with me on getting this museum display ready for this very night. It belongs to you just as much as it does to me."

"I just hope these donors come up with lots of cash. I'm looking forward to having a children's center."

Penelope turned to her trusted assistant, who had become her close friend. "I'm not supposed to tell you this yet because we're waiting to see if we raise enough money. But if we do, the director is going to ask you to be the project manager and oversee the entire building and running of the children's center."

"Are you kidding me? I'm still in graduate school."

Penelope wrapped her left arm around Lucy's shoulder, giving her a gentle squeeze.

"You're almost done with graduate school, and since you have a science degree with a minor in business management, you're the perfect candidate. Well, unless you don't want to work with me full time as my colleague rather than my assistant," Penelope joked.

"Are you kidding? I would love to. I have so many ideas for the children's center," Lucy said.

"I know you do. And that's why I told the director that you were the only logical choice for the job. But you have to act surprised when he offers it to you."

"Thank you, Penelope."

"You are very welcome." Penelope could see Lucy becoming emotional. "Now, you watch *your* mascara," she said with a wink.

They clinked their champagne glasses as the first donors filed through the museum's open doors. Penelope, Lucy, and the rest of the museum staff milled through the rooms, making small talk with each guest as they arrived.

"The museum is absolutely beautiful, dear," Clara said, hugging Penelope. She wore a long, flowing gown the color of mustard with a crystal beaded bodice and sequin-dotted skirt. The light bounced off the crystals, making the dress radiant in a sea of black tuxedos.

"Thank you, Mom. And you look quite dazzling yourself, I might say."

Clara blushed, unusual for her. Her mother was the most confident woman in Penelope's life. She was typically very aware of her beauty. Olivia appeared with a tray of hors d'oeuvres. She had been hard at work catering for the event.

"Olivia, do you need help?" Laurel asked, joining the group.

Olivia smiled. "No, I've got it covered. You can enjoy the gala." A caterer's apron covered the skirt of Olivia's black cocktail dress to keep it clean while she worked.

"I'm afraid to eat anything more I might bust through this borrowed dress," Penelope chimed in.

"You look stunning," Laurel said. "And skinny thanks to all that exercising you do. One canape won't hurt."

"Lucy borrowed clothes and jewelry for us from the bridal store. Your dress is gorgeous, too."

"Blue is positively your color, Laurel," Clara said. "I did my spells for the evening, so the museum should have a great night for donations."

Penelope glanced at her mother out of the corner of her eye. "What do you mean your spells for the evening?"

Clara leaned close and whispered, "The money spells, dear, I did spells so that all these donors will give you so much money for the children's center that you could build two if you wanted." Clara raised her eyebrows and her champagne glass at the same time. "And my spells always work." She winked at Penelope through the glass.

"No, they don't, but thank you, anyway," Penelope rolled her eyes toward Laurel, hoping her friend would see her pleading for help, but Laurel only laughed and ambled into the dinosaur room.

The gala was moving along, and the attendees seemed to have a wonderful time. As guests arrived, Penelope saw more familiar faces. Almost the entire police force was wandering through the museum, including Andre and Ryan. Tristan and his friends showed up and even Robby came by to show support.

"You didn't have to come. I would certainly understand if you didn't." Penelope gave Robby a quick hug.

"Tessa would want me to be here. She bought the tickets months ago when you first told her about unveiling the new display. I must admit that I'm quite intrigued. If there's any way that I can help you with the children's center, just let me know. There might be some fun gemology experiments I can contribute."

"That's generous of you, Robby. I will take you up on that."

Robby's eyes filled with tears. "I'm sorry to go so soon, but people keep mentioning Tessa to me. Katia and Tom said that they would give me a ride home right after you tell us the name of your new mineral."

Penelope understood and excused herself to mingle with the guests before her nine o'clock speech. She was surprised to see Jessie and Betsy at the gala roaming about the biology wing. She had spoken to both briefly about Tessa's murder, and neither seemed overly generous with information.

Laurel hustled over and handed Penelope a second glass of champagne. They leaned back against the wall and surveyed the area.

"Your mother certainly seems to be having fun." Laurel watched Clara spin around the dance floor with one of the eligible men of Sierra Springs.

Penelope chuckled. "At least she's dancing and not doing more spells."

They watched the crowd for a few more minutes, sipping champagne and enjoying the evening that Penelope had hoped for since her first day working at the museum.

Laurel let her eyes wander the room. "Is it just me, or does this ballroom look like your murder board?"

Penelope agreed. "It is a little odd to see all of them here." Almost every suspect on the board had shown up at the gala. "I'm shocked to see Jessie and Betsy here."

"This may be our best chance for answers. I'll go talk to Betsy. You go talk to Jessie. Let's hope they've had enough alcohol to loosen their lips."

"That's probably a good idea. I don't think Betsy would want to speak to me after our encounter at the college," Penelope said. "Meet back here in fifteen minutes and let me know what she says. Then it will be time for my speech."

Mingling through the crowd in opposite directions, they searched for their marks. Penelope found Jessie looking through the ancient clay pot display and silently stood next to her, waiting for her to stop reading about the Incas.

"Thank you for coming tonight, Jessie."

Jessie turned to see Penelope standing next to her. Her shoulders slumped.

"Oh, hi. I didn't expect to see you."

"I work at the museum. You know that."

"I thought you worked for the city, building roads or something."

"My primary job is being the resident geologist here at the Natural History Museum. I'm the one who created the display that is being unveiled tonight. I work for the city in my free time because they don't have anybody else."

"Well, you look fancy. I bet all the men here want to dance with you."

Penelope put her hands on her hips. She was starting to wonder if Jessie had a touch of bipolar disorder. One day she was nice and the next day, a sourpuss. *Why are you even here?* she wondered. Penelope was aware of the hundreds of people nearby. "You said last week that you have been having a tough time. Is there anything I can do for you?"

"I *was* hoping to run into you at some point. I guess here is as good as any."

"Why?" Penelope was curious about the sudden mood switch.

"I think I might have some information about Tessa's murder. I kept wondering how she was killed right next to me, and I never noticed. Because I honestly didn't notice. My therapist tells me I'm too wrapped up in myself." Jessie frowned.

That diagnosis is not shocking, Penelope thought. "What kind of information do you think you have today that you didn't when we spoke last week?"

"My therapist helped me think back through the day, and I realized Tessa had another visitor in the afternoon. I heard her talking to some customers that she sold a few pieces of Robby's jewelry to and one or two of her candles, but then somebody showed up that I think she knew."

"Who?"

"I'm not exactly sure who it was because I never saw them. But I heard them. The voices were muffled, but it was a woman. And I think I would recognize her voice again."

"Did you tell the police?"

"Not yet."

"You need to tell them."

Jessie looked squarely at Penelope. "I'll call them on Monday."

"Several of the police detectives involved in the investigation are here tonight. You should—" The loudspeaker crackled on, indicating that it was time for her display unveiling. Clara breezed into the room with a handsome man on her arm.

"You're up, darling," Clara said, dragging Penelope out of the room, into the foyer, and to the stage.

Penelope looked back at Jessie as her mother whisked her away. "Let's talk after." Penelope saw Jessie nod just before she lost her in the crowd. She would have to find Jessie after the unveiling and take her to see Ryan.

She better not leave, Penelope thought. This was the first actual break Penelope had in the case. If Jessie was telling the truth and Tessa argued with a woman, that conclusively ruled out Robby.

As she waited to be introduced by the museum director, Penelope mentally went through her speech. She had practiced it for three days with Lucy and she wanted it to be perfect. Lucy was impressed with the last few run-throughs and as much as she wanted to impress the attendees, she wanted to do an excellent job for Lucy, who was her biggest cheerleader. The lights were so bright Penelope could see nothing past the first row of donors standing in front of the stage.

"Now I will turn the presentation over to Penelope Lake," Mr. Canfield, the director, said. "Ms. Lake is responsible for everything you see here tonight and has brought to Sierra Springs one of the most unique and inspirational displays her field has ever known."

Penelope accepted the wireless microphone, thanking the director, who then sauntered off stage, leaving her alone to face the crowd. *Girl Scouts. They are all just Girl Scouts.*

"Hi, I'm Penelope Lake. I'm the resident geologist here at the Natural History Museum in Sierra Springs and I'm pleased that you all would take time out of your busy schedules to come here tonight to see our newest display." Penelope took a slow breath and closed her eyes. She let the nerves wash away and a blanket of calm spread over her body. *I wonder if my mother did a calming spell. I'm not usually this at ease,* she thought.

"I first found a sample of the rare Black Top Mountain mineral while I was on a hike during summer break in college. It wasn't until I was in graduate school I realized that I had found something truly unique. In fact, so unique that it didn't even have a name. This discovery led me on a search for the world's most rare samples and we have assembled them here." Penelope told the guests how she conducted her quest for these rare samples and how much the collection meant to her, the museum, and science.

"This collection would not have been possible without everyone that I have worked with over the years." Penelope thanked all of her former professors at the University of North Carolina, her fellow students, and the museum director. "Most of all, I would like to thank Lucy Arden, who worked tirelessly with me on this display while simultaneously raising her brother, earning her college degree, and is just a few weeks away from completing her master's degree." Penelope found Lucy tucked into the crowd, mascara melting across her cheeks.

"And last, my family and friends. My mom, Clara, sister Olivia, and my best friend Laurel." Her eyes searched for each of them as she spoke. Penelope was tearing up now. She cleared her throat.

Penelope pointed to the floor-to-ceiling velvet curtain to her left. "If you would all please move to the entrance of the mineral display room, we will unveil our latest display titled *Rare Crystals of the World* and the new mineral that I discovered, which I named Lamartinite, after my late father, Martin Lake.

Penelope watched the crowd slowly step through the foyer and gather on the right side of the main entrance. She handed the wireless microphone to the sound technicians and carefully walked down the five steps from the stage, moving through the crowd to the unveiling rope.

"Thank you all for coming. I hope you enjoy." Penelope pulled on the satin rope, allowing the navy velvet curtains to open wide.

The crowd filed into the display room and all Penelope could hear were gasps and squeals as people explored the new rocks and minerals. Penelope stood outside the door and simply listened for a few minutes. She closed her eyes, drinking in the evening's excitement. At that moment, she realized how nervous she had been all week worrying that people wouldn't like the new display, but hearing the commotion inside the room, she realized it was a hit.

As she scanned the patrons entering the exhibit room, Penelope's heart skipped a beat. Marlene was here with her brother, Louis. Now was her chance to talk.

"Excuse me," Penelope said, fighting her way through the crowd. "Excuse me."

Penelope inched closer. The gathering had dispersed to the edges of the room. She heard a chorus of "oohs" and "aahs" while the patrons enjoyed her display.

She spied Louis, his graying curly hair sticking up, standing near the fluorescent mineral case.

"Louis," Penelope called, waving slightly as he turned at the sound of his name.

Louis smiled. "Hi, Penelope. Magnificent display."

Penelope's heart raced at the sight of another suspect. She felt an unexpected thrill during her approach, silently planning what strategic questions to ask. Penelope understood why Ryan and Andre enjoyed being detectives. It was fun and exciting.

"Thank you. Thank you for coming." She looked at Marlene, hoping Louis would introduce them. He picked up on her cue.

"Oh, I'm sorry. I didn't realize that you two have never met. Penelope, this is my sister Marlene."

Penelope extended her hand, which Marlene accepted.

"I'm glad to see you both. With all the trouble at the festival a couple of weekends ago, I was worried that people might be too afraid to attend."

Penelope's eyes fixed on Marlene even when Louis replied. "Tessa's murder was awful. I'm not sure how the festival will survive."

"I hope people will come again," Penelope replied, still staring at Marlene, who stood expressionless. "Were you exhibiting at the festival, Marlene?"

"Why would I?" she asked, sipping from a champagne flute.

"Oh, my mother said that you own the Wicked Thyme Candle Company. Since you are local, I thought you might have been interested in exhibiting."

Marlene straightened. "No, I wasn't there," she snapped. "I only sell online."

"Sorry. I didn't mean to hit a nerve."

Louis looked sideways at his sister. "Stop. It's over."

"What's over?" Penelope feigned innocence.

Marlene scoffed. "Tessa and I were in a lawsuit. She stole my candle designs."

"Wow," Penelope tried to sound surprised. "I had no idea that Tessa would steal from someone. You also have dripping candles?"

"No, it was the fragrance core. It was my idea and suddenly, Tessa was selling candles with the same thing."

"So now that she's gone, I assume the lawsuit is over?"

"No. Now I go after her husband for the money she owed me," Marlene said, leaning close. The acrid smell of alcohol was thick as she slurred her words.

The anger in Marlene's tone startled Penelope. According to the paperwork she found in Tessa's files, fragrance cores had been used in candles for years and the idea wasn't proprietary.

"Oh, I hope you'll reconsider. Robby is having a tough time right now and the candle store is closed." Penelope pleaded.

"I don't care," she retorted, tipping her champagne glass and chugging the golden bubbly. She deftly swapped the empty glass for a new one as a server floated by with a full tray.

Louis sighed. "Marlene, take it down a notch. People are looking."

Penelope quickly became annoyed with Marlene's attitude. She tried to hide her anger. As the face of the museum, she needed to be a pleasant host. Penelope wanted to press Marlene but was afraid of a drunken reaction. "When was the last time you talked to her?"

"Are you accusing me of killing her?" Marlene's voice escalated.

"No, not at all," Penelope said, putting her hands up. Her mind flashed to the note on her Hummer and the SUV that had followed her twice. Was it Marlene? If so, this conversation could lead to something more dangerous. For the first time, Penelope felt scared.

Marlene moved toward Penelope. "How dare —"

Penelope jumped backward.

"Okay, that's enough." Louis grabbed Marlene's arm. "We're leaving. I'm sorry, Penelope."

Louis ushered Marlene out of the gala, leaving Penelope shaken. She never expected such a fierce reaction from Marlene, but now, more than ever, she was glad to know that Sandra indeed planned to slap her with a countersuit soon.

Penelope stood in the center of her display room, taking deep, controlling breaths to calm her shaky nerves. Luckily, most of the guests were unaware of Marlene's outburst.

Clara glided to her side. "You did it, my dear." Clara wrapped her eldest daughter in a bear hug. "Thank you for choosing to name your mineral after your dad."

Penelope fought back tears. "Thank you, Mom. It hasn't been easy keeping that secret from you. I can't tell you how relieved I am that people seem to like the display. I just hope it makes them want to make enough donations so we can open the children's center."

"I've been working on that." Clara winked at Penelope.

"More magic?"

Clara smiled bewitchingly. "Not unless you count working my magic on all the eligible single men in this room. My feet are tired from all that dancing."

Penelope laughed and hugged her mother again. "Well, I appreciate your sacrifice for the museum."

Lucy, Laurel, and Olivia came over to congratulate Penelope. According to Lucy's latest tally, generous donations were rolling in for the new children's center and the attendees loved Penelope's new display. A little overwhelmed, Penelope excused herself from the group. She jostled through the crowd, heading toward her office at the rear of the museum, in need of a few moments alone to collect her thoughts. Penelope thanked everyone she passed for coming and for making their donations. She even thanked Andre because he had donated one of the biggest checks of the evening.

"Hey, Penelope." Ryan grabbed her hand before she stepped into the hallway that led from the display areas to the employee offices and labs.

"Hey, Ryan. Thank you for coming. It means a lot." Penelope's mind quickly flipped from the gala to the investigation. "I think you and I need to have a chat later. I spoke to Jessie earlier in the evening and she thinks she has some information about Tessa's murder, and Marlene Black had it out for Tessa, too."

"Penelope, we talked about this. You need to stay out of it and let me handle it. From the looks of the checkbooks I've seen out, it looks like you will be busy with the children's center."

Penelope's feet and back ached. She didn't want to fight with Ryan, so she just nodded and walked down the hallway toward her office. Halfway down the hall, she slipped her satin heels off her feet and carried them dangling off her right index and middle fingers, aiming for her waiting couch. Penelope was just about to enter her office when she noticed a light in the adjoining rock lab and the door was ajar.

"I'm positive I closed that door before the party," she muttered aloud.

Penelope cautiously stepped down the hallway, listening for sounds that somebody was inside. Nothing. Maybe she accidentally left the door open after all. Or perhaps Lucy had come back during the event and forgot to close up. Penelope stepped into the lab, samples and paperwork were strewn across the floor. As she hurried toward the back corner to check the safe was secure, she tripped and fell face-first onto the floor.

"What the heck?" Penelope spun on the floor when a sinking feeling clutched inside her chest. "Not again. I fell over another—"

Penelope looked in dismay at Jessie's lifeless body lying behind the worktable.

Prosperity Spell to Inspire Donations

To enhance your prosperity and gain wealth.

Spell Supplies

*3 Gold Candles | 3 Silver Candles | Green Tissue Paper |
Bay leaf | Basil | Mint | Several handfuls of change and
dollar bills | Green Crystals*

Place the gold and silver candles on either side of a table
and set green malachite and amazonite to complete a
semi-circle. Working inside the semi-circle, fold the green
paper into a pouch by folding top to middle and bottom
to middle. Rotate the paper and repeat.
Place several coins, dollars, bay leaf, basil, and mint into
the paper and fold. Drip candle wax onto the paper to seal
it, being careful not to get the paper near the flame. Recite
five times:
As I wish, I shall receive. Make it so. So mote it be.

Chakra Stones for Prosperity and Wealth

Use these wealth stones in your spell for extra benefit. You
can also wear jewelry made with these crystals or keep them
in your pockets until you get the money you want.

Malachite | Amazonite | Emerald

Chapter Twenty-Three

Penelope scrambled to her feet, fumbling for her cell phone. She found it hiding beneath her desk after tumbling from her hands as she fell. She texted Laurel.

Andre. Ryan. Rock lab. Now. Tell no one.

As Penelope waited for the cavalry to arrive, she checked Jessie for signs of life. She had no pulse, and she wasn't breathing. Just in case, she began CPR compressions. Andre, Ryan, and Laurel burst into the room.

"Help me!" Penelope cried. Penelope's mind was reeling. Not again. She couldn't have found another dead body. Not in her museum. Not in her rock lab. Tears poured down her cheeks as Laurel wrapped her arms around Penelope's shoulders, pulling her back.

Andre and Ryan took over CPR. Penelope sat on the floor in stunned silence.

"Stop," Andre ordered after a few minutes. "She's gone."

Penelope gulped. "You didn't tell anybody you were coming back, did you?"

"No," Laurel said.

"Good. The gala needs to go on." Penelope's brain went into overdrive. The gala and likely the future of the museum could be in jeopardy if the patrons found out what was going on.

"Penelope, we've had a death here. In your laboratory," Andre said.

"Chief." Ryan nodded toward Andre. "This is Jessie Hanlon."

"Did anybody see you come back here?" Andre asked.

Penelope shook her head, pushing herself to stand. "I was talking with Ryan a few minutes ago after the unveiling. And then I came back to my office. I wanted to catch my breath. This area is restricted, so there is no way anybody from the gala should have been back here. But lately, our security guards have been pretty slack."

"Was this hallway locked?"

"The hallway itself isn't locked because we have security at the entrance during the day. But we typically keep all the offices and workrooms locked if no one is back here. I was having trouble with the lock on the lab door yesterday, though. I thought maintenance fixed it."

Ryan stood and pulled his notebook out of the inside pocket of his tuxedo jacket. "Penelope, let's go to your office and we can walk through everything that happened tonight. The Chief can ask the medical examiner to come in the back door where you get your deliveries so that no one from the gala will see."

Andre agreed and asked Laurel to help him lock the doors to the hallway and keep a lookout for people trying to get into the secure area. Andre called the medical examiner and the police forensics team and told them both to respond, but using no lights or sirens and parking in the back of the building, so the guests at the gala remained unaware of the murder. Everything had to be radio silent.

Penelope overheard Andre talking on the phone. "I want plain clothes officers at all the entrances. If the killer is still at the gala, I don't want to spook them," he said.

Andre moved to the service loading bay to await the police technicians and Laurel went to the opposite end of the secure hallway, standing lookout.

Penelope took a seat behind her desk. Ryan pulled a chair beside her. He took Penelope's right hand in his left and asked her to recap the events after the display opened.

"The last person I talked to before I came back here was you." Penelope thought about the last few minutes. Was there someone else in the hallway? Did she see anyone other than Ryan? No. He was the last person she saw or spoke with before entering the rock lab.

Ryan nodded, jotting a note in his notebook.

She cleared her throat. "I talked to you, then walked back to my office. I was going to get a bottle of sparkling water from my fridge when I saw that the door to the rock lab was open and the lights were on. I went to close the door when I realized some samples and paperwork I left on the table were on the floor."

"But you didn't see the body right away?"

"No." Penelope's entire body shook. "When I saw the samples were on the ground, I got concerned about this safe in the back where we keep the more valuable ones. So, I was going to check and make sure that nothing was missing, but before I could get there, I tripped and fell."

"You fell over another body?" Ryan rubbed his forehead.

Penelope snatched a tissue from the box on the desk and dabbed her eyes. "I can't believe it. Please don't tell my mother. She would never let me live that down. I don't know how I didn't see her on the floor other than the project table mostly hid her. I think I tripped over her wrist or her hand when I was going to check the safe." Penelope pulled a second tissue from the box on her desk and blew her nose.

Ryan scribbled detailed notes. "I promise not to tell Clara. You and I can have a couple of secrets." Ryan winked, then quickly looked down at his notebook and kept writing. Penelope waited for him to look up as her signal to keep talking.

"I was trying to help her and then you guys came in."

"Are there security cameras?"

"Yes, but they're not always on back here. They're on timers and motion sensors set to only work when the building is empty."

"Okay, I'll look at the footage, but that kind of system may not have been operating with everyone in the building."

"The museum has never had a theft, so we probably haven't invested as much as we should into security in the back offices."

"Did you touch anything in the room other than Jessie?"

"Tonight? No. But I work in this room every day." Penelope felt the tears return. "Um, do you think it was the same person who killed Tessa?"

"At this point, Penelope, we don't even know that Jessie was murdered. She could have simply wandered back here and had a heart attack."

"Heart attack? Jessie is twenty-six years old."

"Yes, and I agree that it's unlikely. But stranger things have happened. She could've had a congenital heart defect or some other underlying medical condition we don't know about right now. That is what the medical examiner is going to tell us."

The next few hours were a whirlwind as the medical examiner's van and the forensic team showed up in the loading bay. Andre instructed everyone to be quiet and let the gala continue. After the medical examiner removed Jessie's body and took her to the morgue, the forensic techs scoured Penelope's workroom and every other accessible area in the secured wing, including the hallways, the open offices, or anything that a killer may have touched if indeed Jessie was murdered.

Ryan and Andre had instructed Laurel and Penelope to return to the gala and act normally. Penelope found that particularly difficult since she had just found her second dead body in two weeks. She did her best to put on a smile and focus on the patrons. She even let herself find some joy that her mother was dancing with every silver-haired wealthy man in the room. Clara liked to tell Penelope that she was taking one for the team, but Penelope knew better. She loved the attention. Her mother had been lonely since her father vanished.

The gala wrapped up at about one o'clock in the morning and finally, all that remained were the staff and Olivia's catering team. Penelope asked Laurel to slip back to her rock lab and see if the police were done. When she returned with Andre and Ryan, Penelope realized things must be returning to normal.

Andre's eyes locked with Penelope's for a moment, his jaw clenched. He gave a curt, almost imperceptible nod before striding through the foyer and out into the night. Penelope's stomach tightened at his brusque departure, wondering what information he might be withholding. Ryan stopped by Penelope's side to check that she was okay.

"I'm all right. Thank you for asking and for everything you did tonight." Penelope's voice wavered slightly, betraying her exhaustion.

"I would do anything for you, Penelope. But I appreciate you coming out and keeping the gala going. Did you get that list of attendees like we asked?"

"Yes, I emailed it to you earlier." Penelope reached out to grasp Ryan's hand. "Thank you for keeping all of this from the donors and the press."

Ryan's voice softened. "I can see how much this museum means to you. It turns out that the forensic team found a lot of prints that were not yours or Lucy's. They ruled out the staff that worked in the executive wing secure area as well."

"They got an example of Lucy's prints off of her desk?"

"Yes. And they pulled yours from your office too. I'm heading back to the station right now to see if they can do a rush on the identification of the unknown prints."

"That's great." Penelope's mind churned, considering the implications. If she, Lucy, and the other staff were ruled out, the killer must have been a guest.

"I've already talked to the security guard to keep him in the loop with the situation. He's going to gather all the surveillance camera videos for us and send them over to the precinct when the museum clears out."

She released Ryan's hand. "That's good. Although, that guy may not have a job soon. You weren't the first person he let back there this week without telling me first. And now this." Penelope planned to talk with the museum owner in the morning to sort out new procedures for security.

"Other than the owner, please don't tell anybody else about what's going on until we determine if this was murder or natural causes."

Penelope swallowed hard. "I understand Ryan. You can trust me." Her voice trailed off.

"Your mom and Olivia will ask questions, but please, keep the details to yourself."

Penelope's head felt heavy. The tears were returning as total exhaustion was setting in. She agreed to keep the details to herself as much as possible. She was happy that Laurel knew about Jessie's death. That gave her at least one person to talk to.

"Okay, I'm going to head back to the precinct, but I want you to call me when you get home, so I know you're safe. Or I can take you home myself."

"No, thank you. I can get home."

"Okay, I'll talk to you soon." Ryan squeezed Penelope's arm and then left through the front door, leaving Penelope to keep a secret from almost everyone close to her.

She was heading back to her office to get her purse when Lucy stepped out of the shadows. "Why did the police want my fingerprints?"

Chapter
Twenty-Four

"I felt so awful for Lucy," Penelope said, inserting her earbuds and switching to Bluetooth.

"I can't imagine what she was thinking when she overheard you talking with Ryan." Laurel's voice boomed through Penelope's head as she grappled with the volume button.

"Overhearing that conversation without knowing that we had found Jessie dead in the rock lab freaked her out. She calmed down when I explained why the police wanted her fingerprints."

"How long will the police have your rock lab tied up as a crime scene?"

Penelope wrapped the borrowed gown in the dress bag and hung it gingerly in her closet with the jewelry pouch and elegant shoes tucked into the bag.

"Hopefully not long. Ryan said that the crime scene technicians would stay through the night to gather evidence and go through the display area. I hope by tomorrow morning, I'll be able to get in there and clean up the rest."

"That's good."

Jasper was sleeping soundly in the middle of Penelope's unmade bed. Penelope snapped her fingers. "Lucy and I are planning to meet there early and get started if Ryan gives me the all-clear later today." Jasper slowly opened one eye.

"Other than a murder in the back room, how did the gala turn out?"

Penelope snapped again, unable to fully wake the puppy. "Amazingly well. We got a ton of donations for the children's wing."

"Did you make enough for Lucy to get promoted to run the new center?"

"I think so. At least, my mother was certainly trying her hardest with all the men there," Penelope said, pulling the dog onto the floor.

"She was a social butterfly last night. I didn't know she had it in her."

"I wish *I* didn't know that she had it in her." Penelope threw the comforter over the pillows a split second before Jasper again landed in the center of the bed.

Laurel turned quiet for a moment. "Who do you think killed Jessie?"

Penelope sat on the edge beside Jasper and cuddled her. "I have no idea. I thought she killed Tessa."

"She still could have."

"I guess so." Penelope left Jasper sleeping and set her coffee maker to brew a cup.

"Perhaps someone found out that she killed Tessa and then killed her for revenge?"

"The only person who would do that is Robby, and we've ruled him out. He's just not a killer." Penelope leaned on the counter as the last few drops of coffee tumbled into a mug.

"He was at the gala, though."

"I talked to him, and he was getting ready to leave with Katia and Tom right after the unveiling. Plus, Jessie told me Tessa was arguing with a woman."

"Hopefully, Ryan and Andre are figuring out what happened."

Penelope flopped into her overstuffed chair, pulled her fluffiest blanket around her shoulders, and cradled the warm mug. "I hope so. But in the meantime, I have some sleuthing to do on my own."

"You do?"

"Yep. I'm going to have lunch with Nate Sorensen today." After Laurel saw Nate's card fall from Betsy's bag, Penelope immediately called him to meet up for brunch. She hadn't seen him in years, and it would be nice to catch up. Nate became a leading psychologist in the area and specialized in anger management. From the behavior that Penelope observed in Betsy, she needed him.

"Do you think that's a good idea?"

"We were college buddies. I'm just having lunch with an old friend that I haven't seen in a long time." Penelope sipped the coffee, feeling the caffeine energize her.

"He's not going to tell you about a patient."

"I don't need details, just enough to determine if I should rule Betsy in or out as a suspect. She was at the gala, so she could have killed Jessie. Did you get to talk with her last night?"

"No. How are you going to get him to reveal anything?"

"Nate used to ask me out. He wasn't my type, but we were good friends. We keep up with each other when we can."

"Good luck. Call me after."

***

Nate Sorensen was sitting quietly at a corner table at Amelia's, reading at half-past two on a lazy Sunday afternoon. Penelope was right on time but felt late because Nate was always early. Even sitting, Nate's six-foot-five-inch frame dominated the room.

He glanced up from his comic. "Penelope," Nate said, like he wasn't expecting to see her.

"You said two-thirty, right?"

"Yes, of course." Nate stood and hugged Penelope. His embrace made her feel tiny.

"You look great." Penelope admired her friend's newly chiseled muscles. "Have you been working out?"

Nate ran his hand through his hair. "Yeah. I joined a gym. One of those cross-fit meets running meets martial arts places."

Penelope's eyes widened. "Sounds hard. But it's working for you." Nate's gaze met hers. She had forgotten how good-looking he truly was with emerald eyes and curly light-brown hair that he paired with a short, professional cut. His black frame glasses struck a delicate balance between science nerd and sophisticated professional.

Penelope and Nate met at the University of North Carolina when they were in the same Introduction to Psychology course. For Nate, it was the first course in his major, but Penelope was just hoping to get a general education requirement out of the way. He often asked her out, but Penelope was dating Andre even though it was a long-distance relationship. By the time she and Andre broke up, Nate had a steady girlfriend.

"You look great, too."

"I've been doing aquathlons. It's a run-and-swim combination. They're fun. You should try one with me."

Nate shifted in his chair. "That sounds like something you would be good at. I'll come to watch you sometime, but I'm still not much of a swimmer."

Penelope's mind flashed to a college memory when Nate joined her on a run and almost fell off a bridge and into a fishing pond. Even though the pond was only a few feet deep, Penelope worried that she would have to relive her high school lifeguard days and jump in and save him. A small smile crept across her face. "Yeah."

"You are thinking about the pond incident. Stop."

"Okay, fine, but it was funny," Penelope teased. She regretted not keeping in touch with Nate. The older she got, the more she centered her life around work rather than relationships.

"I was trying to impress you that day and it totally backfired."

"It's nice to see you, Nate," Penelope said. The server appeared with their lunches.

"But we haven't ordered."

"Oh, I ordered for you," Nate smiled. The young server set a large chicken pot pie in front of Penelope and a second in front of Nate.

Penelope's eyes widened. "Oh. Yum. You remembered." She smiled up at Nate while her nose dipped toward the golden crust. Penelope inhaled slowly.

"How could I forget? You are the only person I know who loves pot pie as much as I do."

"Here is your iced chai tea." The server had returned with two large frosty glasses. "If you need anything else, my name is Tara." In an instant, Tara was gone, delivering goodies to nearby tables.

"You certainly have an excellent memory," Penelope said, picking up her fork.

"When it comes to you, I do."

A pang of guilt hit her stomach because, as much as she was happy to see Nate, she had an ulterior motive for the reunion. Penelope cleared her throat. Memory lane was nice, but she needed to get information about Betsy and if she could be the killer, even if the reunion was under false pretenses.

Nate stabbed his fork into the top of his pie, crushing the crust into bite-sized pieces. "Is there a mister in your life?"

Penelope gently lifted the top crust and watched the steam spin into the air. "No. I heard you got married, though, and I wasn't invited to the wedding."

"Ah. That was a whirlwind. We met and two months later we eloped. It didn't last long." Nate shifted in his chair. Penelope could sense he wanted to change the subject.

"How is your practice?"

"It's good."

"I heard you are seeing Betsy Peterson."

Nate squinted and shook his head. "How? Why are you asking about her?"

Penelope set down her fork and sighed. "Did you hear about the woman who was murdered at the festival last weekend?"

"Yes."

"Tessa McCaul. She was my friend, and I found her body."

"That's awful, but it doesn't explain why you are asking about my patient." Nate put his fork down.

Penelope leaned forward and whispered. "Because I saw her coming out of Tessa's shop the day before the murder, and she was very upset." Penelope worried she was coming on strong. How do you come out and ask a psychiatrist for information about their patient when they can't legally tell you anything? She should have planned a smoother segue from memory lane to murder.

Nate leaned back in his chair and ran his hands through his hair. "You asked me to lunch to get information about a patient. Even a geologist would know that it's not ethical. And a friend would not put me in this position." Nate grimaced.

"I'm not trying to jam you up." Penelope took a sip of her tea. "I realize it sounds like that, and I'm not trying to get you to do anything that you shouldn't. It's just that it seems someone found out that I have been asking around about Tessa and they have been following me. I'm a little, no, a lot, freaked out."

"Then you should tell the police."

"They're aware. I just...I just hoped that you could put my mind at ease about Betsy. I talked with her, and she became extremely angry with me. My friend owns The Tipsy Java and saw Betsy with your business card the other day, and I hoped you could at least tell me if I should be worried about her or not." Penelope tried to read Nate's expression, but he was exceptionally good at hiding his thoughts.

Nate ran his tongue along the inside of his lower lip. "And here, I thought you invited me to lunch because you wanted to catch up."

"I do want to catch up." Penelope cleared her throat. "Look, I asked Tessa what was going on, but she said it was nothing. I didn't find out until later that Betsy worked for Tessa."

"That doesn't mean that she is a killer."

"Betsy told me that Tessa accused her of stealing money from the business. That is a motive."

Nate stared at Penelope, his lips pursed.

"There was another murder last night."

Nate's eyes popped. "Another murder?"

"Uh-huh. The girl who ran the booth next to Tessa at the festival was murdered at the museum gala last night in my rock lab. I'm not supposed to give anyone details."

Nate shook his head. "That's awful. But I still can't tell you anything about Betsy."

"I'm not asking about her diagnosis. Just if you think she's a killer because I don't want to be next and I kind of poked the bear when I went to see her."

"Look, Penelope, a discussion about Betsy's treatment is off-limits, but I can tell you she is not the killer."

"Why?" Penelope pressed. "What can you tell me? I found two bodies."

Nate groaned. "I hate that Betsy needs an alibi."

"But she has one?"

"I can't give details, but yes. I can provide her with an alibi."

"Dang." Penelope caught herself. "I mean, good."

"She's not the killer. Now, can we finish our pot pies?" Nate waved at the server and asked for two glasses of water with lime slices.

"Thank you for helping, even though I still don't know who killed Tessa or Jessie."

"Jessie?"

"Jessie Hanlon. She was the girl killed in the rock lab last night." Penelope took a bite of the pot pie.

"Jessie Hanlon," Nate growled. He took a sip of his chai tea. "I'm glad that bitch is dead."

"What? You knew her?" Penelope almost choked on the pie crust. She had never heard Nate sound so nasty.

"Jessie is the reason I'm divorced."

"What happened?" Penelope gulped her tea, trying to hide her shock.

"Jessie and I went out on a couple of dates and then I met Gina. I broke up with Jessie to date Gina and we got married. Almost immediately after the wedding, Jessie started doing crazy stuff. She broke into our house. She left a picture of the two of us on our bed so my wife would believe that I was having an affair with her. She left a dead bird in my office and made crank calls to my wife at all hours of the day and night."

"Oh, my gosh. That's awful." Penelope's jaw hung open. "I'm not sure what to say."

"Jessie was an absolute lunatic, and in the end, my wife divorced me because she believed Jessie was telling the truth. She was a convincing liar."

"I'm stunned. I didn't think she was always telling the truth, but I never would have predicted this behavior from her." Penelope recalled the conversations that she had with Jessie. She had the feeling each time that Jessie was lying about something. "Why would she lie to me about Tessa's murder?"

Nate shook his head. "Penelope, she was completely-ly crazy, and that is coming from a psychiatrist. People like that are compulsive. She was likely hiding something about the murder and was playing games with you. Or, she knew absolutely nothing and just wanted attention."

Penelope and Nate finished their lunch and Penelope promised to call him for a rain check to truly catch up soon.

She drove home more confused than before lunch. Betsy couldn't be the killer, and Jessie was still a suspect. But if Jessie killed Tessa, who would have killed Jessie? She sincerely hoped she wasn't adding Nate to the suspect list.

Chapter Twenty-Five

Penelope sat on her couch Sunday evening staring at the murder board. The shock of discovering Jessie's body in the workroom still stung and so did learning that Nate both knew and hated her. Penelope's body felt numb from head to toe.

She scooped Jasper in her arms, then sat back in the chair and curled up with both feet on the cushion. The dog filled her lap. Jasper was growing fast. Penelope grabbed her coffee mug from the table. The murder board made little sense. The suspects, potential alibis, and motives that she and Laurel had outlined a few days earlier seemed completely turned upside down when Jessie turned up dead at the gala. Jessie was Penelope's front-runner to be Tessa's killer, so why did she end up dead if that was the case?

Were there two killers?

How did Jessie end up in the secure area of the museum?

And why was she in the rock lab?

Questions rattled through Penelope's brain. She sipped her coffee, hoping the caffeine would clear her mind and allow her to think more like a cop than a witness. A loud knock on the door startled her. Coffee sloshed from her cup, coating her hand and dripping down her leg onto her foot. Jasper sat at attention but never left Penelope's lap, her crystal blue husky eyes daring Penelope to throw the coffee her way.

"Who is it?"

A muffled voice from the other side of the door was familiar. "It's me, Penelope. I came to check on you."

Penelope shooed the pup from her lap. "It's okay, Jasper, it's just Ryan." Penelope stood and waddled to the kitchen to get some paper towels. She hollered through the door for Ryan to wait just a second.

After cleaning herself off, Penelope sped toward the door. She checked herself in the full-length mirror that hung next to the coat rack. Her hair was a mess in a loose ponytail wiggling on the top of her head. Her workout clothes looked cute, and she hoped the damp coffee aroma would crowd out the stink of her eight-mile late afternoon run through the trails. Penelope swung open the door and invited Ryan inside. He set a drink holder and pastry bag on the coffee table and then pulled one drink from the tray.

"I told Laurel I was coming to check on you and she sent food." Ryan's face scrunched when he read the sticker on the side of the enormous emerald-green paper cup. "Which sounds gross. What is an espresso chai vanilla latte?"

Penelope gladly took the warm drink from Ryan's hand and reclined on the couch, gesturing he should do the same on the other end. "I love this drink. You should try it."

"I don't want to try it. I'll just take my plain black coffee, thank you."

"You're such a cop." Penelope pushed his knee with her bare foot and laughed.

"Why were you coming to check on me?" Penelope asked.

Ryan looked at her quizzically. "You're not serious, right? You found *another* dead body last night. In *your* office. That can take a toll on anyone plus I—"

Ryan stopped talking. He clenched his jaw.

"Plus, you, what?"

Ryan looked away for a moment. His eyes returned, catching Penelope in a stare. "I wanted to ask if you'd go to the movies with me next weekend."

"You wanted to ask me out on a date?" Penelope was surprised. Ryan had been aloof the past week.

"Yeah. Seems kind of crass with everything that's happened. But I was planning on asking you anyway and I wanted to come by and check on you to see how you were doing since last night and—" His voice trailed off.

"And?"

"And also, to see if there was anything else you remembered." He dropped his gaze.

Penelope tilted her head and looked at Ryan. "Ah-ha! So, you want to ask me out, but you're not sure if you should because you're a cop who's taking my witness statement in your investigation?" Penelope could feel herself talking just so she wouldn't have to answer the question. *Should she go out with him? It might be weird, she thought. Would it be weird?* They were friends, but she knew he liked her a long time ago and if Andre hadn't been in the picture, she could have seen herself dating him. They're both single now, too.

"When you say it like that, it just sounds terrible."

Penelope knew she was making him uncomfortable. *'Always throw them off balance,'* her mother would advise when she had boy problems. Ryan sat waiting for Penelope's answer, his foot bouncing off the floor. Penelope could tell he was growing more nervous. Her brain had run out of excuses to say no. "I would love to go to the movies."

Ryan exhaled loudly. Penelope leaned forward and grabbed the bag of pastries.

"Hey, hey the bear claw is mine." Ryan protested as Penelope eyed the desserts.

"Fine." Penelope wrapped a napkin around the massive pastry and handed it to Ryan, then snatched a black cherry turnover for herself. "Oh, my goodness, Olivia hasn't made these in months. They are so good."

"Let me try a bite."

"No way. You got a bear claw the size of your face. Eat that."

"Okay, I will." Ryan took a bite. "We are confident that Jessie is the one who left the note on your car."

"Really?"

"Yeah, we matched a partial fingerprint from the note to her. It still doesn't explain why she left it, but she was obviously trying to warn you about something. Promise me you'll be careful."

"I will. I promise."

"What did you find out from Nate Sorensen?"

A piece of cherry filling lodged in her throat. Penelope coughed. "Why would you ask about Nate? I haven't seen him since college."

"Save it, Penelope. Laurel can't keep a secret. I know you saw him today."

"She told you?" She would fuss at Laurel later.

Ryan took another bite of the bear claw. "Laurel's worried about you. She knows how much finding Tessa and

Jessie has affected you, especially with the black SUV still unaccounted for."

"Well, I'll admit that it hasn't been fun, but I have to help figure out what is going on. Especially since Jessie was found in my office."

"Then you did see Nate today?"

"Yes, I had a late lunch with him at Amelia's restaurant and we had a very interesting conversation."

"Oh? How so?" Ryan dropped a piece of the bear claw in front of Jasper and gave the puppy a head scratch.

"It turns out that not only is he Betsy Peterson's psychiatrist, but he also knew Jessie."

"He knew Jessie?"

"He did. And he didn't like her."

Ryan raised his eyebrows. "How so?"

"Nate dated Jessie for a couple of weeks and then broke it off and started dating his now ex-wife. Jessie went all *Fatal Attraction* on him after he got married. She broke into his house and did all kinds of crazy stuff. Nate's wife divorced him because of it."

Ryan pulled out his notebook and scribbled while Penelope talked. "Was he at the gala last night?"

"You think he's a suspect for killing Jessie?"

"Wouldn't you after everything you just said? I have a feeling that what he told you was barely the beginning of what happened between the two of them. I'll see if there were any police reports filed."

Jasper jumped into Penelope's lap with a thud. "He said that he was glad she was dead. But he wasn't at the gala last night. Although he should have been. He has a lot of money. I'll certainly be inviting him to future donor events."

"No joking, Penelope. He could be dangerous," Ryan said, reaching out to scratch Jasper's chin.

"Nate is not dangerous. I just think he made a stupid choice, and he's paid dearly for it. The Nate I know is no killer. If he was, he would never have told me that story about Jessie. Besides, psychiatrists can't be killers. They're doctors." Penelope was getting tired.

Ryan rolled his eyes. "You can't seriously think just because somebody's a psychiatrist that they can't possibly be a murderer. Ted Bundy had a psychology degree."

Penelope took another sip of her latte. "Fine, but I still don't think Nate had anything to do with Jessie. He seemed genuinely surprised that she was dead."

"All right. I'll check out his alibi and make sure that he was not anywhere near the gala last night. For the sake of argument, let's assume that he was not the one who killed Jessie. What did he tell you about Betsy?"

"Betsy isn't Tessa's killer either."

"Why do you say that?"

"Nate said that he could alibi Betsy but wouldn't say how."

The two sat in silence for a few minutes while Ryan finished jotting in his notebook. Penelope had finished her cherry turnover and was almost out of her coffee by the time he folded and slipped it into the pocket of his jacket.

"I'll look into all of this and speak with Nate. My gut is saying that one person is behind everything. But if Betsy isn't our killer and Jessie isn't our killer—"

Penelope interrupted. "Then we're running out of suspects."

"Yes, we're running out of suspects." Ryan let his hands slide down his face. "Can I buy you some dinner?" Ryan asked, looking at his wristwatch.

Penelope looked out the window and sighed. She dropped Jasper onto his dog bed. "Rain check? I think I'm too exhausted to leave my house tonight."

Ryan picked up the pastry bag and empty coffee cups and put them in the trash can in Penelope's kitchen. She met him at the front door. Her mind was exhausted, but questions lingered.

Was there a connection between Tessa and Jessie that she couldn't see? Was there another upset seller from the festival? The spring festival was the only place that both Tessa and Jessie had in common. Had Marlene been at odds with Jessie, too? Or did Tessa have people in her life that Penelope never met?

"Get some sleep. I'll talk to you tomorrow," Ryan said, twisting the doorknob and letting a warm breeze waft through the living room. "Don't worry, I'll find out who killed Tessa and Jessie."

Penelope thanked Ryan for coming over and closed the door behind him. She leaned against the thick oak wood and listened for his car to pull out of her driveway. Penelope was tired of not knowing what was going on and feeling like she was becoming a target. She trusted Ryan, but her stubborn streak just would not let her lie back and wait like a sitting duck.

Not if I figure this out first, Ryan.

Chapter Twenty-Six

Penelope strolled into the workroom on Monday morning with an intense determination to find the killer who was whirling around her hometown and invading the museum she loved. She assumed it was one killer, but then again, she could be wrong, and it could be two. But it just didn't seem likely that Tessa's and Jessie's murders were unrelated. Penelope stepped into her office to find Lucy waiting for her with a platter of desserts.

"A little early for treats, isn't it?"

Lucy shook her head, pushing a tray across the desk. Penelope settled into her desk chair, eyeing the treats.

"They are left over from the gala."

"Ugh. The gala. It was the best night of my life and then one of the worst nights of my life." Penelope rocked back in her chair.

"I used to think your life is pretty blissful, but now I think you have the worst luck out of all of my friends." Lucy took a bite of a miniature strawberry and chocolate torte.

"Let's not talk about that. Let's talk about you. How does it feel to be in charge of the entire children's wing?" Penelope assumed that Mr. Canfield had already asked her based on the huge smile on her face.

"I'm not sure that it's sunk in yet." Lucy smiled.

"Director Canfield texted me last night saying we received enough donations to fully fund the children's center and boost research grants for everyone at the museum."

"That's amazing." Lucy's eyes widened.

"You're excited, right?" Penelope tried to shake off her exhaustion and find the enthusiasm that the gala's success deserved.

"Oh, yes. Just nervous, I guess. My first out-of-school, real full-time job, and it's a big one."

"It is a big job, but you're not alone. I will help you as much as you need and so will everyone else here." Penelope popped a mini torte in her mouth. Sugar never failed to brighten her day.

"Thankfully, I'll be able to finish my master's degree while the center is being built, so I can focus fully on the programs when we open."

"I bet your brother is proud of you."

"He is. So...does Detective Snow have any idea what happened in the rock lab? Who might have killed Jessie?" Lucy asked cautiously.

Penelope brewed coffee in her single-cup coffee maker for them both, adding oat milk creamer from her mini refrigerator. "I spent the entire weekend trying to figure out who would kill Tessa at the festival and then turn around and kill Jessie here at the museum."

"And kill her in our rock lab. How did they even get back here during the party? That takes guts. Someone could have walked in."

Penelope looked squarely into Lucy's face. "I don't have any clue on either front. Every time I think I know, I'm wrong. I think the police are going back to square one and looking at everyone again." She placed the mugs on the desk.

"Maybe Jessie killed Tessa and Robby killed Jessie for revenge." Lucy was making the same suggestions that Penelope and Ryan had exhausted the night before. Penelope had no more answers. Or ideas.

"That is a theory. It is so hard to figure out. It seems like everyone that I suspected might be the killer has an alibi."

"So, no good suspects anymore."

"Not really." Penelope stood and slung her messenger bag across her shoulder. "I kind of wish it was Marlene Black. She is mean and volatile. But she's so loud that I can't imagine she could kill Tessa with no one hearing her. She's the only one that is on the list that I haven't found an alibi for or evidence against yet."

"So basically, back to square one." Lucy followed Penelope toward the door.

"Yes." Penelope sighed. "I'm going to the rock lab to start the cleanup."

"I wish I could stay and help you, but I have a class and a meeting with my advisor. I'm close to being ready for my thesis defense."

"No problem. The most important thing right now is that you finish that master's degree so you can focus on the children's center and all those little future scientists out there who need you." Penelope gave Lucy a quick hug. "I'm so proud of you."

"Thank you. I guess I need to get more comfortable with large groups of little people."

"Ha-ha, yes you do." Penelope slung her office door open.

"By the way, maintenance fixed the lock on the lab door this morning." Lucy gathered her pocketbook, and they parted ways in the main hallway. When she turned toward the rock lab, Penelope instantly felt a sense of dread fill her body. She pushed her feet toward the laboratory and wondered what mess awaited her. No one had been in the rock lab since Saturday night other than a team of police officers, detectives, and crime scene technicians. Ryan sent a message earlier that the police were done collecting evidence and she could use the room as usual.

Penelope inserted her key and slowly turned the lock until she heard the familiar pop of the latches retreating. If this had been any other day, Penelope would have been excited to get to work in her rock lab. But today was different. Today, she was hunting for a killer who invaded her sanctuary.

Penelope pushed on the weighted door and watched it open in slow motion before her eyes, revealing the mess that the killer and law enforcement had left behind.

I'm going to need more than one coffee for this job, she thought.

Penelope tiptoed through the mess and flopped her messenger bag onto the corner table. Before she started to work cleaning and straightening the room, she wanted to preserve what it looked like. Penelope climbed on top of the project table, retrieved her phone from her back pocket, and snapped over two dozen photos documenting the current state of the lab. When she was satisfied that she had documented the room sufficiently, she climbed down from her perch and got to work.

After three hours of cleaning, sorting, and filing, the rock lab looked normal again. Map drawers sat filled, samples put back into the cases, floors and shelves cleaned, and Penelope's world was right again.

All that remained after the morning hours of tidying were three empty cups and a fistful of crystals that Penelope could not remember where to store. It was curious that she couldn't place these samples right away. Typically, Penelope remembered where every sample was collected and where it was shelved in her lab. When everything else was tidy, Penelope pulled the stool close to the project table and opened her testing kit.

"Why don't these look familiar?" Penelope muttered aloud. She turned on her tape recorder, picked up a handful of the clear stones, and examined them with her hand magnifier. She always ran her tape recorder when she was examining rock and mineral samples so that she could capture every observation while she was working and then transcribe the tapes later for her paper and computer files.

Penelope rattled off a list of mineral properties as she examined each stone. "Hardness of at least eight or nine on the Mohs scale. Clear samples with no inclusions. Cut surfaces with no fracturing. Glassy luster. No streak. No reaction to acid. Orangish-red, ultraviolet fluorescence. Huh. Odd."

Penelope stared at the samples. They looked like diamonds, but they weren't. "I don't have diamonds or anything close in the rock lab either," she muttered.

Penelope realized she was talking to herself, but sometimes she was her own best sounding board. She sat staring at the crystals when an idea struck her like a thunderbolt. Quickly, Penelope threw the crystals into a black velvet pouch, put them and the testing kit into her messenger bag, and ran out of the door. She listened to the solid door thud to a close behind her. The lock's latch echoed through the hallway when it snapped into place.

"Wait, where are you going?" Lucy cried, holding up two bags of hamburgers and fries and watching her boss run through the lobby.

"I have to go to The Crystal Cove. I'll be back," Penelope yelled over her shoulder. She flung open the glass door at the main entrance and sprinted for her Hummer.

****

Just a few short minutes later, Penelope hastily parked her car in front of her mother's store and sprinted for Tessa's Amethyst Falls candles.

"Mom," Penelope called while she zipped through the empty store.

"Penelope, dear. What are you doing?" Clara emerged from the workroom carrying a half-eaten sandwich.

Penelope did not reply. She pulled the original candle Tessa gave Clara from the shelf and began digging into the base with a pocketknife she carried in her bag.

"Penelope, seriously. Why are you destroying my candle?"

Penelope carved the purple beeswax from the base of the handcrafted candle.

"Can you slide one of your velvet pads over here?" Penelope pried loose one of the smaller gemstones in the candle. When the stone escaped its waxy home, Penelope gently guided it to the purple velvet surface that Clara used when she was showing her most expensive samples to prospective customers.

"Talk to me, Penelope. I don't understand why you're tearing up the candle."

Penelope stopped and looked at her mother. "I need to see the stones in the candle."

"Why? Tessa said that they're just low-quality diamonds from the jewelry store."

"I don't think so." Penelope raised her eyebrows.

Penelope carefully pulled three more stones from the candle and placed them on the purple velvet. She set the candle aside, folded her knife, and shoved it into her bag.

Penelope removed a polishing cloth from the mineral testing kit and gently wiped the surfaces of the stones from Tessa's candle. When they were clean, she laid them back on the velvet, then placed a blue velvet pad beside the purple.

"Mom, can you hand me the pouch of gemstones from my bag?"

Clara found the small pouch of gems and spread them onto the blue velvet.

Penelope examined each stone from the candle and compared them to the gems she had found earlier in the day at the rock lab using her hand lens. The stones looked identical. She quickly tested each one as she had with the crystals in the rock lab that morning.

"Tessa must have known more about crystals than we thought."

"So?"

"These are not diamonds. None of them."

"Sure they are. Tessa said that they were leftovers from the jewelry shop. They can't sell low-quality stones."

"These are not low quality. Look closely with your hand lens. Not a single inclusion is present in any stone. They are all perfect and perfectly cut into popular shapes, like square cushions, teardrops, round, and brilliant cuts."

"Then what are they?"

"They're moissanite crystals. They look almost identical to diamonds, but look under my black light." Penelope flipped the switch on her tiny flashlight, using her hand to shield the store's natural light from the stone.

"They fluoresce a kind of orange color."

"Diamonds fluoresce a blueish hue, not orange or red."

"So, they're not diamonds. What does this mean, Penelope?"

"Tessa suspected something was wrong, and she hid these stones in her candles." Penelope sat on the stool behind the register and released an exhale. "Oh, my gosh." Penelope shot up, gathered the crystals into the pouches, and shoved them into her messenger bag. She was halfway out of the front door as Clara was calling behind her.

"What?"

"I know who the killer is!"

Chapter Twenty-Seven

P enelope pulled up to the jewelry store and parked the car in the space directly in front of the door, ready for a confrontation. Her calls to Ryan went unanswered. She sent a text.

Penelope: Meet me at Robby's jewelry store now!

Armed with two bags of gemstones, one from her rock lab and one from the candle, she pushed open the doors and cringed as jingle bells rang out, announcing her entrance. It was lunchtime and nobody was waiting in the showroom.

Maggie must be on her break, she thought. Penelope called out, "Robby!" She waited for a reply or a noise indicating Robby was coming from the back of the store. Standing alone, Penelope scanned through the jewelry displays. The jewelry in the glass cases at the center of the showroom was polished to a high shine, making the emeralds, sapphires, rubies, and diamonds sparkle. The lighting in the store made even the blackest of stones, like onyx, look dazzling when cut and polished just the right way and set in a bracelet or necklace.

One of the diamond displays along the wall sparkled in the light. Penelope estimated each stone was at least four to six carats. Penelope shone her black light on them. It was hard to tell through the glass, but she detected a faint orange glow at the edges. The stones were not diamonds; she was sure. They were moissanites just like the ones in the candle and in her rock lab after Jessie's murder.

As she tiptoed into the interior hallway, Penelope could hear humming coming from the jewelry studio.

Robby must be working with earbuds in, she thought. She had done the same thing many times in the rock lab and knew how startling it could be when someone approached, and you were deep in thought while working on a project.

Penelope moved across the cement flooring, trying not to let her boots echo. As she neared the workroom, she could see Robby bent over his crystal polisher with noise-canceling headphones enveloping his head.

Penelope knocked on the door frame and stepped into the studio. Robby never looked up from the polisher. She stepped closer and waved her hand in the air, hoping to catch Robby's attention and not wanting to scare him.

But Robby never noticed Penelope slowly stepping in front of his polishing machine until she was just mere inches away. Robby jerked and his startled gaze turned into a big smile when he realized Penelope had come to visit.

"Hey, Penelope. I didn't hear you come in." He slid the headphones around his neck.

"No kidding. These headphones have you hidden from the world."

"I like to focus on the work without distractions when I'm designing a new piece."

"I understand that feeling." Penelope watched Robby. Her body felt heavy with dread.

"This new one is in Tessa's honor. Would you like to see the design?"

"Oh, I would love to."

Robby pulled his sketch pad from the top drawer of his desk.

She gasped. Penelope knew Robby was a talented designer, but this new line was more stunning than she could have anticipated.

"I'm working on the necklace first."

The hand sketch was itself a work of art, showing Robby's talent for design and presentation. The drawing showed Tessa wearing the necklace with her red curls dangling on either side of the cushion-cut emeralds and teardrop diamonds that cascaded down rope-like strands of rose gold.

"It's gorgeous, Robby." Tears filled her eyes while Penelope imagined Tessa wearing this necklace to the gala or a night on the town. She slid her bag off her shoulder and onto the table near the bins of crystals.

Robby smiled. "Thank you. A part of me wants to believe that Tessa can see this, too."

"I'm sure she can."

Robby and Penelope stared at the drawing for a quiet minute before Robby cleared his throat. "So, um, what brings you by?" He placed a second chair next to his desk.

As she sat, Penelope quickly wondered how to phrase her question. "I need to ask you about the stones that Tessa was using in her candles."

"In the Amethyst Falls? Those were just some trash diamonds that I couldn't sell, like I told you before."

"Why couldn't you sell them?"

"One of our suppliers tried to slip some low-quality stuff into one of our shipments. I told Katia that she would have to find someone else. That's why she's been out of town so much hunting for a new supplier that wouldn't try to cheat us."

"She's been a good partner? Katia?"

"Yes. She's been great. I was a little skeptical when she first approached me about joining the store, but she and her family have connections all over the world. She has proven herself useful over the last couple of years."

Penelope nodded. "Huh."

"Why?"

Penelope pulled the two bags of crystals from her messenger bag and laid them on Robby's desk.

"What are these?" Robby scratched his head.

"Examine them."

Robby pulled his magnifier over the top of the two sets of crystals. "Moissanites. Where did you get these?"

Penelope held her breath. "One set from the candle that Tessa gave my mother, and the second set from the floor of my rock lab."

"That's not possible. I gave Tessa diamonds for her candles. I don't even carry moissanite. Most moissanites are lab-created and I only use natural stones."

"I know. I've looked through your cases. Most of your gemstones are natural. But the jewelry on the east wall isn't diamond. They are moissanites."

"That isn't possible. I made those pieces myself."

"Robby, I don't have moissanite in my rock lab, either. I think Tessa may have made some candles with the diamond you gave her. But she had at least one with moissanites from *your* shop."

Robby stood and backed away from the desk. "I don't understand what you are saying. Are you accusing me of something?"

"No." Penelope reached for Robby's hands. "No, I'm not."

"She's accusing me," Katia announced. She sauntered into the workroom holding a gun.

Penelope got to her feet and stepped back from the desk. "Wait, Katia." She could feel the blood rushing through her body. Looking at a gun barrel made her feel nauseous.

"Katia? You killed Tessa?" Robby sobbed. "Why?"

"I would never have put it together if I hadn't found the moissanite in my rock lab. It was you. You killed Tessa and Jessie. You were the one following me in the SUV."

"I thought you were the only person who might figure it out. I needed to keep an eye on you," Katia said, inching toward Penelope.

Penelope looked at Robby. "Katia was switching the diamonds out of your designs and replacing them with moissanite. Once you designed the pieces, they went to the front to be sold, and you never saw them again, right? Moissanites look just like diamonds to most people."

Robby glanced from Penelope to Katia. "Is she right, Katia? Did you replace the gemstones in my jewelry? Why?"

Katia scoffed. "Why do you think? Money. Your nosy wife should have minded her own business."

"Is that what happened? Tessa figured out that you were replacing the stones and took some as proof and hid them in one of her candles?" Penelope pressed.

"She came in here one night looking for Robby and found me replacing the stones. I told her I was just fixing a loose stone, but she was suspicious."

"So, she found your stash of moissanite that you were passing off as genuine diamonds and took some when Robby told her to take the diamonds for his candles." Penelope tried to keep Katia talking. *Where is Ryan?* she thought. Penelope glanced frantically around the room, desperate to defend herself from a gun.

"She told me she had proof that I was stealing the diamonds and replacing them with fakes."

"So, you killed her?" Tears fell from Robby's eyes. He turned to Penelope. "Why didn't Tessa tell me?"

"I told her that if she gave me the stones back and kept quiet, I would leave her alone. However, if she told you, I would kill you both." Katia inched closer to Penelope.

"But Tessa put them in a candle, knowing that you would never find them there. Then, she gave it to my mother for safekeeping," Penelope said. It all made sense. The puzzle pieces were snapping into place. Katia asked Clara for the key to the candle shop, hoping to find the crystals that Tessa took. "You saw the Amethyst Falls when you came by and asked for the key to pick up the boxes of candles. Did you figure it out then?"

"I suspected it when I couldn't find the moissanites in the candle shop," Katia sneered. "I was going to steal the candles the night of the gala, but Jessie ruined my plan."

Tears were pouring down Robby's face. "You killed my Tessa?" he asked again.

"She made me do it. She refused to give me the stones."

"Tessa wouldn't let you steal from her husband." Katia's confession angered Penelope. Two people were dead because Katia was greedy.

"No, Katia. How could you?" Robby stepped toward the gun.

Katia glared at Robby and squeezed the trigger. Penelope jumped toward Robby. A bullet whizzed by her head and struck Robby on the shoulder. He fell to the floor with a thud, grasping the wound. Blood flowed through his fingers. Penelope frantically searched for a cloth to stop the bleeding.

"Leave him," Katia yelled.

"You're pretty sloppy with that gun. Where's your frog venom? Oh yes. I figured it all out the minute I found the moissanite crystals in the candle. You visited vendors in South America and that's where you got the Batrachotoxin. You also lied to Robby, saying that you were out of town during the festival, then you set up the meeting between him and the accountant so that you could sneak into the festival to kill Tessa without him knowing you were in the country."

"You think you are smart." Katia turned the gun on Penelope.

"What I've never figured out is how you did it. How did you inject her with the venom? Someone certainly would have seen you carrying a syringe."

Katia held up her right hand. She spun the onyx stone in her ring to the side and a needle popped out. "All it takes is one quick sting. You're coming with me." She waved the gun through the air, and Penelope instinctively rushed toward Katia, knocking her backward into the wall before jumping behind the polishing machine. Her sleeve caught on the power switch and the machine whirred to life.

Penelope heard a shot ring out and a bullet strike the polishing arm before it ricocheted off the metal and into the wall. She crouched lower, trying to make herself a smaller target. The polishing machine filled the air with a deafening whine.

Katia struggled to her feet. "Get out here, Penelope!"

Penelope squatted behind the equipment. She needed an advantage. "You killed Tessa because she had proof that you were stealing diamonds from Robby. But tell me why you killed Jessie?" Penelope yelled over the buzz of the machine.

Katia snickered. "Jessie. That little tramp saw me at the festival booth with Tessa."

"So, you killed her in my rock lab?"

"She tried to blackmail me. She wanted a million dollars, or she was going to tell the police that I was at the festival."

"Jessie told me she didn't see who was in Tessa's tent. She just recently remembered hearing a woman's voice."

"That little sociopath played you. She knew it was me all along. She started blackmailing me the day after the festival."

"So, you killed her, too." Penelope was reeling from Katia's confession. She had watched hundreds of television shows where the murderer grandly confessed their crimes, but she never expected to witness it in real life. Penelope could feel a cold sweat on her forehead. Her stomach churned.

"Jessie said to sneak into the hallway at the gala and leave the money. Instead, I tried to pay her with crystals.

I figured she was stupid enough to believe that I had a bag of diamonds."

"But she wanted cash, not stones." Penelope's palms were clammy. Robby was pale. He was losing blood quickly.

Katia slowly paced in front of the door, blocking Penelope's escape. "So, we fought, and the moissanites spilled onto the floor. But I stabbed her with my ring, and she dropped like one of your rocks. I heard you and that detective talking down the hall. I didn't have time to get my stones, but I didn't think you would notice given the mess Jessie made trying to get away from me. I guess you're not as stupid as I thought."

Now Penelope was angry again. "I guess not." Penelope could see Katia walking toward her on the other side of the equipment. She crept around the gem polishing machine toward Katia. Penelope searched for anything she could use against the gun-wielding psychopath. The room was full of heavy machines and gemstones. That would have to do.

"You should just leave. I called the police on my way here." Penelope threw a handful of crystals into the hallway. The sharp clatter made Katia pivot. Quickly, Penelope charged at Katia, hitting her in the back and knocking her to the floor as the gun flew across the room toward Robby.

Penelope straddled Katia's back, keeping her pinned to the floor. "Robby, do you have any rope or duct tape?" Katia struggled against Penelope's weight, her arms and legs splayed.

"You killed my wife!" Robby crawled toward Katia, blood pouring down his arm. He picked up the gun and pointed it at Katia as Penelope heard sirens pulling into the parking lot.

"No, Robby. Stop. The cops are here." Penelope jammed the heel of her hand into the small of Katia's back to stop her from wiggling free.

Robby ignored Penelope.

Katia flailed her arms.

"Stop it." Penelope dug her hand deeper into Katia's back and pulled on her hair, making her squeal.

Robby inched the tip of the gun closer to Katia's face. "You killed the love of my life for money?"

Katia raised her head, glaring at Robby. "And freedom. From you."

"Penelope," Ryan called as he ran down the hallway.

"Back here," Penelope yelled. She leaned toward Katia and whispered, "No freedom for you now."

The next few seconds were a blur. Ryan and Andre stormed into the workroom, taking the gun from Robby's shaking hand and placing handcuffs on Katia. Penelope allowed Ryan to help her off the floor and into a waiting chair.

"Watch her ring. It has frog venom in it," Penelope warned, gasping for air.

She sat with Robby while the emergency medical staff tended to his wound. She watched them load him into an ambulance, assuring her it was just a minor wound that bled a lot, but Robby would be out of the hospital soon.

Penelope could feel the pent-up anxiety flowing through her body as she went over the events that got her here—finding Tessa's body, finding Jessie's body, searching for clues, and then finding the most important one in her rock lab. But it was Tessa who ultimately led Penelope to her killer. Hiding the moissanite in the Amethyst Falls candle and giving it to Clara was the brilliant move that caught Katia in the end.

Penelope spent the next twenty minutes at the jewelry store recounting the events for Ryan and Andre.

"How did you know to bring these officers with you?" Penelope asked.

"I was on the phone with your mom when you texted. She told me about the two sets of crystals. When I got your text, the clues started clicking into place. We could never verify that Katia was out of town during the festival. I figured that if Katia killed two people, she wouldn't hesitate to go after you or Robby."

By the time she was done with the police, Laurel, Olivia, and Clara had arrived to take care of Penelope. Katia was on her way to the police station and Robby was safe with the doctors.

"Come on," Olivia said. "I think you need some cheesecake."

"And wine," Laurel chimed in.

"Lots of wine," Clara declared. "And an aura cleansing spell."

"No," Penelope, Laurel, and Olivia cried in unison.

Aura Cleansing Spell

After a traumatic event, use crystals and meditation to
help cleanse your aura and reset.
*Clara's note: You can also use smudging to cleanse a space,
but Penelope doesn't like it when I do that in her house.*

Spell Supplies

*Opal Ring or Necklace | Chakra Crystals | Candle in your
favorite color*

Light the candle and place the chakra crystals around the
candle.
Wear the opal jewelry and recite:
*Healing light, wash over me. Healing light, now set me free.
So mote it be!*

Chakra Stones for Aura Cleansing

Use these cleansing stones to cleanse your aura. You can
use them during meditation.

Selenite | Amethyst | Tourmaline

Chapter Twenty-Eight

B y the next evening, Penelope's nerves had settled and the adrenaline rush gave way to an exhaustion that was gripping her muscles. She was grateful that Tessa and Jessie's killer would now face justice, and Penelope was relieved that the police had shown up in time to escort Katia away before she hurt anyone else.

"Robby," Penelope called as he entered through the door of The Tipsy Java. She jumped up to usher him to their table.

"Oh, Robby, dear. I'm so glad that you're okay." Clara patted the empty chair beside her.

Robby eased into the seat. "Thank you. I was lucky the bullet went straight through my shoulder and didn't hit anything major."

"Phew," Penelope said. "I was so afraid when she shot you. How long do you have to wear the sling?"

"Just a month or so."

Laurel set a large cup and a plate of scones in front of Robby. "Sugar-free hazelnut and vanilla latte, just the way you like it."

"Thank you, Laurel. You make the best in town." Robby looked at peace for the first time since Tessa died.

"I wonder what will happen to Katia now?" Olivia placed a platter of assorted desserts in the center of the table. She and Laurel sat opposite Robby.

"I hope she rots in jail," Robby said.

"Here, here," Penelope chimed in, raising her mug.

"I'm sorry it turned out to be someone that you trusted," Clara said.

"That does hurt." Robby's phone buzzed. "Huh," he said, checking the text message.

"What is it, dear?" Clara asked.

"That was a text from Sandra Phillips. Marlene Black dropped her lawsuit. I can keep producing Tessa's candles."

"Why?" Clara asked.

"Sandra showed her the five million dollar countersuit and Marlene realized she didn't want to fight. I'm glad it's over," Robby said, turning off his phone.

"That's fantastic news," Penelope agreed.

As they sat and let the events of the last two weeks sink in, The Tipsy Java filled up with its nightly regulars.

"The wine crowd is arriving," Laurel said. "Back to work for you and me, Olivia."

Olivia grunted and pushed her chair back from the table. "All work, work, work with you, boss," she laughed.

"Ha, ha," Laurel replied, throwing a dishtowel at her belly.

As the two ladies headed behind the counter, Penelope spied Andre stepping inside the cafe. He made eye contact. Penelope met him by the front windows.

"I wanted to check on you. Are you okay?"

"I'm fine. Thanks. You didn't need to check in on me."

Andre shuffled his feet. "No matter what, we're um...friends. Right? And I—"

The cafe door flung open. Ryan hustled to Penelope's side and clenched her in a bear hug.

"Wow, detective," she said.

"The killer is in jail. I'm just Ryan tonight," he said, holding onto her arms.

Andre took slow steps backward, keeping his eyes on Penelope and Ryan until he reached the door and slipped into the night.

Penelope struggled to escape Ryan's grip. She could see Andre lingering and watching through the window in her peripheral vision.

"Wow, that's quite a death grip you got there, Ryan," Penelope said, pushing back against his arms.

Ryan stepped away slightly. "I'm sorry. I just feel awful that you were in danger."

"You came just in time."

"Thank goodness."

Penelope and Ryan rejoined Clara and Robby at their table. Laurel and Olivia were just arriving with a fresh bottle of wine and burgers.

Clara leaned toward Penelope. "It looks like my love spell worked," she whispered.

"Ah," Penelope sighed. "Don't start."

"I figured it was time for some proper food," Laurel announced.

"Did Katia confess to everything?" Olivia asked.

Ryan nodded. "She did. She had been slowly replacing the diamonds in Robby's jewelry with moissanite for months and then selling the diamonds overseas and keeping the profits."

"I guess I wasn't paying close enough attention." Robby shook his head.

"She was good. The theft ring involves her entire family from here to Russia and she even had some of her contacts in South America in on it. She never meant for you or Tessa to find the moissanites. But Tessa came into the store and saw her alone in the workroom and got suspicious. So Katia stuck the crystals into the cabinet, meaning to come back and get them."

"And those were the crystals that Tessa took for her candles?" Laurel asked, pouring each of them a glass of pinot noir.

"Yes," Ryan answered, taking a sip.

"You didn't notice that they weren't diamonds, Robby?" Clara asked.

Penelope glared at her mother and followed with a swift kick in the shin.

"I didn't look at them. I had a handful of poor-quality diamonds, and I told Tessa that she could have them and said just to get them out of the cabinet. She must have taken both the diamonds and the moissanite."

"Katia said that Tessa confronted her about the crystals when she realized that some of them were too clear to be poor-quality diamonds. Tessa realized Katia wasn't repairing the jewelry but replacing diamonds with moissanites."

Robby shook his head. "Tessa suspected her right away."

Ryan continued. "She did. So, Katia told you she was going out of town, but instead, she went to the festival and used a small syringe that she camouflaged in her ring to inject Tessa with the Batrachotoxin."

"Devious," Clara commented.

"All she had to do was spin the ring around so that it was on the inside of her hand and grab Tessa's arm," Ryan explained.

"Then Jessie tried to blackmail her and ended up just like Tessa." Penelope was shocked at the lengths Katia would go to for money.

"Wow. Cold-blooded," Olivia said.

"Katia will be in prison for the rest of her life, thanks to you," Ryan said, eyeing Penelope. "But from now on, how about I catch the killers?"

"How about next time I promise to wait for you before I confront the killer?"

"Next time?" Clara asked, raising her eyebrows.

Penelope smiled. "Oh Mom, what are the odds that I would find a third dead body in my lifetime?"

www.ingramcontent.com/pod-product-compliance
Lightning Source LLC
Chambersburg PA
CBHW050547190726
48283CB00007B/2035